Ruby stepped between Dick Prescott and the door of his pickup, blocking his way. He raised his hand as if he were about to push her away from his truck. "God, woman. Lay off, will you?" He shifted on his feet. "Just lay the hell off."

Prescott's hand held, six inches from Ruby's arm, his tendons taut. He wanted to shove her, knock her down, she could feel it. She didn't budge and he licked his lips, then dropped his hand. "You'd better move," he said in a quiet voice.

Ruby waited long enough so it wasn't a concession, then stepped aside. The hound snapped its teeth at her as she passed.

She stood in the sandy track until Dick Prescott had slammed his truck into gear and roared out of the clearing, throwing up a cloud of fine sand. . . .

*Also by Jo Dereske*

**SAVAGE CUT**

# CUT and DRY

## Jo Dereske

A DELL BOOK

Published by
Dell Publishing
a division of
Bantam Doubleday Dell Publishing Group, Inc.
1540 Broadway
New York, New York 10036

If you purchased this book without a cover you should be aware that this book is stolen property. It was reported as "unsold and destroyed" to the publisher and neither the author nor the publisher has received any payment for this "stripped book."

Copyright © 1997 by Jo Dereske

All rights reserved. No part of this book may be reproduced or transmitted in any form or by any means, electronic or mechanical, including photocopying, recording, or by any information storage and retrieval system, without the written permission of the Publisher, except where permitted by law.

The trademark Dell® is registered in the U.S. Patent and Trademark Office.

ISBN: 0-440-22222-2

Printed in the United States of America

Published simultaneously in Canada

September 1997

10  9  8  7  6  5  4  3  2  1

OPM

I'm indebted to many people for sharing their expertise with me. They include: Ray Dereske, Mary Dereske, Kerry Harris, Billy Cox, Jeff Niese, Walter Robinson, and entomologists of the North Central Forest Experiment Station.

I'm especially grateful to my editor, Marjorie Braman, and my agent, Ruth Cohen.

And most of all, I thank my husband and best friend, Kip Winsett.

# Chapter 1

Ruby Crane lay on her back on the sandy bottom of Blue Lake, four feet from shore, naked, her hands buoyant and her reddish gold hair furling gently around her head as the water lapped toward the narrow strip of beach in front of her cabin. Only the oval of her face and the tips of her toes protruded from the water.

It wasn't much help. The temperature at ten-thirty in the morning was already ninety-three degrees and the air above water was thick and dripping, a damn close match to the liquid below.

Water nudged the corners of Ruby's eyes but she held them open, blinking when her vision of the pale summer sky was washed by Blue Lake's lazy movement. Even the lake was too hot to make waves.

The sky was cloudless, the air already hazed with humidity. Two crows flapped high across Ruby's view, featureless black wings like a child's drawing. She watched them without moving her head, lazily wondering if it was cooler up there, unable to remember what she'd learned long ago in science classes, if she even had. It *looked* cooler.

Fine bottom sand, amber colored and silky, cushioned her hips and shoulders. "Sugar sand," they used to call it, and as children, she and her sister Phyllis had dug for it on dry land to prove to themselves that the Great Lakes really did once cover all of Michigan's Waters County, that their own backyard had once been beachfront property. Bands of the tawny sand lay beneath the black topsoil like veins of gold.

"Mom, he's looking over here again," Jesse said from the dock, her voice reaching Ruby in a wavery underwater warble, like alien music.

"It's okay, sweetie," Ruby answered her daughter without moving.

"He has binoculars," Jesse added, but not as a warning; Jesse never warned, was never surprised, as if those capacities had been forever lost. Jesse observed. Detail by detail, always scrutinizing for cause and effect, for logic, and if Jesse couldn't discover the logic in what she saw, she freely invented it, relating it with convincing certainty, unable to rest until she found a reason for what she observed.

Ruby sat up, then stood, water sheeting from her body, the hot summer air instantly warming the droplets on her skin. She leisurely reached for the purple towel she'd dropped on the wooden dock earlier. If he was such a dedicated Peeping Tom that he'd taken to watching them with binoculars, then he shouldn't be surprised by anything he saw.

Jesse, in her blue two-piece suit, lay propped on her

# Cut and Dry

elbows on an orange beach towel spread at perfect angles across the dock. A book lay flat in front of her, open to color illustrations of dragonflies whose wings shimmered like rainbows. Jesse gazed intently toward the old Barber cabin, her forehead creased with two deep vertical frown lines. Her slight body was brown, appearing dry and cool in the temperatures that made Ruby wish she could bury her sweaty self in the mud like a frog. Jesse's left foot rhythmically trembled, as it often did when she concentrated.

Ruby tucked her towel around herself like a sarong and sat on the dock beside her fifteen-year-old daughter, facing the Barber cabin and dabbling her feet in the tepid water.

"So who is he?" Ruby asked. She longed to touch the heel of Jesse's trembling foot, to still it, but instead she pulled Jesse's red-gold hair off her neck and rebound the wavy strands in a rough ponytail, pinning it on top of her head.

Jesse's hair was too long. Ruby had tried to convince her to keep the short, simple style she'd worn after the accident, but Jesse was recovered enough to turn up her nose at "boring" short hair, although not enough to care for her hair beyond a routine brush every morning.

Jesse closed her insect book before answering, aligning it with the edge of her towel. "He's an old sailor," she said slowly, enunciating each word. "His binoculars are all he kept from his boat. He sits on his porch all day, remembering, looking out at the water—and us."

Ruby squinted at the Barber cabin a couple of hundred yards across a scoop of Blue Lake, nestled among oaks and beech trees in late June greenery. A willow tree draped over the water where the dock had rotted away. The Barber cabin was built of logs like her own cabin behind her, the Crane cabin. Vacation homes surrounded Blue Lake, more every year; summer people came and went, but the man who'd taken up residence at the Barber cabin didn't fit the summer mold.

For one thing, the Barber cabin had been empty and neglected for years, according to Mrs. Pink, who'd spent half a century on Blue Lake. Three weeks ago, there'd been a flurry of activity that echoed across the water, dawn to dusk: sawing and nailing, the rumble and grind of a bulldozer scraping earth, workmen's boisterous cursing. When silence returned, a new chained gate stretched across the driveway off Blue Road that led through the trees to the Barber cabin, padlocked and hung with a freshly painted KEEP OUT sign. And two days later, the man appeared on the cabin's front porch.

An old sailor, Jesse had decided. *Old* to Ruby's daughter was a relative term. From this distance his features were indiscernible, but from the silver in his hair when the sun touched the porch of the Barber cabin, Ruby guessed perhaps late sixties.

Ruby wouldn't have given the stranger a second thought if Jesse hadn't noticed him and begun to puzzle over his situation, watching him watching them—if that was really what he was doing—whenever she was outside. Always alone, he rarely left the porch during daylight, and who knew if he remained there after dark, sitting for hours, a silent, vigilant figure who apparently preferred people from a distance rather than have them journey up his chained and padlocked driveway.

Ruby wasn't as convinced as Jesse that the man spent his hours watching them specifically. So obsessed had her daughter become that Ruby had asked Mary Jean, her realtor friend in Sable, for gossip.

"You're not the first to wonder," Mary Jean told her. "The Barbers still own the cabin, but all I've heard is that he's not a Barber, although he paid for the cabin's improvements." She'd raised her stylishly arched black eyebrows. "Cash on the barrel: crisp one-hundred-dollar bills, so he's got bucks. Unless he's running a forgery ring over there; *that* would explain the locked gate. If I were you," Mary Jean had advised, "I'd ask Mrs. Pink. She'll know for sure what's going on. And when you find out, let me in on it, would you?"

Ruby hadn't had a chance to ask Mrs. Pink yet. The old woman was a watcher, too, and appeared at Ruby's cabin when the mood struck her, emerging by night from the shadows where she lurked, spying on the inhabitants and tourists of Blue Lake. Ruby grinned, picturing the watching stranger and the lurking Mrs. Pink; a match made in heaven.

"If he's a sailor," Ruby asked Jesse now, spreading more of the coconut-scented sunblock on Jesse's tanned shoulders, feeling her fragile bones under the taut skin, "why didn't he go to the ocean, or even Lake Michigan, instead of coming here?"

"Because he's not *that* rich," Jesse answered without hesitation, as if she'd already unraveled his tale. "He wanted to be more private." She smiled impishly. "And he thinks you're pretty."

"If I'm pretty, then you're beautiful," Ruby told her daughter, kicking up a spray of water over Jesse's back with her bare foot.

"Not really," the always literal Jesse said. "But I have nice hair."

"Definitely," Ruby said, smoothing back a tendril of Jesse's hair, which was beginning to mirror Ruby's in color but with redder highlights, thicker and curlier. "Speaking of hair, what do you say to a haircut?"

Seeing Jesse's nose wrinkle, Ruby hastily said, "Just some of these split ends. That's all, I promise."

"Will Alice do it?" Jesse asked.

Alice Rolley owned the Wak 'n Yak, the only beauty parlor in the small town of Sable, two miles from Blue Lake. Alice's styling skills were still anchored in the early 1970s: bouffant hair, back-combing, and glossy hairspray. When Ruby lived in Palo Alto, she would have avoided a beauty parlor like the Wak 'n Yak, except to roll her eyes over its name.

But when Ruby hit tough times the winter before, Alice Rolley had collected local money and gently battered open social service doors for Jesse's physical therapy and special education, getting them through a bad winter with such generosity and grace that Ruby had been stunned by the depth of her own gratitude,

# Cut and Dry 7

unable to recall such kindness during all her adult life. Now Ruby was a loyal client of the Wak 'n Yak, keeping monthly appointments with Alice, then immediately rushing home after a cut-and-style and standing in the shower until she'd washed away every vestige of hairspray and curl.

"Sure, Alice will cut it if you want her to," Ruby said, jumping on Jesse's agreeable moment. "Let's go up to the cabin and call her now."

"Okay."

Ruby waited while Jesse folded and refolded her towel into a square and then folded it again over her book, smoothing the edges together. Everything even. Before she stepped from the dock to their narrow sandy beach, Jesse turned and waved to the man sitting on the porch of the Barber cabin. He didn't return the wave, but Ruby caught the glint of light as he lowered his binoculars. Caught in the act.

The binoculars were a new element as far as Ruby knew. She decided to ask Sheriff Carly about the man staying at the Barber cabin. She hadn't felt a sense of threat from the stranger, but his increasing curiosity made her uncomfortable.

"How about an ice-cream cone after your haircut?" Ruby asked.

"Chocolate," Jesse said. She walked easily beside Ruby toward the cabin, barefoot over the sandy lawn, holding her folded towel close to her chest, no sign of the drag of her left leg that appeared when she was tired. She'd grown over the long and snowy winter, and despite the thinness that made her appear so small, she was nearly as tall as Ruby.

Ruby had inherited the Crane cabin after her mother's death four years ago. It sat on an acre of land that projected into Blue Lake like a miniature peninsula, the oldest cabin on the lake, built of logs seventy years ago, back when straight, clear white pine was still plentiful and cheap. After nineteen years away from Sable and despite firm intentions of never *ever* returning to this place, Ruby had brought Jesse home to Blue Lake after her accident, planning only to stay until Jesse recovered. They'd now spent ten months in the Crane cabin and Ruby had yet to take the golden building and the property it sat on for granted. *Her* cabin.

Stepping beneath the shade of the red oaks near the cabin was a slight relief after the hot morning sun. No breeze stirred off the lake; the oak leaves hung limp and curled, protecting themselves from the heat. Deep in the branches above them a bird twittered as groggily as if it had been disturbed after dark.

"You first," Ruby said, holding open the door that led onto the cabin's screened-in front porch. The plank floor was gritty with sand Ruby didn't bother sweeping out. Sand was dappled throughout the cabin, in the bathroom, the tub, beneath their chairs, even at the bottom of her sheets. Years ago, Gram had told her, "Leave it. You can't fight it. Sand belongs to the summer, just like mosquitoes and sunburns."

The door inside the front porch entered the cabin's main room, dominated by a fieldstone fireplace, open

## Cut and Dry

to the kitchen, with Jesse's bedroom and the bathroom through a doorway between the two spaces, and a loft above the main room. The cabin was log, inside and out, and hadn't been updated since the twenties, and Ruby had no intention of changing it. It was perfect the way it was.

As they entered, Spot opened her eyes and looked up without raising her head from her refuge beneath the kitchen table. The big collie lay on her side with legs extended, her tongue out. Jesse set her towel precisely on the corner of the kitchen table, edge to edge, then crawled beneath the table and joined Spot, stroking her head and crooning. Spot slowly thumped her tail against the floor.

Ruby poured two glasses of iced tea from the pitcher in the refrigerator, leaned over and handed a sweaty glass to Jesse, then looked up the Wak 'n Yak's phone number in the slender Waters County phonebook.

She dialed the number on her old-fashioned black rotary phone, leaning against the kitchen counter, still wrapped in her purple towel and rubbing the sole of her left foot against her right calf, brushing more grains of sand to the floor. Rumors were that the Sable Telephone Company finally intended to provide Touch-Tone service next spring. Nobody really believed it.

"McCutcheon here," a man's voice answered: curt, officious, and loud.

"I'm sorry," Ruby said, frowning and glancing out

the window toward the shimmery waters as a motorboat buzzed past. "I was calling the Wak 'n Yak."

"Yeah?" he asked, suspicious now.

Ruby recognized his voice, that proud-to-be-a-lawman arrogance. "Mac?" she asked. "It's Ruby. What are you doing there? What's happened?"

The direct frontal assault, especially from a woman, threw sheriff's deputy Howard "Mac" McCutcheon off for a few heartbeats. "Because . . ." he stuttered, then regained himself. Ruby pictured him straightening his spine and raising his knobby chin, puffing out his chest like a lizard in a show of self-inflation. "This is official business," he said. "Police business."

"Let me talk to Carly," she said, making a quick assessment and guessing that something serious had happened, doubting Mac McCutcheon would be answering the telephone in Sable's beauty parlor without persuasion, and that persuasion was most likely in the form of Sheriff Carl Joyce, Junior.

"He's not available," Mac said, his voice rising.

"That's fine," Ruby said amiably, as if she'd misunderstood Mac. "It'll only take a minute. Put him on."

She heard Mac's exasperated breath hissing through the phone line. "I'll see," he finally said.

Men's voices filtered through the muffled mouthpiece, only men's, no women's. Where was Alice? Or Fanny and Katrina, her beauticians? Then the phone bumped against something solid and she heard different, calmer breathing.

"What can I do for you, Ruby?" Carly asked.

"How's your investigation going?" Ruby asked,

guessing again, wondering if the Wak 'n Yak had been robbed. "Any leads?"

Carly gave a short bark that held no humor. "Quit bluffing, Ruby. This hasn't had time to get out yet."

"Don't be so sure," Ruby told him. "But just so I don't spread false rumors, tell me what happened."

There was silence as Carly considered her request. Her question wasn't totally out of line. The two of them sometimes chatted about their respective careers: his as county sheriff and hers in forgery detection, each intrigued by the other's profession and not having many other people to discuss their pursuits with. "You're on the right side of the law now," Carly liked to say, making it sound like Ruby was a reformed felon.

"What happened?" she prompted again, recognizing his hesitation. "Was it a break-in?"

"This is a bad one, Ruby," he said somberly. "It's Alice. Fanny found her when she came to work this morning."

Ruby closed her eyes against the image and turned her back so Jesse couldn't hear her. "Alice?" she asked softly. "Alice Rolley?" as if there were another Alice, picturing the smartly dressed and coiffed silver-haired owner of the Wak 'n Yak. "Alice is dead?"

Carly didn't answer. Ruby ran her hand through her thick hair and leaned against the log wall. "Damn it, just damn it. How did it happen?"

He hesitated. "Keep it under your hat awhile, will you? She was strangled. In the back room."

Questions bubbled in Ruby's mind. She bit her lip, asking only one—for now. "Why?"

"It's too early to say," Carly said, hedging a little. "Maybe robbery, maybe not."

Waters County experienced one or two murders a year, or at least one or two deaths that were acknowledged as homicides. Rumors and suspicions invariably surrounded every unexpected death, proving good late-night conversation for years to come.

"But Alice?" Ruby asked, half to herself, keeping her voice low. "You know Alice; if anybody needed money, she'd just hand it over to them. Half the time, she left the beauty parlor unlocked. Who would bother to rob her? Or . . . kill her?"

"I've got to go, Ruby," Carly said. "Did you call for a specific reason? Is everything okay out at the lake?"

"No, no. We're fine. I called to make an appointment for Jesse's haircut," she told him, feeling foolish as she said it.

Hair appointments were obscenely mundane as Alice Rolley lay dead, murdered. Life cruelly did go on for the rest of the world; there should at least be a pause, Ruby thought, maybe a brief flash across the sky to mark a passing, a reminder of how damn quick it all ended.

"Call back in a couple of days. I don't know whether Fanny and Katrina will open the shop," Carly said. "Jumbo and the kids will have to decide what to do."

Jumbo was Alice's husband. Alice's "kids"—Roseanne and Franklin—were both in their forties.

"I will. Thanks, Carly. And I'm sorry."

# Cut and Dry

"Yeah. Me, too. I'll talk to you later, Ruby."

Ruby hung up and stood for a few minutes, her hand still on the solid black telephone receiver, thinking about Alice Rolley, Sable's premier beautician for over forty years. Like a longtime schoolteacher, Alice had seen the children and grandchildren of her first customers pass through her front door. Hers was more than just a business. What woman didn't spill the details of her life to her beautician? And often, if Alice could wangle a way to help somebody out of a spot, she'd do it. She was one of those rare people able to give another person a hand without making them feel beholden.

Alice dead; it didn't make sense. And robbery made even less sense. Ruby considered the triplet favorites of her former boss, Ron Kilgore: Misguided Love, Greed, and Revenge. "The primitive urges," he liked to say. "That's what moves us, no matter how civilized we pretend to be." He was right too often to be ignored.

Neither misguided love nor revenge were easy fits on the memory of Alice Rolley. And greed was pointless; what Alice had, she passed around. She gossiped, yes. But otherwise Alice could be defined by all the positive adjectives, standing a few inches taller than the masses.

Ruby raised her hand from the phone and turned to watch Jesse, who now lay stretched on the floor with her head resting on Spot's flank, her eyes closed, the thin veins showing on her lids. Spot's tail continued to thump sporadically against the wood floor in contentment. The big dog's left front leg had been amputated last fall following a gunshot wound, but after a period of adjustment, during which Spot stumbled and wore a perplexed expression, she'd learned to get around on three legs as easily, if less gracefully, than before the surgery.

Ruby opened the refrigerator and pulled out the pitcher of iced tea, absently refilling her glass and wondering what Jesse was thinking. Every event in Jesse's life needed an explanation, and Ruby surmised her daughter wasn't asleep but inventing a scenario to go with Ruby's hushed tones over the telephone.

She would hear the details of Alice Rolley's death—the truth, not the rumors that would be wildly circulating by noon—from Carly later, maybe even offer her own opinions, but now she braced herself, waiting for the shocked calls that would be quickly followed by news regarding the funeral, a luncheon, all the local forces marshaled and grief sublimated into the rituals necessary to deal with death.

# Chapter 2

Despite having spent the first seventeen years of her life at either the gray house a block off Sable's main street or the Crane cabin on Blue Lake, Ruby still considered herself an outsider. For the first fifteen years she'd been a child who didn't understand Sable's subtle workings, and after Gram's death she'd been a rebellious teenager who didn't care, nursing a raging passion to escape Sable, Waters County, and Michigan itself.

So less than a year after her return, it was disconcerting to find herself fielding calls and questions regarding Alice Rolley's death.

"But you know about these things," Enid Shea persisted. "You must have some idea. Poor Alice." The older woman's voice caught in a sob. "I still can't believe it."

"It's a horrible shock," Ruby agreed, the phone pinned between her ear and shoulder while she put away breakfast cereal and milk. "But I don't know any more than you do, Enid. I'm sorry."

"Then who does?" Enid complained. "Carly hasn't

said a word and he's the sheriff. He should be telling us what he's found out, keeping us informed. That's why we elected him. There's a murdering thief on the loose, right here. *Now.* It's just unbelievable. We could all be strangled in our beds and he isn't doing one single thing to protect us."

Ruby wiped off the counter, pushing crumbs into her hand and dropping them in the sink. "Carly's still investigating. Once he's made some progress, I'm sure he'll get the word out." Telephones were invented for people like Enid Shea. She wasn't shy about asking who was pregnant, and how soon after the wedding, if there was madness in a family, if tales of infidelity were true, or which spouse was at fault when children didn't come quickly enough. Enid didn't hold conversations with people; she held interrogations.

"That Carly," Enid said, with a sniff of disdain. "I don't trust Carly to figure this out. Between you and me, he hasn't got the marbles or the starch to be sheriff, let alone solve a murder. Not like his dad. Carl Senior would have already made an arrest. We'd all be able to sleep at night."

"He's doing his best." Ruby defended Carly, certain it was true. Carly wasn't one to jump to conclusions, an attribute many people would have preferred to his plodding through the evidence. What his father had done with flair and instinct, Carly did with long and tedious investigation that looked to outsiders as if he were a slow-witted amateur.

"He hasn't done anything yet that I know of," Enid said huffily.

# Cut and Dry

"It's only been twenty-four hours since Alice was killed," Ruby reminded her. With her wrist, she wiped at a drip of perspiration sliding down her temple toward her ear, feeling the sweaty phone receiver against her neck. Why hadn't she bought an air conditioner that spring instead of replacing the storm windows? Right now, winter felt light-years away.

"He'll just shilly-shally around until somebody else figures it out for him—like you did the last time."

"That was an unusual situation," Ruby told Enid, keeping her voice even and as neutral as possible, refraining from pointing out that Enid herself had been instrumental in blocking justice "the last time."

Enid sniffed again and Ruby pictured her tight lips and speculative eyes, and the gray sausage curls Alice Rolley probably could have sculpted with her eyes closed.

"Maybe," Enid said in an ominous tone touched by sanctimony. "But if Carly expects to be reelected sheriff this fall, he'd better get on the ball."

"I'm leaving for town in a minute," Ruby told Enid, trying gently to extricate herself from the conversation, "so I'll have to hang up."

"Oh. That reminds me why I called," Enid said loudly in Ruby's ear, back to business. "I've taken charge of Alice's luncheon. You couldn't expect Roseanne to know the first thing about putting together a luncheon. Could you make a nice Jell-O salad? The grocery store's having a sale on that good chunky canned fruit cocktail, the kind that has sliced bananas in it, so you could pick some up while you're in town."

"I'd be glad to," Ruby told her, grateful the conversation had evolved beyond Carly and Alice Rolley. "Anything else?"

"No. I just want it to be nice for poor Alice. Franklin makes the best pies in town, but with his mother lying in the funeral parlor murdered, I don't suppose he'd be working in the bakery, would he?"

"Probably not," Ruby agreed.

After Ruby hung up, she sat at the kitchen table opposite Jesse, who was lost in one of her insect books, her lips moving as she read, and added *fruit cocktail* to her grocery list.

Enid Shea hadn't been the first person Ruby had heard voicing doubts about Carly's abilities as county sheriff. Waters County voters couldn't forgive Carly for the mean trick he'd played on them. They'd elected him to be the sheriff his father was and he hadn't measured; no way had he come within a mile of his dad in the eyes of the voters.

Ruby picked a toast crumb off the table on the end of her finger and licked it off. Alice had been a pillar of Sable, a good woman whose senseless death left everyone reeling and feeling vulnerable. Emotions were high. Enid was right: Carly had better be on top of this one.

Sable was a stubborn town—and successful—because it ignored all progress in the rest of Michigan, not caring what the rest of the country did, either. Most of its businesses had been founded and continued by families who didn't expect to get rich, just to get by. Sableites shopped where their parents had shopped, with no patience for the flashy choices of Wal-Marts, suspicious of every chain store except Dairy Queen and NAPA Auto Parts.

The only substantial changes that had taken place in the two-block downtown's 150-year history came whenever a store burned down and was replaced by a more modern building. Despite its stubborn self, Sable was becoming "quaint," lost America, the kind of town that made a good backdrop for television spots about the good old days: streets without parking meters, pots of flowers on every porch, and American flags decorating the street corners. It was only a matter of time before some national politician pulled into town with a crew lugging lights and cameras.

The town's name was pronounced—without apology or explanation—"Sobble," not "Sable," and strangers were rarely corrected; they just became the object of smug glances, branded as outsiders. Logging of hardwoods and CCC-planted red pine still flourished in the county, but Sable lived by the seasons: in summer, tourists stopped by on their way to Lake Michigan or the surrounding inland lakes; in autumn, sightseers drove through in search of colorful fall leaves, then came the deer hunters. Snowmobilers buzzed along the winter roads, and in spring came the morel mushroom hunters. The residents of Sable depended on outsiders for the money that let them live there and resented the necessity of catering to the whims of outsiders to get it.

Ruby pulled into an angled slot in front of Mary

Jean's real estate office. "I'll get your door from the outside," she told Jesse. Mystifyingly, her Pinto station wagon was becoming a "classic," drawing even a few admiring glances, but the passenger door hinge had begun to rust out and it screeched, resisting movement.

The street was quieter than usual. Three women talked urgently together in front of the dime store's Fourth of July display. A young mother pushed a stroller past. Ruby entered through Mary Jean's office door, which was blocked open by a ceramic pig; Jesse was beside her, hugging her beetle identification book.

Insects were Jesse's consuming summer passion. She read all the books she could find and then reread them, memorizing and reciting orders, families, and species, suddenly announcing bug facts in a dreamy voice. It was the exactness of entomology that drew Jesse, Ruby believed, the predictability of the science. Jesse didn't want to collect and pin the insects; she only wanted to make sense of their tiny ordered lives.

Mary Jean, her curly dark hair falling into her face, was huddled over her computer, frowning, fingers racing over the keyboard. She'd moved into this office six months ago and still couldn't afford to replace the orange shag carpet or the fake wood paneling, relics of the past.

"Boy, am I glad to see you two," Mary Jean said, glancing up from her computer and rolling her eyes. "Barbara is driving me crazy and I've threatened to send her to one of those church camps. Right now

## Cut and Dry

she's trying to find my checkbook so she can figure out if it's an empty threat or if I can really afford it."

"Can you?" Ruby asked.

Mary Jean snorted and lifted a thick manila folder from her desk. "If the sale of the Carters' farm falls through, I won't even be able to afford macaroni and cheese for dinner. I'll have to grovel to Pete for help."

Mary Jean had the happiest divorce Ruby had ever seen. She'd left her husband, Pete, six months ago, the day she'd received her real estate license, and moved her daughter, Barbara, and herself into the apartment over her new office. Now Pete pursued her with teenage enthusiasm. A month ago they'd been caught making love in the old bandstand by the high school. Charlie Jones, who'd seen them with his own eyes, had announced to everybody in the Knotty Pine restaurant the next morning that "they weren't doing it the normal way." The town didn't know what to make of them.

Mary Jean called over her shoulder toward the back of the office, "Jesse's here, Barbara. Put my purse away." She touched Jesse's shoulder. "Go on back, honey."

In high school, Mary Jean Scribner had been a plain wallflower, the last to be picked when choosing up sides, overlooked for giggly girlish friendship. She'd never left Sable, but in the intervening years she'd cast off her shyness and developed a forthright voice and cynical worldliness. Since Ruby's return to Waters County, the plumpish dark-haired woman had become her closest friend.

"Business is at a standstill in town," Mary Jane said as she switched off her computer. "All anyone can talk about is Alice Rolley. Who and why. Do you have any inside info?"

"Not yet," Ruby said, dropping her bag on a wood-and-Naugahyde chair.

"Tell me, is it normal to feel guilty about every mean thing you've said when a person dies?" Mary Jean asked, running both hands through her shoulder-length hair, flattening it to her head.

"I think so," Ruby told her. "Yes, I know it is." Through her mind ran a few trite but true phases about not knowing until it's gone gone gone.

"Well, that's a relief. Alice was so damn *good* I confess I sometimes doubted she was for real. Doubted it out loud and in public and now I wish I'd kept my mouth shut." She waved a hand toward the coffeepot beside her desk. "Have some, if you want. It's only an hour old, the third pot today. People keep drifting in and out, everyone's in shock about poor Alice." Her face saddened. "People don't like to be alone when something this awful happens."

"What are they saying?" Ruby asked as she poured coffee into a styrofoam cup, thinking how Alice's name was hardly mentioned now without that adjective: "poor" Alice.

"Mostly they're asking. Who could have done this and why and how horrible it is." Mary Jean shook her head. "And it is, too. Horrible, I mean. There are a few people around here who'd make more plausible victims than Alice. I've heard some complaints about

# Cut and Dry

Carly not having caught the killer yet, and doubting he ever will."

"Carly don't get no respect," Ruby said. She sipped her coffee, wondering what made coffee so satisfying, so *necessary*, even in the heat of summer.

"Ain't it the truth?" Mary Jean countered. "But we need somebody to blame until the murderer's found and Carly's our best target. There are a few theories, none too wild—yet. A lot of talk about how Alice's family is bearing up. I heard Roseanne couldn't stop screaming when Carly told her her mother was dead. He had to call Dr. Doyle to give her a sedative."

"What about Franklin?" Ruby asked. She sat on the edge of the chair so her bare skin wouldn't stick to the Naugahyde.

Mary Jean nodded across the street toward the yellow awning on the bakery where Franklin was renowned for the best pies in the county. "I guess when Carly sent Mac McCutcheon to the bakery to tell him about poor Alice, Franklin punched Mac in the mouth. Laid him flat out on the floor in the middle of the pots and pans. Mac probably deserved it. I hate to think how he broke the news. Some days Mac's a bastard and some days the bastard is Mac. And Jumbo . . ." Mary Jean shook her head and refilled her ceramic cup. Its inside rim was brown with coffee stains. "That family."

"What about Jumbo?" Ruby asked.

"I don't know, but it's weird, isn't it, that Fanny found Alice's body when she showed up for work? The word is that Alice was killed the night before.

You'd think Jumbo would have missed his wife when she didn't come home all night long."

"You'd think so," Ruby agreed turning her styrofoam cup, seeing the teeth marks she'd absently made around the edge.

"Unless he was used to her staying out all night. Alice was good-looking for her age but I've never heard she had a love life going on the side."

"Maybe Jumbo didn't miss her because *he* didn't come home," Ruby suggested.

Mary Jean's eyes brightened. She picked up a pencil from her desk and turned it between her fingers. "*That* makes more sense, doesn't it? Jumbo's always had a nasty reputation for fooling around, you know."

Ruby did know. But he and Alice had remained together for forty-five years; it couldn't have been too serious.

"Are you going to the funeral?" Mary Jean asked.

"Enid Shea's assigned me the job of making a Jell-O salad so I'll attend the luncheon."

"Me too. I'm supposed to bring pickles, 'nice dills'. Give that woman a chance to boss people around and she's in heaven. Will Hank be there?"

Ruby shook her head. "He's busy on a hardwood management job by Cadillac. He'll be back Friday night."

Mary Jean took Ruby's left hand and studied it, bare except for Ruby's mother's silver baby ring on her pinky. "No commitments?"

Ruby laughed and pulled her hand from Mary Jean's. Her nails needed trimming. "Not yet."

"If you get bored with him, there's a line-in-waiting. I might even throw over Pete and join the chase."

Hank Holliday, a consulting forester, had arrived in Waters County a few months earlier than Ruby. He'd aroused suspicion in the rural area with his revolutionary ideas of managing forests on private land: cutting trees while *saving* forests, assuring that the landowner received good money besides. At first an outcast, once he'd proven himself he'd become a man of interest among the female population. But by then Ruby and Hank, the two outsiders, had already found each other.

"Leave Jesse here tonight and I'll bring her to the luncheon tomorrow," Mary Jean suggested. "Maybe I'll take the girls to Lake Michigan after I close up this place. It'll be cooler on the lake. Barbara has an extra swimsuit she can wear."

"I don't know . . ." Ruby began.

"Don't worry about her. I'd call you and the doctor the instant anything went wrong. You first."

"I know, but . . ."

Mary Jean squeezed Ruby's arm. "It'll be okay. Give her a little more room, Ruby; she's ready."

When Ruby left Mary Jean's office, tamping down a stab of unease as she left a willing Jesse behind, the blue sheriff's car was parked beside her Pinto. Carly leaned against the hood, gazing down at a torn sheet of paper. Sheriff Carly Joyce was in his early forties, thin and upright, wearing a hat even in the heat because, people said, he was self-conscious about his balding head. He'd been called Carly all his life to distinguish him from his father, Carl Senior. "Carly" had stuck, even though his father had died seven years ago.

"Hi, Carly," Ruby said.

"Ruby," he acknowledged somberly. Her face reflected back at her from his glasses, her nose distorted. He held out the torn paper. It was an announcement printed from a computer, using various styles and sizes of type. SAVE AMERICA! it cried out in Roman caps across the middle of the page and went on to announce in italics a meeting for citizens who love the constitution. *Join the First Americans.*

"What is this?" Ruby asked, scanning the page. With all its various styles of type, it looked as if a kid with a new printer had experimented with all his print fonts. "The First Americans? Is that a Native American group?"

"Not at all," Carly said. He touched the words *First Americans*. His hands were long and narrow. "They're referring to the first Americans after the Constitution was signed, back when George Washington was our leader. Constitutionalists, they call themselves sometimes, wanting to get back to the letter of the law. Saving America for Americans."

"Those groups have been around awhile, haven't they?" she asked. "I didn't know they had a name. 'First Americans,'" she repeated. "They're not organizing like the militia, are they? Here in Sable?"

"Not quite the same. Similar ideas but supposedly without the violence. There are literally hundreds of

# Cut and Dry

these groups in the country. Around here, up until recently, it's been a bunch of guys complaining over their beer and pigs' feet, and I guess some of their complaints are legitimate." He snapped the paper with his thumb and forefinger. "Now these meetings . . . The organizers come in from outside the county, spread the word along with a healthy helping of dissatisfaction, and hightail it out of here before the repercussions."

"Who around here would attend meetings like these?" she asked, noting the date and time: seven-thirty tonight at the River Park shelter.

"You'd be surprised." He folded the paper into quarters, then once more, and slipped it into his shirt pocket. "But this is the least of my concerns." Carly's cheeks had a perpetual sag to them, pulling down the corners of his mouth and making his thin face hangdog morose.

"Were you waiting for me?" she asked.

"Yeah. I saw your car and then got sidetracked by this notice lying in the street. How are you?"

"Fine. But this is a sad thing about Alice."

He nodded, sticking a finger inside the rim of his cap and wiping away perspiration. A young boy walked past, glancing at Carly and holding his hand behind his back.

"Roger, have you got illegal fireworks again?" Carly asked.

"No way," the boy said, and took off running down the sidewalk, glancing back as if Carly were hot on his tail.

"Can I talk to you for a minute?" Carly asked Ruby. "Maybe in my car?"

"How about mine?" Ruby suggested. "Yours looks a little too . . . serious."

Carly moved the passenger seat back in Ruby's Pinto so he had more room for his legs. "Damn hot," he said. "I don't suppose this antique has air-conditioning."

"Only windows," Ruby said, rolling hers down all the way. After she'd burned her thigh on the hot plastic seats, she'd covered them with towels. "Any progress?"

"Not enough to suit anybody, including me," Carly said, tapping his fingers on his knee. He smelled of peppermint Lifesavers.

"*Did* Alice die during a robbery?" Ruby asked.

"It looks like burglary was the intent, but Alice had already deposited the day's receipts. She must have come back to the shop for something and surprised a robbery in progress."

"And she was strangled?"

Carly nodded. "In the back room. This part isn't out, at least I don't think it is: Whoever did it used a hair dryer cord from an old dryer she kept in back."

"I hadn't heard that," Ruby told him.

"Good. Maybe we can still keep a few things out of the public gossip mills."

"Were there signs of a struggle?" Ruby asked, picturing Alice. She'd been attractive, slender, but in her early sixties. What chance had she had against someone younger and stronger?

## Cut and Dry

Carly nodded. "Some. Supplies had been knocked from storage shelves. A chair was on its side. Not much, really."

Carly shifted uncomfortably on the seat; it wasn't just the heat or the conversation about Alice's death.

"What was it you wanted to discuss with me?" Ruby asked, pulling one leg onto the seat and facing Carly.

He fingered a split in the plastic of the padded dash, waiting at least thirty seconds before he spoke, and then the words were careful, rehearsed. "You've probably heard there are people who hope I lose the sheriff's election this fall," he said, gazing through the windshield at nothing.

"Something like that," Ruby told him.

"Some people believe I'm already a lame duck and they're not being as cooperative as I'd like." He was red-faced, uncomfortable, and Ruby tried to help him out.

"And you'd like me to keep my eyes and ears open," she finished for him.

He turned back to her, his face a mixture of relief and embarrassment. "Yeah, I guess that's what I'm trying to say. Nothing too active or investigatory, just let me in on whatever you hear. My budget's pared to the bone and I don't have much of a staff."

"Is Mac working on the case?" Ruby asked.

Carly's face darkened. "Not as much as he'd like to be," he said in a quick burst of words. "I've assigned him to other duties."

Ruby changed the subject. She ran her hands around the steering wheel, feeling the gummy buildup where her palms usually gripped the wheel. "Where was Jumbo?" she asked Carly. "Why didn't he notice Alice was gone all night?"

"He says they've kept separate rooms since Franklin moved out a couple of years ago. He claims it wasn't unusual for him and Alice to miss seeing each other for days at a time, what with his long hours at the mill and her shop and clubs and charities."

Ruby found that hard to believe; she knew what a house felt like when one of its occupants was missing, whether he or she was visible or not: achingly empty, hollow.

"Who was the last to see Alice alive, then?"

"As far as we know, Fanny and Katrina, her beauticians. Babs Prescott and her granddaughter were the shop's last appointment for the day. All three women and the little girl left together around five-thirty. After that, nothing."

"What about the bank teller?" Ruby asked. "Didn't you say Alice deposited the day's receipts?"

"In the night deposit." Carly reached behind him and pushed open the Pinto's rear window. "The bank's drive-up window closes at six so it was sometime after that. I'm thinking around seven or after."

"Was Alice molested?"

Carly shook his head and looked away. "The coroner checked."

A woman passing by with a bag of groceries glanced at the sheriff's car and then squinted into Ruby's, halting on the sidewalk for a better view. Her mouth formed an O. Then she gave her head a perplexed

## Cut and Dry

shake and hurried on, looking back at them once more.

"Well," Carly said, watching the woman. "Now I've fed the rumor machines a little more fodder. Sorry, Ruby."

"I don't care," Ruby said, and that was true, she didn't. She hadn't for years.

"I'll talk to you later," he said over the screech of the hinge as he opened the car door. He stood and straightened his pants legs, then leaned down and said through the open door, "In fact, I'd like to. Do you mind?"

"Because I'm on the right side of the law, you mean?" she asked, only half teasing.

"You've had some good ideas before," he told her, and then, more self-consciously, "I admire that. So what do you say? Is it okay?"

"Sure, call me whenever you want. I wouldn't mind," she told him, watching him salute her with his finger to the brim of his cap.

Ruby drove home by way of the strawberry field near her grandparents' old farm, intending to buy a quart of strawberries, but the unpainted plywood stand in front of the field stood empty. A sign scribbled on cardboard with a felt-tip marker was nailed to the front. CLOSED DUE TO DEATH, it read. Another family connected to Alice Rolley, she was sure.

She passed one of her favorite childhood spots: the little woods a mile from Gram's old place, full of slender dogwood trees growing beneath the oaks and maples. Every spring the creamy white star-shaped flowers had appeared on the naked branches before the rest of the larger trees leafed out, while the spring mud was still cold and ferns were still curled and pussy willows just budding—eerily white among the dark tree trunks, luminous on dusky spring evenings.

She'd taken Jesse for a ride that spring to see the flowering dogwoods, choosing a clear evening at twilight, anticipating Jesse's reaction to the sight.

But the dogwoods were gone. Not a single white flower bloomed in the little forest. Ruby couldn't help it; she'd cried in frustration and grief, thinking the trees had been cut down. But Hank had told her no. "Anthracnose," he'd said, the same sorrow in his voice that Ruby had felt. "A virulent form of necrotic blotch. One of those diseases that seem to come out of nowhere. It showed up about twenty years ago and raced through the species. Seventy percent of the wild dogwoods in the country are already affected."

The cabin without Jesse's presence was too silent. Ruby put away her groceries and then turned on the radio but it blared out too loud and gave her an uneasy sense that it hid unseen goings-on beneath its innocent music: an intruder; maybe even, she thought in a nervous unbidden fancy, Alice Rolley's killer searching for another solitary woman.

It was too hot to work on one of Gram's quilts, definitely too hot to exercise, and she was too restless to read. She abandoned the cabin for the sunny dock, but even the wooden boards felt blistering hot be-

# Cut and Dry

neath her bare feet. Across the lake, she spotted the stranger on the front porch of the Barber cabin and realized she'd forgotten to ask Carly about him. Next time, definitely.

Finally, Ruby retreated to the cooler cabin and called her old boss, Ron Kilgore, in California, eager to talk to someone who didn't know about Alice Rolley's death, a respite from all the unhappy discussion.

But it was DeEtta Becket who answered. Ruby had helped DeEtta leave Sable the autumn before, recommending her to Ron as a receptionist for his detective agency.

"Oh, Ruby," DeEtta said. "Mom told me all about Alice's murder. Are you working on it? You should be. I can't believe it. She was so good to everybody."

After holding a conversation identical to those she'd been having the last two days, Ruby asked, "Is Ron there?"

"Uh-uh, he went to the city for the afternoon." Ruby smiled to hear DeEtta refer to San Francisco as "the city." Already she was sounding like a Californian. "Did you get that last job all right?" DeEtta asked. "I think Ron called it the Darrow job?"

"I did. Tell him I'll get it back to him next week."

Ron provided Ruby with her main source of income. He'd expanded his agency, concentrating more of his business in forgery and dropping most of his divorce cases. "I want to get out of the motel back lots with my camera," he'd said. No longer just handling wills, bad checks, and threatening notes, now he'd moved into authenticating historical documents. With

Americans' mad passion for collecting, when baseball cards and porcelain banks in the shape of cartoon characters could bring hundreds of dollars, the business in historical documents and signatures was booming.

After a rocky and reluctant start, Ruby had taken to historical documents with as much passion as she had present-day forgery crimes. The sensuousness of vellum and early laid paper, the deterioration of inks, the elegant penmanship, the possibility that the note written by a historic personage was *real;* she loved it all. In her loft right now waited a purported bill of sale for *one used oak desk,* written in pencil by Clarence Darrow, the "Darrow job" DeEtta had referred to.

Historical and criminal documents weren't all Ruby examined. Whenever a famous—or infamous—person died, Ron was approached by collectors to authenticate autographs that suddenly might quadruple in value, death being the greatest personal and career enhancer. "Death is an elevator," Ron said. Documents went back and forth between Michigan and California by FedEx, their authenticity determined in Ruby's lab in the cabin's loft.

"Mom says it's hot back there," DeEtta said.

"It's this miserable humidity," Ruby told her. "How is it there?"

"Oh, I guess it's nice."

Ruby caught the wistfulness in DeEtta's voice. "Are you homesick?" she asked.

"Not really, but when something bad happens, I

## Cut and Dry

feel I should come back for . . . I don't know, just to be there." She sighed. "Hug Jesse for me, okay?"

Ruby said she would and then, giving herself up to the heat, went to her kitchen to create the Jell-O salad requested by Enid Shea.

# Chapter 3

The generous luncheons that came afterward were as much a custom in Waters County as the funerals themselves. Held in the VFW hall or the Elks' lodge or a church basement, long tables of food, more long tables covered by white paper for the mourners, filling whatever room was chosen. Through hamburger casseroles and gelatin salads, sadness was transformed into a philosophic acceptance of death, even gaiety.

Alice Rolley's luncheon was held in the community room of the Presbyterian church, the church she'd faithfully attended since she was a baby. It was too small for the crowd, really, but the rear double doors were open to the newly paved parking lot, and people milled between the community room and more tables set outside in the killer sunshine.

Ruby had skipped the funeral—she'd endured all the funerals she intended—and arrived at the luncheon in time to pay her respects and eat a piece of cherry cobbler.

"Why not somewhere with air-conditioning?" Mary Jean Scribner asked Ruby irritably. "What's Jumbo

## Cut and Dry

got against a little cool air?" She pulled out the neck of her navy dress and blew down onto her shiny skin. "It's not like he couldn't afford it."

"You don't know that," Ruby said. She wore a cotton dress, loose enough that underwear was unnecessary.

Mary Jean snorted and released the neck of her dress. "*Everybody* knows that. The Rolleys have never hurt for money." She leaned her curly dark head closer to Ruby, and Ruby smelled expensive perfume.

"And the insurance," Mary Jean went on softly. "Nothing to sneeze at, I heard. Jumbo could quit Northern Timber tomorrow and buy himself a nice Winnebago and a lifelong supply of gas and spend the rest of his life seeing America. That's great cherry cobbler, isn't it? Enid Shea made it." She waved her fork at Enid, who bustled between tables, dishcloth in one hand, dirty cups in the other. "Being a great cook is almost compensation for having the meanest mouth in the county."

"Green is more traditional for funerals," Enid had told Ruby when she'd delivered her salad to the church kitchen, doubtfully eying Ruby's fruit-studded peach Jell-O. "I wish you would have used lime. I thought you knew."

Two squealing toddlers impervious to the heat chased each other between Ruby and Mary Jean, and behind Ruby a woman said, "It's because of the hole in the ozone layer. The sun just falls straight through the atmosphere and overheats the earth. That's why all the frogs are dying, too. Ask Roseanne; she'll tell you."

Ruby glanced over at Jumbo Rolley, Alice's husband, who'd been holding the same untouched plate of apple pie for the past half hour, standing near a green felt banner of Bible verses. He towered over everyone in the room, standing six inches above the man he was talking to: timberman Silas Shea, a big man himself.

The two men, and most every other man at the luncheon, had removed their ties and jackets, and the underarms of their white shirts were circled dark with perspiration. Jumbo and Silas spoke earnestly and Ruby guessed they weren't discussing Alice's death, more likely the falling price of beech logs or the stand of dead oaks along Bell Road killed by gypsy moths. Any expression beyond a few words of sympathy would be inappropriate, at least here at the luncheon, where dwelling on sorrow was considered bad taste.

Ruby had forgotten Jumbo's real name until she read it in Alice Rolley's obituary: Leo. He was in his early sixties, called Jumbo for as long as anybody could remember. Always the biggest, her father had once said, from day one. "His mother used to tell him the other kids would catch up, but nobody around *here* ever did."

Jumbo looked a good ten years younger than his age: straight-backed, his hair thick and steely gray. Energy emanated from his big frame; Gram would have said Jumbo was a "doing man," not a "sitting man." He ran the headsaw on the hardwood line at

## Cut and Dry 39

Northern Timber, a job that had kept him fit and slender beyond his years but now had been mechanized to laser beams and button pushing, not much more physically strenuous than a desk job.

A cigar protruded from Jumbo's shirt pocket. He paused in his conversation with Silas Shea and raised his head as if he'd heard someone call his name. His eyes were small and deep-set, his skin tanned. Aside from his eyes, every other feature was . . . well, jumbo. Large flat forehead, high cheekbones, protruding nose and ears, a long chin that jutted forward, a wide mouth.

Jumbo scanned the room, his brows raised in question, and settled on Ruby, tipping his head and gazing at her quizzically. He pressed his lips together, his eyebrows relaxed, and he held her gaze for a few seconds without smiling. Then he nodded slightly and turned back to Silas.

Beside Ruby, Mary Jean asked, "What was that all about?"

Ruby shook her head. "I don't know. Probably nothing."

"That didn't look like 'nothing' to me," Mary Jean protested. "It looked like Jumbo had something up his sleeve." She shook her head and tsk-tsked. "And Alice barely cold."

"*That's* ridiculous," Ruby told her mildly. Since her divorce and rekindled romance with her ex-husband, Mary Jean had developed an abiding interest in all subjects salacious.

"Mmm," Mary Jean murmured. "Everybody knows

Jumbo was testing the waters long before Alice died. Living with a saint has its stresses. Likes them young, they say."

A woman leaned close to Mary Jean and said in a harsh low voice, "Mary Jean Scribner, how could you talk like that here? And *now*?"

It was Roseanne Rolley, Alice and Jumbo's daughter. Her face blazed red. She was a big woman who scorned makeup and wore her hair pulled back in a severe ponytail, with hands and facial features large like her father's. Her tan emphasized her straight white teeth. Roseanne, who was rarely seen in clothing other than jeans and shirts, today wore a blue dress printed with roses, and shiny black flats.

Mary Jean looked up at Roseanne steadily, no sign of embarrassment or apology on her face. "Are you eavesdropping, Roseanne Rolley?" she asked.

"I couldn't help overhear you," Roseanne began angrily, striking one thick hand into the palm of the other. "My father's one thing, but my mother . . ." She sniffed and her eyes filled with tears.

Mary Jean's face softened. She reached forward and took Roseanne's shaking hand in both of hers, her own eyes damping up. "I forget myself sometimes. It's my big mouth." She dropped Roseanne's hand and made zipping motions across her lips. "Forgive me, okay?"

Roseanne nodded, her lips tight, and turned to Ruby. "And you, Ruby Crane. Listening to this talk after all the help my mother gave you."

"I'm sorry about your mother, Roseanne," Ruby

said, wanting to touch her as spontaneously as Mary Jean had, but stopped by the coolness in Roseanne's eyes and by a regretful little part of herself.

"Thank you," Roseanne said stiffly.

Ruby and Mary Jean watched her walk away. The fabric of Roseanne's dress strained across her upper back. "I could kick myself," Mary Jean said. "I spent so many years inside my little shell scraping and grinning, it's like the words just leap out of my mouth now." She shook her head. "I didn't mean to . . . Damn it."

Roseanne sat down heavily on a folding chair at the end of one of the long paper-covered tables and in a moment was surrounded by murmuring and consoling women, one of them Ruby's great-aunt Magda.

"I've seen her name in the *Waters County Proclamator* the last few months," Ruby said. Roseanne had been three years ahead of Ruby in school, in her sister's class, a solitary, overemotional girl passionate about horses but indifferent to her studies.

Mary Jean nodded. "Roseanne's finally found her mission in life: evangelical environmentalism. At least it got her to move out of her parents' house." She sighed. "But as usual, Roseanne took it to the limit."

Ruby had read Roseanne's name in connection with protests regarding wetlands, deer kills, and clear-cutting. One of those nonscientific crusaders who spoke from the heart and made good copy. Roseanne's protests weren't unreasonable, and in fact were mild by the California standards Ruby had known. But here in

Waters County, Roseanne's stood out as a single strident voice: extreme and flaky.

"Her views must put Roseanne at odds with her father," Ruby said, "when his livelihood depends on mowing down as many trees as possible."

"They already were at odds," Mary Jean told her. "He treated her like the redheaded stepchild." She took two swallows of iced tea. "I forgot to tell you. I promised Barbara and Jesse we'd take them to the fireworks over Lake Michigan on the Fourth."

"Are they any good?" Ruby asked, remembering the fizzling displays years ago.

"My dear, Pere lets its backstreets go to hell in order to finance these fireworks. Schools go without textbooks, libraries without book budgets. Anything to reel in the tourists."

Pere, situated on Lake Michigan, was the largest town in Waters County, and the feeling was that county taxes went disproportionately to Pere to entice tourists.

Mary Jean beckoned Ruby farther into a corner, away from the bustle of the luncheon. They stood behind two older women who were sharing a piece of pie. "I saw you talking to Carly outside my office yesterday. What did he say?"

"He said Alice probably died during a robbery," she told Mary Jean, not saying any more than Carly had already made public. "Alice made the beauty parlor's night deposit at the bank and Carly thought she might have gone back to the parlor for something she forgot.

## Cut and Dry 43

Whoever killed her didn't realize she'd already removed the money from the shop."

"Do you believe that?" Mary Jean asked.

"Which part?" Ruby asked.

"That it was a robbery?"

"It's as good a place to start as any," Ruby told her.

"What did he say about Alice not being found until the next morning?" Mary Jean asked, glancing over at Jumbo, who was nodding solemnly at a comment of Silas Shea's, his pie plate dangerously tipped. "I mean, *was* Jumbo home?"

"We didn't get into the details," Ruby said to Mary Jean, noncommittal despite Mary Jean's grin and expectant eyes. Whatever Carly told Ruby went no further; she valued his confidences too much.

"And she did it," one of the elderly women in front of them was saying gleefully, sotto voce. "She went out there after dark and peed right on his grave," and the two broke into muffled laughter, bumping shoulders with one another.

Mary Jean's eyes widened. She met Ruby's eyes, and Ruby could see the laughter bubbling there, mirroring her own. She grabbed Mary Jean's arm and pulled her toward the food table, trying to suppress a giggle.

"Here," Mary Jean said, shoving a napkin in Ruby's hand. "Wipe your face. Oh God," and she clutched her chest.

"But with my coloring," a voice said close to Ruby's shoulder, "would you recommend more of a beige-toned base?"

She turned to see a red-haired woman standing in front of Fanny and Katrina, Alice Rolley's two beauticians, who studied the woman's face critically before nodding their heads and whispering to one another.

"The two fates," Mary Jean murmured. "Or maybe Mutt and Jeff." She tipped her head. "Or Laurel and Hardy, Cheech and Chong."

"Stop," Ruby demanded, catching another giggle rising in her throat. Every description of Mary Jean's was perfectly apt. The two beauticians were as unlike as possible and as inseparable as twins, sharing a car, a job, even a house overlooking the river.

Katrina was tall, thin, elegant, and black, the only black person in Sable. "But she's light black," Enid Shea had said, as if her blackness were an excusable flaw, like an unfortunately placed mole.

Rumor was that Katrina was the secret daughter of some Sable man's dalliance. Rumor was she'd run away from a drug dealer in Detroit who'd beat her. Rumor was she'd had an affair with a Sable man who'd been job hunting in Detroit and had followed him home.

But Ruby had observed Katrina and Fanny's fond glances and habit of touching one another and guessed the opposite. Katrina had arrived in Sable a year ago, she'd heard, a month after Fanny had attended a stylists' conference in Detroit.

Fanny was tiny and plump with freckles and big hair that used to be the color of maple bark. Both young women were well liked, their lives a series of small adventures that were either "great" or "not so great."

## Cut and Dry 45

Finished with their consultation, Fanny and Katrina turned to Ruby and Mary Jean. "That's a great color on you, Mary Jean," Fanny said, touching her sleeve. "It brings out your eyes."

"Mmm-hmm," Katrina agreed. "All those little blue flecks."

"Thanks," Mary Jean said, smoothing her dress front. "You're keeping the shop open?"

Fanny nodded, raising her hand to finger one dangling earring, her eyes troubled. "We didn't plan to open right away, so soon after, I mean, you know, but people kept calling us at home and asking us to do their hair for the funeral. So Jumbo said to go ahead and open up." Fanny leaned close to Ruby. "Can you believe it?" she whispered. "Alice left the shop to *us.*" She put her finger to her lips. "It's not official yet but Jumbo said that's what she put in her will. We were so surprised!"

"Congratulations," Ruby said.

The tears spilled and Katrina handed Fanny a tissue. "Don't mess up your eyes," she warned Fanny gently, and to Ruby she added, "No congratulations, please. We've dreamed of having our own shop, but not like this."

There was no recrimination in her voice, but Ruby apologized anyway. "That was thoughtless; I'm sorry."

"We all do it, talking without thinking," Fanny said. "The things I've said . . ." She blew her nose and patted Ruby's hand before she walked off toward the dessert table with Katrina.

Mary Jean grinned at Ruby. "Neither one of us is in top diplomatic form today, I guess."

The crowd began to thin out as the afternoon wore on and the temperature nudged one hundred, the mugginess weighting every breath. Makeup ran, foreheads glistened and ankles swelled, flesh and clothing stuck to furniture. The coffee urn was still three-quarters full, but the iced tea had run out and been replaced by ice water in sweaty glasses. Conversation dulled. In a corner beneath a fan, Mary Jean's daughter, Barbara, and Ruby's Jesse had curled up and fallen asleep on a paper tablecloth they'd laid on the floor. Ruby gazed at the two still and perfect young faces and searched for a word. Estivation, that was it: hibernation during summer.

"You stop by in a couple of days," Ruby's aunt Magda said as she headed for the door, an empty casserole dish in her hand. "The raspberries are coming on in all this heat." She nodded toward Jesse. "They'll be good for her."

Aunt Magda was Gram's youngest sister, eighty-eight years old and still driving. She was bald from a bout of rheumatic fever as a child and wore a chestnut wig in public; she wore a tam—or went bareheaded—at home.

"I will," Ruby told her. "Tell Uncle Mack hello."

Aunt Magda waved her hand at Ruby and left, her back bent forward from osteoporosis. Ruby watched her, unconsciously straightening her own shoulders and spine.

Mary Jean poured a fresh glass of water, taking time

## Cut and Dry

to fish a few of the melting ice cubes from other glasses. "I saw Babs outside," she told Ruby, holding up the glass. "I'm taking this to her," heading toward the door of the community room and mumbling, "That damn Dick." Ruby spotted Enid Shea coming toward her and hastily followed Mary Jean through the double doors. The talk was that Babs Prescott, Alice's last appointment on the night she died, was taking it hard.

Outside, five men stood around the bed of Dick Prescott's new blue pickup parked in the dappled shade of a poplar tree, hands folded over the rails. Two beagles lay on burlap bags in the bed, against the shade of the sides, a plastic bowl of water between them. Ruby blinked in the sunlight and slipped on her sunglasses. The paved parking lot shimmered; a spot in the asphalt near the poplar looked soft, oily.

"All this legislation is what's wrong," a heavy man with rolled sleeves was saying, his voice rising in fervor, finger jabbing rhythmically on the metal rail. "It comes from the federal government right on down the line without us getting a word in. No say. Law on top of law. They put all those laws in effect and never repeal a single one of them. We're the bottom of the food chain. More of our rights disappear every day."

Heads nodded and the man went on. "The little guy loses out. He also said the Sixteenth Amendment was never legally ratified; the IRS is illegal and nobody wants *us* to know it. They kept it a secret from the taxpayer."

Mary Jean glanced at Ruby, her eyebrows raised.

Ruby shrugged, wondering who "he" was. The First Americans organizer Carly had talked about? Whoever had put up notices of the meeting at River Park?

"You should've been there, Dick," another man said, nodding to Dick Prescott. "He would have had something to say about your wetlands mess."

"I'll give the lawyer a chance first," Ruby heard Dick say.

The driver's door of the pickup stood open. Inside, Babs Prescott sat on the passenger side, her hands folded in the lap of her black dress, gazing straight ahead, the personification of long-suffering patience. Her eyes were bagged with dark circles and her dyed blond hair was stiff with hairspray that saved it from flattening out in the humidity.

Mary Jean ignored the men and leaned across the steering wheel, handing the glass to Babs, who jerked a little, startled, but took it, swallowing half the water in deep gulps. Babs was well preserved in a country way: her hair curled and back-combed out of fashion, her eyeshadow parakeet blue and lipstick a berry slash. She was bosomy, the kind of woman who, thirty years earlier, had driven boys crazy by wearing tight sweaters, someone who'd been held up to Ruby as a warning when she was a teenager, a girl who "had" to get married. Ruby had already known how to avoid *that* situation. She had always suspected the warning *hadn't* been that if you fooled around you might "have" to get married, but that you might mess up and "have" to marry somebody like Dick.

Bab's husband looked up from the tailgate of the

## Cut and Dry 49

pickup and frowned at Mary Jean. "You don't need to wait on her," he told Mary Jean who merely looked at him over the pickup bed without expression and waited for Babs to finish the water.

Dick Prescott was, as Mary Jean said, a dick. A blustering ruddy-faced man who kept rabbit dogs, bird dogs, and retrievers and hunted whatever he felt like whenever he wanted, any time of year, in season or out. He was a blocky man, not overweight—yet—but solid, his brown hair in a buzz cut, receding so that in the sunlight he appeared bald.

Ruby stepped up beside Mary Jean and smiled at Babs, who sat panting in the heat of the cab, her flushed face shining with perspiration. The faux leather seats of the truck glistened in the sun, soft and smelling of baking man-made materials.

"How are you, Babs?" Ruby asked. Ruby had heard that Babs blamed herself for being in a hurry to get to her granddaughter's piano recital, for not staying and chatting with Alice like she usually did.

"I'm all right," Babs said in a whispery, girlish voice. "I'm just waiting for Dick." Her hands turned, one over the other, the knuckles white. "It's hot today."

Ruby left Mary Jean and Babs and went around the pickup to Dick Prescott, who was complaining about the building permit process. She stood behind him and touched his elbow, interrupting him. "I don't think Babs is feeling well," she said quietly.

"Jesus," the beefy man said, clapping a baseball cap on his head. "Women." But he wasted no time. "See you guys later," he told his friends, hauling himself into the cab and starting the truck while the men still leaned on the bed.

Mary Jean stepped back beside Ruby, holding the empty water glass and watching the shiny blue truck pull away. Ruby thought she caught a glimpse of Dick touching Babs's hair, but she wasn't sure. The gun rack behind the driver's seat blocked her view.

"At least he left the door open," Mary Jean said, "but I bet he wouldn't have let a single one of his dogs sit inside so long in the heat. I can't figure out why Babs . . ." She stopped. "To each her own, I guess," she continued as they headed back inside.

As Ruby walked toward the two sleeping teenagers to wake Jesse, Jumbo Rolley crossed the room toward her, extending a hand to stop her. He smelled of Old Spice aftershave and sweat, and his small eyes were red, his expression still slightly stunned. The plate of pie he'd held earlier was gone, replaced by a sodden white handkerchief that he mopped across his forehead before he spoke.

"Are you going to be home later?" he asked Ruby, his raspy voice low, nodding to the north, toward her distant cabin.

"I plan to be, why?" she asked him. She had to raise her head to look into his big face. Otherwise she'd find herself staring into the center of his chest.

"I might stop by," he said.

"Is it something we could discuss now?" she asked, but he waved his hand and shook his head, swaying it like a caged bear's, then walked away, saying again, "I might stop by."

## Cut and Dry

❖ ❖ ❖

"Stop, Mom," Jesse said. She said it without urgency because Jesse rarely spoke with urgency, a fact that Ruby was accustomed to and why she immediately hit the brakes. Their little car shimmied on the gravel of Blue Road and shuddered to a stop, raising dust. As soon as the car came to rest, the open windows were useless; no more breeze. A gnat flew inside, as if it had been racing alongside the car waiting for this very chance, and bumped at Ruby's eyes. She swatted at it and asked, "What is it?"

"Back there," Jesse said, pointing into the trees behind them. They were a quarter mile from the wooden bridge that crossed the narrow little swamp that separated their driveway from Blue Road.

Blue Road traveled all the way around Blue Lake, cabins to one side and hardwood trees to the other. The leaves of milkweed, yellow rocket, and sassafras bushes were layered with road dust, the oiled gravel worn from the road's surface.

Ruby backed the Pinto, stopping at the end of the driveway that led to the Barber cabin, where the man who sat all day on his front porch lived. "Here?" Ruby asked Jesse. The Barber cabin was invisible, blocked by trees.

Jesse didn't answer, but she stared at the chained and padlocked bar across the driveway. The KEEP OUT sign hung crookedly. Using signs for target practice was a common sport in Waters County; the stranger's notice had already acquired three bullet holes and now resembled most every other rural sign in Waters County.

"What do you see?" Ruby asked her daughter. Grass and dandelions grew down the center of the two-track driveway. She couldn't spot any fresh tire prints in the soft sand.

Jesse looked long and hard at the shady lane that led through the trees to the Barber cabin; a sheen of perspiration glistened on her upper lip. The day was still: no breeze, no clouds, no relief.

"We can go now," Jesse finally said, turning in her seat and facing straight ahead.

Ruby put the Pinto in gear and slowly headed toward home, knowing that sooner or later whatever Jesse had seen would be explained; encouraging her to talk before she was prepared only frustrated her and lengthened the process.

Jesse sat with Spot beneath an oak tree, and Ruby was inside the cabin, washing dishes, fondly remembering her automatic dishwasher in Palo Alto, when she heard a vehicle approaching on the long driveway from Blue Road. Spot barked twice, halfheartedly doing her duty. The car was coming slowly through the trees, carefully taking the curves and ruts. She should have the narrow lane graded; she'd forgotten what four seasons did to a driveway.

Ruby glanced once more at Jesse gazing out at the quiet lake, then returned the crusty cereal bowl to the dishwater and dried her hands as she crossed the kitchen to the door.

## Cut and Dry

A red Ford pickup pulled up next to Ruby's Pinto. She recognized the big truck as Jumbo Rolley's: the tied-down CB antenna, the way the cab was raised off the lugged tires, not for looks but because it suited Jumbo's size. She checked her watch; they'd returned from Alice Rolley's luncheon only an hour ago. Jumbo had said he might stop by "later." He hadn't wasted any time.

Ruby rebuttoned her shirt and stood beside the cabin in her bare feet on a soft carpet of soldier moss, watching as Jumbo climbed heavily down from his pickup, his funeral clothes exchanged for jeans and a yellow polo shirt with an alligator on the pocket.

"Hello, Ruby," he said with a touch of formality, nodding once and asking, "How are you?" as if he hadn't just spoken to her an hour ago.

"I'm fine. Would you like a glass of iced tea?"

"No thanks." The big man glanced uncomfortably over Ruby's head, gazing along the pitch of the cabin's roof. Ruby waited.

"Alice collected all that money for you and your daughter last winter," he said. "Arranged transportation for your girl to attend that special school."

"I'll always be grateful," Ruby told him. "It would have been tough, impossible really, without her help."

"Mmm-hmm," Jumbo said. He nodded, rocking back on his heels. "I want to hire you," he said abruptly.

"To do what?" Ruby asked, genuinely puzzled.

Jumbo gave her a sharp, slightly irritated glance,

narrowing his small eyes. "To find out who killed my wife. How much do you charge?"

"Talk to Carly," Ruby told him. "I'm not a detective."

"That's not what I heard," Jumbo said. He stood before her, a few feet farther away than most people did, as if he understood the power of his size, one hand in his jeans pocket. "Everybody says you solved the Asauskas deaths last year."

"Mina was my friend," Ruby told Jumbo, feeling as she always did at the mention of Mina's name, a slow beat of pain in her chest.

"I'll pay you good," Jumbo continued, confident he'd overcome any reason she had for saying no, not used to being denied.

"Carly will do a thorough job," Ruby said. "Besides, I'm *not* a detective. I'm a forgery specialist, a handwriting analyst. I don't have the training or license to be anything else."

Jumbo made a *pfft* sound with his lips and waved his hand in dismissal. "We do things around here without licenses and fancy de-grees. It's what you know that counts."

"And what do you think I know?" she asked him.

Jumbo shrugged. "Women, maybe." A deerfly landed on his arm. Ruby winced, imagining its digging bite. Jumbo didn't even flinch.

"Women?" Ruby repeated.

Jumbo nodded. "Alice's friends, the beauticians in the shop. They might tell you things they won't tell Carly."

"Did you love Alice?" Ruby suddenly asked.

Jumbo flushed and Ruby bet he'd rarely mentioned the word *love* when Alice was alive, if ever. "She was a good wife," he said.

"But did you love her?" Ruby persisted.

"I'd like her to be alive," he said, kicking at a clump of quack grass with his huge foot. "And . . ." He stopped.

Ruby held her breath, sensing that Jumbo was about to get to the real reason he wanted to hire Ruby's services. She remembered what Mary Jean had implied about Jumbo fooling around on Alice. "Is there something you hope I'll find out before Carly does?" she asked.

His eyes shifted into the trees and he wiped at his mouth with the back of his hand. "Maybe."

Every fiber of her body told her to keep her nose out of Jumbo's business. She wasn't a detective and couldn't claim to be; she'd been a high school dropout who'd become a detective's secretary who'd become a forgery specialist. Her expertise lay in disguised handwriting, papers and inks. She sat at her table tucked in the cabin's loft and solved paper puzzles, not murder and mayhem.

But Ruby Crane also possessed an abiding curiosity, and she knew it. She was being offered the opportunity to hear Jumbo Rolley's secret, maybe a hint as to why Alice Rolley had died. The hook dangled in front of her.

"If I were to do a little looking," Ruby said slowly, cautiously, watching Jumbo's eyes, "only a little, and if

I came up with information that would help Carly, I'd give it to him. He's the law, not me, and I won't stand in his way."

"I understand that," Jumbo said, nodding. "I'd respect that. And in fact, that would be a good idea."

"Why?" Ruby asked, suspicious.

Jumbo shifted uncomfortably. "There's somebody I don't want Carly to come down on too hard. I thought . . . well, maybe if you talked to her and then told Carly what she had to say, he'd leave her alone."

"Jeez, Jumbo," Ruby said, folding her arms. "Are you saying you really *weren't* home the night Alice died? You were with another woman and you didn't tell the sheriff?"

"I wasn't thinking too fast," Jumbo said. "The shock and everything. You know how it is."

Ruby did, but she didn't care to remember. "Who was the woman?"

"Will you take the case?" he asked, sounding too TV-ish.

"I'll look into it, yes," Ruby said. "So who was it?"

He looked down at his feet, an oversize boy admitting to wrongdoing. "Tracee Ferral," he said in a low voice.

Ruby couldn't help it. "Tracee Ferral?" she repeated. "You've been having an affair with Tracee? She's younger than your own children."

Ruby saw Tracee in her mind: an ex-Miss Color Festival in her early thirties, married at least once, overweight and giggly, perpetually suntanned, her blond hair streaked. Ruby remembered seeing Tracee

## Cut and Dry 57

in the chair in the Wak 'n Yak. "Didn't Alice do Tracee's hair?" she asked Jumbo.

Jumbo shrugged, but she could tell from his face that he was aware his dead wife had frosted his lover's hair. What was a young woman like Tracee doing having an affair with a man as old as Jumbo Rolley?

"Talk to her," Jumbo said. "Then tell Carly."

"It sounds like you're more concerned about having an alibi than discovering who killed Alice," Ruby told him.

"That's not true," he said through tight lips. "I'm just suggesting you begin with Tracee."

"I will," Ruby said. "But I can't promise you I'll go any further than that."

"That's fine." Jumbo turned and put one hand on the door handle of his pickup. "I appreciate this, Ruby, and I know how this looks to you, but I did . . . care about Alice."

Ruby watched Jumbo's pickup disappear into the trees that closed in around her driveway. Alice Rolley had been murdered while her husband was having an affair with a woman half his age?

What kind of woman went to her lover's wife to have her hair done? She tried to picture Alice standing over Tracee in the styling chair. Had she known? If Ruby had been Alice, she'd have strangled Tracee with the hair dryer cord. *That* would be a murder that made perfect sense.

She shuddered and rounded the cabin toward the oak where Jesse had been sitting. Jesse wasn't there. Neither was Spot. Ruby felt panic rising into her throat. She turned and ran to the cabin, through the porch and into the big main room. "Jesse?" she called. "Spot?"

The cabin glowed in the afternoon sun, the toffee-colored log walls fragrant in the heat, but there was no one inside. It was empty. She ran back outside and called Jesse's name as she raced toward the shore of Blue Lake. There was no answer.

# Chapter 4

As soon as Ruby reached the narrow beach she realized that the twelve-foot canoe she'd bought for Jesse that spring was gone. Ruby herself had left the green canoe tied to the dock after a quick paddle at dawn that morning instead of overturning it on the beach as she usually did. She raised her hand to her forehead, searching the flat water of Blue Lake for the little craft.

"Spot?" she called again, but there was no answer. The dog had gone with Jesse. Spot was protective, but the image of the big three-legged dog in Jesse's narrow canoe wasn't much reassurance.

A speedboat motored leisurely past farther out on the water, a young woman in a brief red suit sitting on its foredeck. A half-dozen kids swam off a raft in front of a group of family cabins on Strawhill Point, their voices magnified over water. But she couldn't spot the outline of her daughter paddling a canoe anywhere on the lake.

Blue Lake was a large body of water, though, roughly shaped like a lumpy fist with an extended thumb, and not all of it was visible from Ruby's dock. Ruby flipped over the old aluminum rowboat lying in the grass and shoved it into the water, the sand scrunching and protesting against its bottom. She jumped in, steadied herself, and pushed away from shore with an oar against the disturbed bottom sand, then sat down and secured both wooden oars in the locks.

Jesse was probably fine, just out of sight along one of the scallops of shoreline, but as Ruby pulled with all her strength on the scabby oars, scanning the water, she failed to convince herself.

Jesse sometimes accused Ruby of being overprotective; Jesse didn't know the half of it. There were nights when Ruby descended five or six times from her bedroom in the loft just to check her daughter's sleeping form, to reassure herself.

It was nearly a year since Jesse had been injured in the car accident that had killed Stan, Ruby's ex-husband. Jesse's only injury was invisible: a head injury. Against everyone's advice, even her own, Ruby had brought Jesse home to recuperate at the cabin on Blue Lake. In the midst of fear for her daughter's life, Ruby had longed for the familiarity of home, even if it was a home she'd once sworn she'd rather eat dirt than return to. Her instincts had been right; this place had been good for Jesse—and good for her, too, she reluctantly admitted; by living here she'd removed the sting of its memory, tamed it.

Jesse's healing was an uphill climb made by fits and starts and, frequently, heartwrenching backward

## Cut and Dry    61

slides. There was still more recovery ahead, but Jesse had recently plateaued, nearly there. Ruby thought of her daughter as Jesse-with-a-Difference. Subtle changes had taken place in her personality and abilities; once Ruby grew accustomed to them, they might alter again. Spontaneity had been traded for deliberateness, teenage sloppiness for a curious geometrical orderliness. Jesse was sweetly trusting, yet at times observed the people around her with piercing insightfulness. She sometimes forgot what was said to her in the midst of a conversation, but remembered the color of the dress she wore to her first day of kindergarten. "Expect anything," the doctor had said, and after a year, Ruby did.

Sweat poured from Ruby's body, attracting gnats and stubborn deerflies; her arms were slick against her sides. She hauled backward on the oars, turning to view the lake in every direction, the sluggish rowboat lumbering through the water as if it hauled an anchor. The oarlocks screeched with each pull. Why hadn't she bought Jesse a flaming red or bright yellow canoe, instead of forest green?

Just as she felt the cold nudges of panic in her chest, the certainty of disaster, she turned her head to the left, toward the shaded shoreline in front of the Barber cabin. There, partially hidden by the graceful branches of the willow tree, was Jesse's green canoe, pulled partway on shore, its stern end bobbing gently in the water.

On the porch of the Barber cabin, she spotted reddish gold hair and then recognized Jesse sitting in a lawn chair beside the stranger who'd been spying on them. Spot lay between Jesse and the man, her head raised and watching Ruby.

The oars went lax in Ruby's hands, bumping against the sides of the rowboat and floating flat in the water. She let out her breath in relief and leaned over the side to splash cool water on her perspiring face and down her neck, then she rinsed her arms.

She let the rowboat drift toward shore, dipping one oar then the other to guide it toward the willow tree. Her heart calmed and settled into a steady beat, the knot in her throat dissolved. As she drew closer she could see Jesse and the man on the porch regarding her, both of them silent and grave as if observing an approaching stranger and wondering, friend or foe? Spot, her tail joyously wagging, limped toward Ruby: it's about time you showed up.

Neither stood or waved or called out while Ruby tied the rowboat to a rotting post that rose from the reeds, the remains of the long-vanished dock. She stepped into the water and splashed the three feet to shore, rubbing Spot's ears and patting her back before she climbed up through the weeds and crabgrass of the sloped lawn to the cabin.

The man on the porch was younger than she'd surmised from her glimpses across the lake. Maybe in his mid- to late fifties. He wore light pants and a sweat-darkened blue cotton T-shirt, crossed by wide red-and-yellow-striped suspenders. He didn't rise from the metal lawn chair as she stepped onto the golden boards of the newly repaired porch of the Barber cabin, but she could see he was a tall man by how far his legs stretched across the porch, by how tiny Jesse looked next to him. He was slender, almost thin, with that shade of gray hair that was once black. He had a thick brush mustache and blue eyes that sloped downward at the outer corners.

"Hello," Ruby said to him, holding out her hand. "I'm Ruby Crane. I see you've met my daughter, Jesse."

"Hi, Mom," Jesse said.

He leaned forward from his chair and shook her hand, and as he did she felt his cool blue eyes observing her, sizing her up, forming his opinions regardless of what she said, looking at her from head to toe. There was only observation, nothing sexual or personal in his inspection. It was a technique Ruby knew and recognized. The calculated indifference, even suspicion. She didn't know why the man was here on Blue Lake, but she'd bet she could name his occupation.

"Johnny Boyd," he said, his voice deep, neutral.

"John," she acknowledged.

He shook his head. "It's Johnny. That's what my mother christened me and that's what it says on my birth certificate. I fought more than a few battles for the right to be called Johnny without a snicker."

And he waited until Ruby acknowledged his name, self-consciously using the diminutive on this silver-haired man. "Johnny," she said.

"Say it a few times and it gets easier." He grinned.

"Jesse and I were discussing the benefits of canoeing. She has a nice even stroke."

"Do you canoe?" Ruby asked him. She undid the band from her damp hair and rebound it, catching the loose strands.

"Never had the pleasure," he said.

Behind him through the open door of the Barber cabin, Ruby made out a stack of cardboard boxes against the wall of the shadowed kitchen. *Dinty Moore* beef stew, read one, *Spam* read another, *Libby's* sliced peaches. Still another, the top box on the stack, its flaps open, read *Jim Beam,* "World's Finest Bourbon." An empty glass sat on the plank floor beside Johnny Boyd's foot, a half-empty bottle was visible behind his chair, along with a stack of paperback mysteries and a pair of binoculars.

"Are you vacationing on Blue Lake?" Ruby asked him. The cabin's repairs were extensive and obvious: new boards here and there in the floors, a patched roof and new chinking between some of the logs. The steps were new, even an unpainted flagpole beside the porch, rising above the treetops but without a flag.

He raised his silver eyebrows. "I'm here for a couple of months," he said. "Jesse said you live in your cabin year-round?"

Ruby glanced at Jesse who avidly watched Johnny Boyd, her head tipped like a curious bird's. The time to chastise her for leaving the cabin had passed; it would mean nothing to Jesse now. Ruby would have to reinforce later that her daughter shouldn't leave without telling her first.

"We do," Ruby told him. "I didn't know she was here. If she does this again, would you ask her to call me?"

"No phone," he told her. His slight smile was cool, distant.

She noted there was no sign of a car around the cabin, either. Ruby's own attempt to hide out when she'd returned a year ago had included ordering an unlisted phone number, which had been given out willy-nilly by Peggy Dystix at the Sable Telephone Company. "I didn't think you meant you wanted it unlisted *locally*," she'd told Ruby, which of course was *exactly* what Ruby had meant.

Again Ruby glanced inside the small cabin at the boxes, the sparse furnishings. No television or radio that she could see, two halogen lamps and a microwave. Books, a lot of books, in tidy rows and stacks, on the floor, on the table, neatly lining the windowsills.

"You're not local," she said.

"No, I'm not," he said, not offering anything more. His voice had the slightest lilt to it, a rise she caught at the end of his sentences.

"You're retired from the force?" Ruby asked.

"Are we talking *Star Wars* here?" he asked mildly, raising one side of his mouth.

"When I find my teenage daughter on the front porch of a male stranger's home, I have a right to know the particulars," Ruby told him. She was prying and she knew it.

He didn't falter, didn't appear offended by Ruby's implications, only gazed at her with that telltale inscrutable appraisal that made her feel that every single one of the defenses she'd carefully constructed over the years had been flicked aside. She fought the childish urge to squirm.

"And you're Irish," she said, leaning against one of the posts that held up his porch roof. It was newly replaced, a pale four-by-four. "An Irish cop. I thought they only existed in books and old movies anymore."

He nodded as if grudgingly approving of her quick appraisal. "Where I grew up," he said, "a boy had three career choices: a priest, a cop, or a criminal." He paused. "Maybe all three."

"Where was that?" Ruby asked.

"I came here to be alone," he said.

"So did I," Ruby told him. "This is the wrongest place you'll ever find for solitude. People creep in to find you. Bar your driveway," she said, waving a hand toward his disused driveway that led to Blue Road, "and they'll come from the sea," and she pointed to the canoe and aluminum boat on his shore.

"You have a history here," he said. "I don't."

"How did you know that?" Ruby asked him. A crow landed on his roof and cawed before flapping away, answered by a second caw deeper in the trees.

He shrugged, a slight flush for the first time marring his aloof composure.

"See, I told you," she teased. "You're already boning up on local news."

"Some of it filters through," he acknowledged. "Even without TV, radio, telephone, or newspaper."

"Then you've heard about Alice Rolley's death?"

## Cut and Dry 67

she asked, guessing that Sheriff Carly Joyce had probably dropped in on Johnny Boyd to assess a new addition to the county, conducting the same sizing-up of Johnny Boyd that he in turn was now doing of Ruby.

"Briefly," he told her.

"The funeral was today. Her death is unsolved, but the sheriff thinks it was a botched robbery."

He nodded in the way of a man who politely preferred not to listen.

"So your main form of entertainment is your binoculars?" she asked, nodding to the black instrument on the table beside him.

"Now who's watching who?" he asked her.

There was the stockpile of food, the locked gate, the complete withdrawal from the media. "What are you hiding from?" Ruby asked.

"He's sick, Mom," Jesse answered for him. "You're being rude."

Johnny Boyd looked at Jesse in surprise and then gave a slight shake of his head, grinning at her and giving her a thumbs-up sign. Ruby studied him again, bearing in mind this new bit of information. He was thin and, yes, beneath the slight tan, pale, a certain tightness around his eyes and mouth. And he hadn't risen when she'd arrived, behavior at odds with his otherwise polite, almost courtly manner. All his movements were brief, compact, as if to conserve energy.

"Sorry," Ruby told him while Jesse noted her apology with an approving smile.

"Curiosity is one of our natural vices, I suppose," he said.

"Then you're here on Blue Lake to recover?" Ruby asked, and when he didn't respond, she raised her hands in surrender. "Okay, no more rude questions. But can I ask if you have *some* connection to the outside world? A way to get out of here? Anybody who stops by? It's a mile to town."

He waved a hand toward the trees beside the Barber cabin. "Only the old lady who spies on me from the trees sometimes."

"That's Mrs. Pink," Ruby told him. "She's always done that, even when I was a girl. She's harmless."

"I figured as much."

"Do you need anything?" Ruby found herself asking. "Let me know and I'll bring it over."

"The driveway's padlocked," he said.

"I'll paddle it over," she told him. "From the sea." She turned to her daughter. "Come on, Jesse. Let's go home and fix dinner."

Jesse rose and touched Johnny Boyd's shoulder. "I'll come back again," she said, raising her paperback book. "I'll tell you about the walkingsticks. They can regenerate their body parts."

"Lucky dogs," he said, raising his hand and lightly touching Jesse's. As he did, Ruby saw the outline of a small pistol beneath his T-shirt, just above the waistband on his right side. He was left-handed and she wondered if his handwriting was a typical leftie's: backward-leaning and difficult to read.

"They're not dogs," Jesse corrected him. "They're insects. Order Phasmida."

## Cut and Dry

They were nearly to the boats, Jesse walking close to Ruby, their arms occasionally brushing, when Johnny Boyd called out from the porch.

"Tabasco sauce," he said. "A big bottle."

"Got it," Ruby called back to him.

Ruby and Jesse leisurely crossed the corner of Blue Lake toward the Crane cabin. Spot lay in the bottom of Jesse's canoe, as still as a carving, even when a duck flew twenty feet above their heads, its wings whistling. They didn't talk. Jesse still needed to concentrate on one task at a time, whether it was physical or mental. Interruptions disrupted her whole process and forced her to begin again from the beginning, or sometimes dissolve into mechanical rocking as if she'd fled her body and left it on idle. Jesse had developed the ability to zero in on a subject to the neglect of all else, a skill of Ruby's as well. Interruptions weren't always even *possible*.

Since Ruby was facing backward in the rowboat, she watched Johnny Boyd. He sat unmoving in his chair on the Barber cabin porch, watching them; still judging her, she'd bet.

He'd half admitted he was an ex-cop, and Jesse had claimed he was ill, a claim he hadn't denied. But Ruby wondered why he'd cloistered himself in the cabin, pulling in and locking the gate behind him. And he carried a gun. Even sitting on the porch and gazing over the gentle waters of Blue Lake, his gun was at the ready.

∘ ∘ ∘

"Look, Mom," Jesse said as they maneuvered the two boats alongside their own dock, aiming toward their scoop of beach.

Ruby turned in the direction Jesse pointed. The blue sheriff's car was parked beside her cabin and Sheriff Carly leaned against it, smoking a cigarette and watching them.

# Chapter 5

Carly ground his cigarette into the earth under his heel and strode down to the dock, his hat pushed high on his forehead. He was in his sheriff's uniform and he walked the way a man who's been in the military walks whenever he finds himself in uniform, for all of his life.

"Ruby," he acknowledged, and leaned from shore to grab the bow of Jesse's canoe and gently haul it on land. A white envelope protruded from the pocket of his shirt.

"Hello, Jesse," he said. As he reached into the canoe for Jesse, Spot jumped neatly past him and landed on the strip of beach without getting her paws wet.

"Hi, Sheriff Carly Joyce, Junior," Jesse greeted him, naming him completely as he lifted her and her tightly held book to shore.

"I didn't know you smoked," Ruby said as she moved a lawn chair a few feet from the water for Jesse to sit in.

"Took it up again," he said tersely. He helped Ruby

pull the aluminum boat all the way on land and turn it over, dumping gallons of water into the sand, the result of a slow leak that Ruby kept meaning to patch.

"Can I talk to you for a few minutes?" Carly asked Ruby.

"Sure," Ruby told him, shoving the oars beneath the upturned boat and wiping her wet hands on her shorts. "Grab two of those plastic chairs and let's sit on the dock."

She left her rubber thongs on the shore and led him onto the dock, its wood as warm as flesh beneath her bare feet. The vibrations of their steps sent water bugs skating out from under the shade of the boards, leaving triangular wakes behind them.

Carly set the white chairs so Ruby had a clear view of Jesse, who'd turned her lawn chair so she could watch the Barber cabin, where Johnny Boyd still sat on the front porch, once more a featureless figure across the lake.

"The radio said there's a chance of thunderstorms tomorrow," Carly began. Always there was the necessity to establish a sociable foundation before the talk could turn to the business at hand. The ungodly heat, this year's mosquito population, grandchildren, benign subjects that forged a common ground.

"A storm might cool it off," Ruby said, glancing out at the hazy air that gave the green trees surrounding Blue Lake a silvery cast.

"That's the worst of it," Carly told her, crossing his legs, then uncrossing them again. "The temperature's supposed to hold in the nineties. It'll be like taking a steam bath." He shrugged. "Not that I've ever taken one."

"I met Johnny Boyd," Ruby said, nodding toward the Barber cabin across the water. "Did you know him before, when he was a cop?"

Carly shook his head. "Can't say I did. He's a friend of one of the Barber sons. He traded fixing up the cabin for letting him stay there until . . . as long as he wants."

"I understand he's been sick," Ruby gently prodded, not really knowing. "He's a long way from family and friends."

"Cleveland's not so far," Carly told her, and Ruby tucked that piece of information away. Cleveland.

"He's carrying a gun," she continued. "A pistol in his waistband."

"He has a valid permit." Carly flicked away a fly buzzing close to his ear. "I checked him out, Ruby. There's no reason for you to worry about Johnny Boyd. He'll keep to himself. That's why he came here."

"That was my reason, too," Ruby reminded him. "But it didn't work out that way."

"Never does," he said, contradicting himself. "They say if you want to make God laugh, make plans." He scratched his neck, glanced up at the sky as if searching for the predicted thunderstorm, and pulled the envelope from his shirt pocket. It was legal-size, unsealed and thick. "I've got a favor to ask you," he said, his voice uncertain or apologetic, maybe both.

"Does it have anything to do with Alice Rolley's death?" Ruby asked.

"More or less." He lifted the envelope's flap and bent it backward, creasing it with his thumb. "Could you take a look at a couple of documents for me?"

"Handwriting?"

Carly nodded.

"Is that what's in your envelope?"

Again Carly nodded, and Ruby winced as he pulled two unprotected pieces of paper from the white envelope. She never touched a job without donning disposable gloves, and even then the questioned documents were protected by clear plastic enclosures. But here Carly sat, on a dock over water, removing the papers with his bare hands and smoothing them flat on his pant leg as if they were last week's grocery lists.

"This is a page from the beauty parlor's appointment book," he said, pointing to the larger sheet. "From the day Alice died. I've put a tick by all the listings in Alice's handwriting. It's your . . ." He frowned. "What do you call it: the person's actual handwriting to check against?"

"The standard," Ruby told him.

"And this"—Carly lifted a smaller rectangle of paper, a bank deposit slip printed with the Sable Great Lakes Bank logo—"is the ticket found in the bag when Alice made the night deposit that evening."

"Did you make a copy of this deposit ticket?" Ruby asked hopefully.

"Front and back," Carly assured her.

"What am I looking for?" Ruby asked.

"This is just one step in the investigation," Carly told her, tapping the toe of his black shoe against the dock. "Could you verify that everything on the deposit ticket was written by Alice Rolley?"

"Is there any doubt?" Ruby asked.

"None whatever. But I intend to be as meticulous as possible in this, with proof backing up every damn thing I say, no matter how minor it is. Alice was the closest thing Sable had to Mother Teresa and people are demanding answers—quick. Folks who've never locked their doors are scrambling around in their junk drawers looking for old keys. I can't afford to let anything go wrong in this case."

"Because of the sheriff's election this fall?" Ruby asked. She moistened her dry lips and tasted salt.

Carly continued smoothing the papers on his leg. There was a thin line on his right thumb like a paper cut, a knob on his middle finger common to people who spent a lot of time using a pen or pencil.

Ruby couldn't stand the casual way he swept his hands across the documents, how close they were to the water. One sudden breeze . . . "I'll take those," she offered, motioning to the pages. He handed them to her and she held the papers by the edges, then folded the envelope in half and wrapped it around the two documents like a file folder and held them that way close to her body.

"Not just the election," Carly said. "Alice Rolley was an important member of this community. She helped a lot of kids, a lot of people." He nodded toward Jesse. "Including you. It was a senseless death."

"Who's running against you?" Ruby asked.

His foot tapped harder. "It isn't official yet, but Mac McCutcheon's been mentioned."

"Mac, your deputy?" Ruby asked incredulously, remembering the arrogant lawman's voice on the phone when she called the Wak 'n Yak.

"That's what I heard. Unrest in the ranks. He'll have to declare pretty quick."

Ruby nodded, thinking that Mac McCutcheon was the type who'd give the citizens hard-and-fast answers, none of Carly's careful investigations. He'd likely close his eyes to a few transgressions, too. Waters County wanted law and order but not interference. If you kept your crimes to yourself, the feeling went, they were nobody's business, especially not the law's.

"You didn't come to the funeral luncheon," Ruby said.

"I was working. Donna, the jail's secretary, brought a plate of food back for me."

"I think I heard a few potential members of the First Americans out in the parking lot discussing the world."

"A lot of huffing and puffing about taxes and big government?" Carly asked. He took a pack of cigarettes from his shirt pocket and shook out a cigarette, then changed his mind, putting the pack away again.

"That's right."

"The talk will heat up for a while and then die

# Cut and Dry 77

down. It's happened before around here. The First Americans have just brought it out in the open more."

Carly rubbed his jaw. "A man needs an enemy. If we don't have the Russians, we have to find one closer to home to spar with and the government's a better target than your next-door neighbor. It's human nature. Ignore it."

"You're saying it's harmless grousing?"

"In my opinion." Carly shrugged. "These guys have some legitimate complaints and not much recourse. They want to be heard."

"You sound sympathetic," Ruby said, thinking of the desire not just to be heard, but to be the loudest.

Carly looked out across Blue Lake, following a pair of ducks traveling low across the water. "I am, sometimes. They're mostly good men who want the world to be black and white. Pure and simple." He grinned briefly. "So to speak."

Jesse had turned her attention to her insect book, bent over the pages, her hair hiding her face. Spot leaned against her legs, her tail dipping in shallow water.

"Do you still believe Alice died during a robbery attempt?" Ruby asked.

Carly rubbed his hands together. "So far. Everything points to Alice returning to the shop and surprising a robbery in progress."

"But her body was found in the back room," Ruby said. "Is that right?"

"Just off the shop area," Carly told her.

"And what was taken?"

"He, she, or they, were after cash. The cash drawer was open—it didn't even lock, just a drawer under the counter, like my wife keeps the silverware in."

"Most local people know that Alice emptied her cash drawer every night."

Carly nodded. "Right. It could have been somebody passing through."

"Carly," Ruby said. "People don't just 'pass through' Sable. Since the bypass was built, it's been off any main roads. And the closest freeway is fifty miles away."

"That remoteness," Carly said, "makes the town an easy target. Unlocked doors, trusting people."

Ruby didn't consider the population of Sable all that "trusting." It was just less effort to stay honest because when everybody knew your daily habits for all of your life, it was too easy to get caught. "Jumbo came out to see me this afternoon," Ruby said.

Carly sat up straighter and frowned at her. His foot stopped tapping. "He wants you to investigate Alice's death?"

"He thought my womanly experience would open doors in the beauty parlor world," Ruby said, deciding to keep the Tracee Ferral part of the story quiet for now.

"Plus, Jumbo doesn't believe I have the wits to solve a stolen bicycle case," Carly said, his voice dropping, foot gone back to tapping. "He doesn't let me forget he caught me skinny-dipping in his cow pond when I was eight. 'Neck-deep in cow piss,' he likes to say."

"I warned him I'd share whatever I discovered with

you," Ruby told him, watching Jesse lift her head from her book and move her lips, making no sound.

"Thanks. What did he say to that?"

"He thought it was a good idea, that it might speed up finding Alice's killer."

"Is he paying you?" Carly asked.

"It was mentioned."

"Well, charge him California prices, would you?" Carly stood up and so did Ruby, carefully protecting the envelope and papers that held Alice's handwriting.

"I'm not licensed to do any detective work here," she reminded Carly, just as she had Jumbo.

"I won't report you," Carly said. "And Jumbo's probably right; women will be more open with you than me. Alice Rolley knew a lot of local secrets."

"Do you think that's what got her killed?" Ruby asked. "Knowing somebody's secret?"

Carly shook his head. "I'd put my money on robbery. Alice was the kind of woman who'd give anybody what she could but I think she'd try to resist a burglary."

Ruby agreed. Alice had been generous but not one to be taken advantage of, a woman with a strong sense of right and wrong. "How soon do you want a report on these?" she asked Carly, holding up the papers.

He flushed. "Is tomorrow too soon?"

"Tomorrow afternoon?"

"Okay. Oh, we'll pay you professional fees for your opinion. I can at least get you that much."

"I appreciate *that*," she said. Money was a never-ending problem. There weren't enough forgery and historical document cases coming from Ron Kilgore, not enough money in the occasional receptionist work she did for Mabel Parker, the local photographer. If it hadn't been for Alice Rolley's help last winter, Ruby wasn't sure what she'd have done.

"Thought you might. I'll talk to you tomorrow then."

Carly carried the two plastic chairs off the dock and halted beside Jesse's chair, hunkering down for a moment to tell her good-bye. Jesse solemnly shook his hand.

Ruby held the papers Carly had given her away from her body, feeling the old familiar eagerness at the sight of Alice's penmanship, even if Carly didn't doubt the authenticity of the documents. Every job was a subtle puzzle, a challenge and opportunity to uncover a charlatan, an impostor. Forgers always slipped up; they couldn't help it. The misplaced connection, an unusual lift of the pen, misproportions. She was hot to examine the papers in her lab.

Hank Holliday phoned while Ruby was slipping Alice Rolley's papers into clear protective plastic sleeves. She was in the cabin's loft, which doubled as her bedroom and lab, although her lab had a tendency to spill beyond its L-shaped confines: tables, an outdated but perfectly adequate computer, high-intensity lamps and a light table, the locked metal cabinet that held past jobs and her stereoptic microscope.

The loft was open to downstairs, separated by a railing and a staircase not much better than a ladder.

## Cut and Dry

She'd wired a telephone extension in her loft herself a month ago; another heavy black rotary phone.

"I'm stuck here for another couple of days," Hank told her, "waiting for a Forest Service bug man to give me his opinion on this gypsy moth infestation. We might try introducing that new fungus. It works on the caterpillars like Ebola. Pleasant thought, eh?"

It was a good year for gypsy moths, a bad year for Michigan's trees. Acres of oaks stood stark and leafless as the caterpillars methodically ate their way through the leafy canopy. So far that spring and summer, only patches of trees had been attacked in Waters County, but they stood in brown devastation in the midst of summer green. If they had the time and strength, the trees would put out another growth of leaves—a second spring—but the effort weakened the trees, frequently to death.

"I thought you *were* a gypsy moth expert," Ruby said. Hank ran his own forestry consulting business. He'd published an article on the gypsy moth cycles in a forestry magazine three months ago.

Hank laughed. "One of the primo best. But my client wants an opinion sanctioned by an employee receiving a paycheck from the U.S. of A. How's life in the country?"

"Alice Rolley's death is still the main news: whether it was a robbery; who did it; who's next. That sort of thing."

Hank was silent for a moment, then asked, "Are you getting involved?"

"Not really. Jumbo's asked me to make a few

woman-to-woman inquiries, and Carly doesn't mind, so I'll ask around tomorrow. Jumbo offered me hard cash so how could I say no? It sounds like Alice did some saintly deed for most everyone in Waters County so I'm only expecting to hear canonization testimonials."

"*Somebody* thought otherwise," Hank reminded her.

"Carly believes it was an outside robbery and Alice resisted." As she said it, Ruby realized how much she doubted that version of Alice's death. She had no reason to be skeptical; hers was a gut response. But if Alice had been resisting a robbery, why was she killed in the back room? Why not in a struggle out front where the money was kept?

"You still there?" Hank asked.

"Sorry. I was thinking. Have you heard of the First Americans?"

Hank groaned. "They're here, they're there, they're everywhere," he said.

"So it's not a new group?"

"A couple of years old, I think. They were around when I lived in the thumb," he said, referring to the way Michigan was shaped like a mitten, the "thumb" jutting into Lake Huron. "They'd like to see the country go back in time a couple hundred years. Nonviolent revolution, supposedly. Waters County has its own chapter?" Hank asked. "I can see how it would be fertile ground."

"You mean because we're already a hundred years out of step?" Ruby asked. "What's another hundred?"

# Cut and Dry

Hank laughed. "Who's involved?"

"I don't know. I've just heard talk. There was a meeting the night before Alice's funeral."

"I'll nose around when I get back," he told her, "if you really want to know. Right now, I'd better get moving. Stay out of trouble. I'll see you the day after tomorrow, for sure."

"I'll be here," Ruby assured him, smiling as she hung up, seeing before her Hank's sharp eyes and cynical grin. They weren't quite a couple, but almost.

She set aside Alice's papers and looked over the railing at Jesse downstairs, sitting at the kitchen table practicing multiplication, her summer homework for her tutor. Through some curious connections in Jesse's brain, she was recovering all her mathematical skills except for one: If the numbers weren't written in front of her, if she had to pull them out of her own mind, she was capable of it, but she had to start from the beginning, from the number one. If she were asked how old she was, she counted from one upward until she arrived at fifteen. She'd only recently learned to count silently, sometimes using her fingers, until she reached the number she knew was correct.

Ruby crossed the plank floor of the loft and stood by the window for a few moments, gazing at the still leaves and bright water of Blue Lake, the reeds and cattails along its shores, letting the old familiar view quiet her mind. Her first memories were of this place.

Then she sat at her table and began studying the papers in front of her, the rest of the world receding as she concentrated.

The page torn from the Wak 'n Yak appointment book held three different specimens of handwriting: a barely legible scribble; a childish round hand with open loops and *i*'s dotted with circles; and a finer hand in a modified Spencerian style that Ruby would have identified as Alice Rolley's without the check marks Carly had placed beside each entry.

It wasn't that Alice was older than the other two penmanship authors that gave away her ownership, but that handwriting fell into classes: styles learned in school at a young age. Even with the personalized embellishments and shortcuts a person developed as he or she grew further from those first penmanship lessons, traces of the original style invariably remained.

Looking at the angular connections, the elaborate capital letters, Ruby thought Alice had probably been taught the Palmer method by a teacher who'd learned the Spencerian style of handwriting herself. Elements of both styles existed in her entries, especially in her numerals with the shaded tail of the 5 and the graceful hooked upper line of the 7. There was more evidence of the tightness of finger movements rather than the freer strokes of wrist and forearm movement of later handwriting methods.

Ruby carefully examined the names in Alice's handwriting, from Enid Shea's wash and set at nine A.M. to Babs Prescott's tint at four, all of it consistent, orderly, unhurried. She studied Alice's schedule as a whole but didn't dissect the penmanship—yet. Ruby had discovered long ago that simple observance sometimes caught barely perceptible anomalies of rhythm

# Cut and Dry

and line and placement that were lost in close observation.

Finished with the appointment book, she turned to the deposit ticket that Carly had removed from the night deposit bag. On the back, Alice had listed the day's receipts that had been paid by check, each accompanied by a name: nine checks, matching several of the appointments. Enid Shea's name wasn't there; she'd probably paid with cash. Prescott was the last name listed: Babs's tint.

All were in Alice's handwriting, consistent in every way with the appointment book entries. On the opposite side of the deposit slip, the currency and coin was listed, along with the date and a total of the entire deposit.

Before she even understood why, Ruby felt a twinge at the base of her neck, a shiver of excitement, like glimpsing the glow of eyes in a night forest. She had spotted something unexpected, abnormal.

She carefully smoothed the deposit ticket, squinting and pulling her high-intensity lamp closer. The date was in Alice's handwriting. But the numbers listing currency and total lacked Alice's customary flourishes. The angles were similar, but there was no closed loop at the bottom of the 5. One of the 7's had a smear and under the scrutiny of a magnifying glass, showed evidence of a pen lift. These numbers also showed heavier pressure, as was frequently common when a forger was using caution, trying too hard to imitate every movement of the victim's pen.

Perhaps the totals had been written by Fanny or

Katrina, Alice's beauticians. Ruby turned back to the appointment book. Whichever woman wrote with a childish hand, and Ruby guessed that would be Fanny, hadn't written the numbers, and unless Katrina had concentrated on making her slashing numerals readable, it wasn't her penmanship either.

Ruby sat back and turned her pencil in her sweaty, glove-encased hands, letting her excitement subside before she continued. Who else could have filled out the deposit ticket? According to Fanny and Katrina, Alice had been the last person to leave the shop.

There was another oddity she hadn't noticed before. The amount of money deposited seemed too little for the number of customers listed in the appointment book.

Ruby grabbed her calculator and ran down the list of customers. An amount for the service was listed beside each name. She added the numbers twice.

Not only were the currency and total amounts not in Alice's hand, but the total deposit was exactly $150 short of the day's take.

# Chapter 6

"I'll bring it to your office in about an hour," Ruby told Carly. "As soon as I type it up." She'd been surprised when Carly himself had answered the phone at the sheriff's office. It was seven o'clock and she'd planned to leave a message, expecting to hear one of his deputy's bored voices as he began his long night manning the phones.

"I thought you wouldn't be finished until tomorrow afternoon," Carly said, his voice scratchy with weariness.

"I found something."

She heard the scrape of furniture, the clearing of his throat. "On the deposit ticket?" Carly asked, all fatigue gone from his voice.

"Yes," she told him.

"I'll come out."

"My report's not complete," Ruby said, holding up her scribbled notes as if Carly could see them. "I need to stop by the store for milk anyway."

"Can you tell me what you found?"

"I'll show you when I get there." Ruby had learned

to never give a verbal report; words were misconstrued too easily. Only after her analysis was read by the client did she provide any additional comments.

She wasn't certain of the deposit ticket's significance, maybe it meant nothing. Katrina might have cleaned up her handwriting and totaled the deposit for Alice. Alice might have laid aside $150 cash for herself. There was nothing wrong with that; it was her business. The one indisputable fact was that Alice hadn't filled out the entire deposit ticket herself. The numbers on the slip had been written by two different people.

"Would you like to visit your grandfather for an hour?" Ruby asked Jesse after she hung up.

Using a finger of each hand, one to the eraser end, one to the lead point, Jesse laid her pencil beside her sheet of multiplication problems—parallel to the side edge of the paper, equidistant from top and bottom—before she answered. "Yes, please."

"You can call him," Ruby told her, and pointed to the telephone number written in large block print and taped to the log wall above the phone.

Ruby's father lived in Sable, in the same house where she'd grown up. Her communication with him was because of Jesse, a cautious civility that Ruby accepted would never truly warm up to true affection. She didn't grieve over the distance, didn't long for the all-forgiving, teary-eyed embrace. She and her father both preferred the polite acknowledgment they'd managed to attain, anything more would be hypocritical. It was Jesse her father loved unstintingly. That's what continued to bind Ruby and her father together. Without Jesse, there wouldn't be any contact and Ruby doubted that either of them would mourn the loss.

As Jesse conducted a slow and precise telephone conversation with her grandfather, Ruby heard the sounds of another vehicle approaching on her sandy driveway. She might as well be living in town, she thought as she stepped outside into the still bright evening light. It wouldn't be completely dark until ten o'clock.

A Volkswagen convertible repainted the color of pink cotton candy, its top down, buzzed toward her out of the trees, dust swirling behind it, the driver's blond hair flying.

Ruby knew who owned the car. It was Tracee Ferral, Jumbo Rolley's supposed partner the night Alice died. Ruby glanced toward the lake, the trees beside the cabin. No quick place to hide. Spot sat down beside her and leaned against her leg, watching the Volkswagen approach.

The driver's door was thrown open before the engine had completely died and out leapt Tracee, wearing oversize mirrored sunglasses, her lips a grim red line.

"Does that dog bite?" Tracee demanded.

"Not usually," Ruby told her, patting Spot's head.

"Fun-nee."

Tracee Ferral was all tightly contained plump flesh. Belted white shorts cut her figure in half, topped by a green low-cut sleeveless shirt with a lace inset between her breasts.

She dramatically pulled off her sunglasses, flinching as she caught the wing of a dangling gold angel earring. Her eyes were darkly enhanced with liner that curled upward at the outer corners of her eyes. Ruby had a vision of Tracee made up to look the same at age fifty as she did at thirty, as she probably had as Miss Color Festival at age seventeen.

"I know Jumbo was here," Tracee spat out in a high-pitched voice, pointing her sunglasses at Ruby, drops of moisture flying from her lips and catching the sunlight on the word *was*. "And this is none of your business. You ignore that old coot and just stay out of it."

"Who frosted your hair?" Ruby asked calmly, noting Tracee's becomingly windblown blond hair.

Tracee pulled herself up defiantly and placed her hands on her rounded hips. "Alice did. So what?"

"So didn't you feel uncomfortable with your lover's wife fussing over your hair? Holding all those chemicals right next to your eyes like that?"

"Alice did the best job. What did you expect me to do? Drive all the way to Muskegon?"

Ruby shrugged. "Did Alice know you were fooling around with her husband?"

"Certainly not." Every move Tracee made or sentence she uttered was accompanied by a dramatic gesture: a flick of the wrist, a swivel of hip, raised eyebrows or tipped head.

Secrets were rarely kept in Sable for any longer

than it took to catch a breath and dial a phone number. Certainly Alice could have sniffed out a situation as momentous as an affair involving her own husband.

"Jumbo said he was with you the night Alice died. Is that true?"

Tracee leaned down and brushed a speck of dirt from the strap of her white sandal. Her toes were as beautifully manicured and polished as her fingernails. Ruby glanced down at her own plain and slightly dirty bare feet.

"Yes," Tracee said, eyes still on her sandal.

"All night?" Ruby asked.

"That's none of your business."

"But it might be Carly's business—or one of his deputies'." She thought of the least appealing of Carly's men. "Maybe Mac will be questioning people for Carly."

"Mac McCutcheon gives me the creeps," Tracee said, her penciled eyebrows gathering in disgust. "I dated him for a little while after I won my Miss Color Festival title, can you believe it?" She paused and shuddered. "He blows his nose on his fingers."

"*Was* Jumbo with you all night?" Ruby asked again.

"Kind of. From about six-thirty on. He hadn't eaten supper because Alice wasn't home. . . . I made him spaghetti, with meatballs."

"He worked late?" Ruby asked. "He came directly from work to your house at six-thirty?"

"I don't know. He doesn't tell me everything. I'm not his wife, you know."

"I know," Ruby said. "Where do you work?"

"At the auto parts store. A lot of people fix up their cars in the summer. We're really busy right now." Tracee frowned at Ruby. "What difference does it make where I work or if Jumbo worked late? Neither one of us knows anything about how Alice died. Nothing."

"She was strangled," Ruby reminded her.

"That's not what I mean and you know it. You're just being mean because you think you're so much smarter than everybody else."

"I didn't even finish high school, Tracee," Ruby told her before she thought, surprised by Tracee's charge. Thinking she was smarter than *anybody* had never been one of Ruby's conceits.

"But you left here, you went to California where things *happen*." Tracee's voice rose crankily.

"What I did is called running away from home and I don't recommend it. Now tell me again how long Jumbo was with you the night Alice died."

Tracee sighed and touched each corner of her mouth with her pinky finger. "From six-thirty at night until about five in the morning. He went home to get ready for work."

"The two of you met at your house?" Ruby asked.

Tracee rolled her eyes. "Well, we wouldn't have gone to a motel in *this* county, that's for sure. I live in my uncle Joe's old house, you know, by the river. He left it to Mom." She paused and hastily added, "But I pay rent."

"So Jumbo did return to his own house in the morning?"

# Cut and Dry 93

"To change clothes. But he and Alice didn't . . . you know, so he never noticed she wasn't home. He's real broken up about her dying."

"Are you?"

Tracee turned and gazed over Blue Lake. A misty line of perspiration clung to the downy hairs of her upper lip. "I am. I really am sorry. I worked for her when I was in high school, kind of like an apprentice. I got high school credit for it, learning to cut hair and stuff. But putting my hands in other people's hair just grossed me out." Tracee's voice softened. "Alice helped me with my hair and makeup for the Miss Color Festival pageant. She was good to me."

"But not so good that it stopped you from having an affair with her husband."

"That didn't have anything to do with Alice," Tracee said, looking at Ruby as if she were dense as concrete. "They weren't *really* married anymore; they just lived together. They didn't, you know, *sleep* together, not for years."

"Where were you between the time you left work and six-thirty when Jumbo arrived at your house?" Ruby asked.

"At home." Her eyes narrowed. "Wait a minute. Don't start thinking anything funny about *me*. I don't kill anybody or anything."

"Not even flies?" Ruby asked.

"That's right. No way."

A breeze stirred the oaks, rustling the leaves with a faint whisper. Together, Ruby and Tracee turned toward the trees, as if facing the slight movement of air might coax it to them. But the breeze died away, leaving the oak leaves trembling and unrefreshed.

"Can I ask you something personal?" Ruby asked Tracee.

"Isn't that what you've been doing?" Tracee asked sullenly.

"You're an attractive young woman," she said, watching Tracee's eyes light up in agreement. "Why have an affair with Jumbo? His children are older than you are."

"He's not so old, not the way it counts," Tracee said, readjusting her sleeveless top. "Besides, he treats me nice."

"He's generous?" Ruby said, further defining the draw to a man twice Tracee's age.

"Mm-hmm," the plump young woman agreed.

"I see." She looked at the shiny little convertible. "Did he buy your car for you?"

"He only helped me with the down payment. And I'm going to pay him back." Tracee drew herself up into a dramatic version of sternness. "So now are you going to tell everybody in town about Jumbo and me?"

"I'm not interested in spreading gossip," Ruby told her, wondering who in town *didn't* already know.

"Just don't connect our names with Alice's death."

"That's the sheriff's business, not mine," Ruby told her.

"But you're going to tell him I said Jumbo was with me all night? So he won't come around to ask me any questions? Mac neither?"

"I'll tell him. But he may want to talk to you himself for the details."

"I'd rather you did," Tracee said, pushing back the cuticles of her left hand with her right thumb. "You're a woman, and besides, you're having an affair with Hank Holliday so you know what it's like."

"Neither one of *us* is married," Ruby reminded her.

Tracee passed over that fact as if it had no bearing. "People around here can be so uptight about anybody having a little fun."

"Was Alice?"

Tracee screwed her mouth to one side, an aid to thinking. "I couldn't say. She talked gossip. But it was like, you know, promotional."

"Promotional?" Ruby asked, confused.

"Sure, just like free coffee and donuts. When you had your hair done, you knew you'd hear some good dirt on somebody."

"Where did Alice get all this 'good dirt' in the first place?" Ruby asked. Behind Tracee, a finch landed on the folded-back convertible top, pecked at a shiny hinge, and flew away, leaving behind a white smear.

"From other customers. You know how it is: When people start fussing with your body and making you look nice, stuff just falls out of your mouth. You feel all warm and trusty."

Tracee placed her hand on the door handle of her car. "So now you know everything I know, okay? Forget about snooping around for Jumbo. Pass on what I told you to Carly, but don't try to play big-city detective. I mean it." She slid behind the wheel and said with a touch of proprietary smugness, "You forget to do any snooping and I'll tell Jumbo to pay you anyway."

"I think if I'm going to be fired, I'd prefer that Jumbo did it, not you."

Tracee disappeared behind her sunglasses, sniffing. "Well, *I'm* telling you that you're fired and Jumbo does what *I* say."

Ruby stood beside the cabin and watched Tracee's pink car speed away into the trees toward Blue Road, buzzing like a lawn mower being pushed too hard.

The town of Sable closed at five-thirty, all except the grocery store and Jimmy's bar, so the street was empty but for the cars parked at angles in front of those two establishments.

Ruby drove past the post office and turned a block off the main street, stopping in front of the gray house where her father sat on the porch swing, his head sunk into his collar like a turtle's. When he spotted her car, he straightened his back, raised his head, and pulled on a face of energy. He was old and ill, and if he hadn't harbored so much animosity toward the world, he'd have died long ago. Her mother had, and Ruby believed it was because that was the only way the timid and overrun woman could escape him.

"Bye, Mom," Jesse said. She got out of the car, already waving to her grandfather, who was slowly balancing his cane to rise to his feet.

"Tell your grandfather I'll pick you up in an hour,"

# Cut and Dry

she told Jesse, giving her father a brief wave before driving off.

The Waters County jail and sheriff's office was halfway between Sable and Pere, a low brick building with a few parched yellow petunias in raised beds.

Ruby reached for the handle of the plate glass door and saw Mac McCutcheon sitting at the desk in front of the police radio, so she was prepared for the way he leaned back and rocked in his chair, regarding her from the lower rims of his eyes.

"The office is closed," he said, lacing his fingers behind his head like a TV character. When he spoke, pointed canine teeth appeared, overlapping his lower teeth. "Have you got an emergency?"

Mac had been a game warden before he'd lost his job for unspecified reasons and was hired on as one of Carly's deputies. He'd grown up in Sable, younger enough than Ruby that her only memories were of a boy amid a pack of bicycles zipping down Sable's sidewalks.

He wore his brown hair short, nearly shaved, unknowingly stylish if he lived in other parts of the country, merely utilitarian here in Waters County. He was a tall, lumpy-faced man with a knobby chin and cheeks that protruded as if he had round bones beneath his flesh. If he was really planning to run for sheriff against Carly, he already had the self-assured, intimidating manner that Carly lacked, the movie tough-guy sneer. Even sitting down, there was a swagger to Mac's demeanor.

"Carly's expecting me," Ruby told him.

"I'll check," Mac said, not moving, still staring at Ruby, his eyes moving down her body. "I hear you're nosing around again. In Alice's death this time. Care to sit down and tell me all about it?" He nodded toward the chair beside his desk. "Right here."

"Never mind," she told him. "I know my way."

Mac grunted as Ruby passed the desk toward Carly's office and she felt his eyes on her until she'd shut the door. The sheriff's office smelled of cigarette smoke and french fries. A Dairy Queen cup sat beside a photo of his wife, Georgia, and their two daughters.

"What did you find?" he asked, wiping the grease from his fingers on a DQ napkin and holding out his hand for the manila folder Ruby removed from her bag.

"Hello to you, too. Is Mac McCutcheon working on Alice Rolley's case after all?" she asked.

"Nope," Carly said, his eyes on the folder in Ruby's hand. "He's in charge of the office for a few weeks."

So Carly could play politics too. Keeping Mac occupied while he investigated Alice's death at least kept Mac out of the limelight. She gave him the folder. "Read it first and then we can discuss it."

While she waited, she sat in the chair opposite Carly's desk and removed from her purse a small notebook she carried with her to list unfamiliar words she read or heard. Her education had been spotty, most of it self-imposed. When she was twenty-five, she'd discovered books, and along with books, the excitement of words. Now she stored them away, learning their definitions and pronunciation. It didn't

# Cut and Dry

matter that she hardly ever used them; the power came in *knowing* them.

*Deshabille, arcane, megrimish, vitiate.* On *persiflage*, she heard Carly say, "I'll be damned."

Ruby looked up to see Carly staring at the empty wall above her head, his eyes distant and frowning. Then he nodded to himself and turned to Ruby. "So Alice didn't complete the deposit ticket herself?"

"No," Ruby told him. "She listed the checks on the deposit slip as they came into the shop during the day. The handwriting matches the names in her appointment book, but the numbers in the currency section and the total amount of the deposit, on the opposite side of the slip, were written by someone else."

"Who?" he asked, but only rhetorically, bringing his hands together, fingertips touching, over Ruby's report.

"Katrina or Fanny might have an idea."

"You checked the numbers against their handwriting?"

Ruby nodded. "They definitely weren't written by Fanny, and I don't believe Katrina wrote them either, although I'm not as certain about that." Ruby had decided not to mention the $150 shortage until she discovered whether Fanny and Katrina had a simple explanation. If not, she'd tell Carly.

"We thought that Alice made the night deposit and then returned to the shop and was surprised by a robber." He spoke softly, half to himself. "The coroner said she probably died sometime before midnight and I narrowed it to between six forty-five or seven and midnight, but if she didn't write the deposit ticket . . ."

"It may have been written by the murderer," Ruby finished, "who then deposited the receipts at the bank to make it appear Alice died later than she did."

"Her last appointment was at four," Carly said.

"Babs Prescott's color touch-up," Ruby provided.

"And Babs had her granddaughter with her. They left the shop about five-thirty, the same time as Fanny and Katrina. The last they saw of Alice, she was sweeping up hair."

"But no one spotted Alice making the night deposit? The box is right beside the bank's front door."

Carly shook his head. "No one's come forward to say they did."

"So Alice could have actually died as early as five thirty-five or five-forty?" Ruby asked.

"Possibly. I'll talk to Katrina and Fanny about the deposit slip. If neither of them knows who wrote the ticket . . ."

Ruby nodded, and then told Carly about Tracee's visit and her claim that Jumbo had spent the night at her house.

"He was with her from six-thirty on?" Carly asked.

"That's what she said," thinking the same thing Carly probably was, that if Alice Rolley could have been killed as early as five thirty-five, Tracee wasn't much of an alibi for Jumbo after all. Or Jumbo for Tracee.

* * *

## Cut and Dry

It was dusk when Ruby picked up Jesse. She parked in front of her father's house and waited while Jesse said good-bye and walked to the car, her left leg dragging a little the way it did when she was tired. She turned at the car door and waved to her grandfather once more before she got in, smelling of 6–12, the same old oily insect repellent that came in a glass bottle, which Ruby's mother had smeared on her as a child. It wasn't even on the market anymore. The last stash of 6–12 in America might be sitting in the back of her father's medicine cabinet.

"Did you have a good time?" Ruby asked her.

"He showed me how to tie knots," Jesse told her. "I can almost tie a half hitch."

"Good for you."

"Aunt Phyllis called while I was there."

Phyllis was Ruby's older sister, an engineer in Albuquerque. Ruby hadn't seen her in thirteen years. They spoke rarely, mostly just a few brief and wary words when she called to talk to Jesse.

"Did you talk to her?" Ruby asked Jesse.

"Mm-hmm. She sounded different."

"In what way?"

"I haven't decided yet," Jesse said calmly, and Ruby let it go.

Ruby parked in front of the grocery store ten minutes before it closed. The beat-up wooden door of the bar across the street was open, and as she got out of her car she could hear a country music song about too many broken hearts wafting into the street from the dark interior of the bar.

"I'll be right back, sweetie," she told Jesse, who frowned in concentration, her head tipped toward her open window as she listened to a musical line regretting "one last drink on the fast lane of love."

All she needed was milk; the cooler was at the rear of the store, forcing her to thread through the chips-and-pop aisle, past a display of Nutter Butters, her favorite. She grabbed a half gallon of 2% from the cooler and turned, nearly bumping into Enid Shea, who was pushing a wire cart filled with grocery basics: no mixes or frozen dinners or canned meals in Enid's cart, only "real" foods.

"The weather's going to change," she told Ruby. "My leg's been knocking up all day long."

"How's Silas?" Ruby asked, hoping to deflect the conversation from heading toward Alice Rolley's death.

"He's home in the good barn, where he always is, working on that old plane." She squeezed her lips together in a thin line of resignation.

For thirty years Enid's husband, Silas, had been building a Blériot monoplane that *his* father had begun in the 1920s, and it was nearly finished. Silas, who'd flown in a commercial jet once in his life, and then to visit his dying sister, had announced he'd taken to studying a 1930s pilot's manual, determined to take off from his back pasture in his Blériot before the opening of deer season.

"Wasn't that a nice luncheon?" Enid asked Ruby,

# Cut and Dry 103

eying her bare legs. "I didn't get a chance to shop until now." She sighed. "All that cleanup I had to do."

"You did a good job," Ruby told her, edging around Enid's cart toward the front of the store. "Everything was delicious."

"It was the least I could do for poor Alice. We'll never see a woman like her again." She shook her head and gazed into the middle distance before she said, "You know I don't always approve of you, Ruby, but I'm relieved to hear you're working for Jumbo, looking into Alice's death."

Ruby stopped midstep. "Who told you that?"

Enid's chin raised. Her protruding eyes challenged Ruby. "Well, aren't you?"

"My daughter's waiting in the car for me," Ruby told her. "Excuse me; I have to leave."

As she hurried past the shelves of potato chips toward the checkout, Enid called after her, "You be sure you do your best job. Alice deserves that much."

Ruby was grateful to be in the privacy of her own car, pretending not to see Bruce Becket and his wife as she backed out of her space. Did everyone in Sable know Jumbo had asked her to investigate his wife's death? Had he announced it at the bar? Held a town meeting?

"Do honeybees smell sweet?" Jesse asked, breaking into Ruby's thoughts.

"They might," Ruby told her. "They're carrying all that nectar home to their hive so they can make honey."

Jesse closed her book; it was too dark to read.

"Grandpa said they do. He said a honeybee stung him on the nose once and he smelled it. Did he tell you that, too?"

"No," Ruby told Jesse. "He didn't."

On their way home, they drove past houses where the occupants sat on screened porches or beside hissing and popping bug lights. Dusk was the dominion of the mosquitoes, when humans took cover or doused themselves with protection. Ruby glimpsed couples and families caught in artificial light, like stage appearances, tableaux of family life.

At the cabin, after Jesse had gone to bed, Ruby stood in the dark on her own screened-in front porch. She raised her glass of whiskey to the west, toasting Alice Rolley, silently promising to do her best to help find Alice's killer. The Barber cabin was dark and Ruby wondered if Johnny Boyd also watched in the darkness, as she did, drinking his Jim Beam. Around the lake, bonfires dotted the shore revealing the dark human shapes gathered around the flames, keeping back the night.

# Chapter 7

Before her ten o'clock appointment at the Wak 'n Yak, Ruby dropped off Jesse to meet Mary Jean's daughter for a softball league game sponsored by summer school. Jesse didn't play yet, but she watched with increasing interest.

"If only Dad would park his truck in back," Barbara was complaining to her mother when Ruby and Jesse walked into the real estate office, "instead of leaving it out on the street all night where *everybody* can see it."

"My love life is embarrassing my precious daughter," Mary Jean said to Ruby. "Can you believe it?"

"Mo-om," Barbara whined. "It's *Dad;* it's so gross."

"Dis-gusting," Ruby told Mary Jean.

Barbara rolled her eyes and tossed her head with the same flourish as Mary Jean tossed hers when she was offended. "Cut it out, you guys. Come on, Jesse. Let's go. Mothers are *so* boring."

Jesse stood, considering Ruby and Mary Jean. Finally, she asked, "Is that because you're old?"

"Definitely," Ruby told her, kissing her forehead.

Mary Jean sat at her computer scanning through screens of property descriptions. After the girls had left the room, she turned to Ruby. "You on your way to sleuth at the murder scene?"

"And I need a trim."

"Efficient." She tapped her finger on the screen. "Do you know how scarce chunks of property over twenty acres are becoming? I could sell them by the bushelful."

"Bushels of acres?" Ruby asked. "Buyers are looking for timbered property so they can sell off the trees?"

"There's that, but what's *really* hot right now is hunting property. Your own corner of the wild world that you can fence off and then blast away at Bambi. No competition. Downstaters eat it up. And if it's already logged, that's okay; no bad old trees to jump in the way of your shot."

She stopped scrolling and grabbed her pencil. "Aha. I wonder if I could talk the Barvicks boys into selling off a corner. They quit farming years ago."

Mary Jean was the only realtor in Sable and she gleefully pursued her business, expecting the bonanza couldn't last; another realtor was bound to move in sooner rather than later.

The Wak 'n Yak stood a street off the northern end of Sable's two-block downtown, originally a milliner's shop tucked between a warehouse and a boarded-up building with a faded eighty-year-old sign advertising Clark's needles and threads.

## Cut and Dry

First, Ruby circled the block that held the Wak 'n Yak, swerving past three children coaxing a black dog to pull a wagon filled with empty pop bottles and cans.

The back side of the block was lined with white clapboard houses dwarfed by huge leafy maples, the sidewalk raised and broken by the trees' scavenging roots. Ruby knew who lived in a few of the houses: Mrs. Bert the seamstress had been there since Ruby was a child. Next to her, the Durbases, notable for raising a dozen children, all boys. Mac McCutcheon's mother lived on the corner, a frazzled tree-swing still hanging from the maple in her yard. Carly had already questioned the residents whose houses backed the alley across from the Wak 'n Yak; nobody had seen or heard anything unusual the evening Alice died.

Then she drove through the gravel alley, pausing behind the beauty shop and noticing how the back door stood open, protected by only a wooden screen door that Ruby doubted was even latched. Streetlights at both ends probably cast very little illumination on the middle of the alley where the door was.

Anyone leaving the building after dark could easily conceal themselves. But if Alice had been killed earlier than Carly had first thought, it would still have been broad daylight. Ruby glanced at the peeling paint of the garage on the opposite side of the alley and the tall, morning glory–covered fence; it would be a snap to conceal yourself during daylight, too.

A crime taking place inside the shop during the daylight hours would actually be more easily disguised: no inside lights to expose the act to anyone passing by; a lot of street activity and noise to mask any screams; windows in daylight usually reflected sunshine, making them difficult to see through.

She parked out front and walked up to the shop on the painted red sidewalk, pausing to study a photograph of Alice that hung in the window, surrounded by black crepe paper bunting. Alice's silver hair was, of course, perfect, swept up from her face, her skin smooth. Gram would have said that Alice had good bones.

Mabel Parker had taken the portrait and because Ruby had done some part-time office work for Mabel, she wasn't surprised to note the way the photographer had caught Alice's personality: three-quarter face, smiling but looking off-camera, eager to get on with business. Snap that photo and let me out of here.

When Ruby pushed open the glass door, the bell that normally jangled with each customer's entrance bumped dully against the plate glass, its clapper wrapped in black cloth.

Otherwise the shop was exactly the same: a woman's retreat. Three hair dryers, three sinks and chairs, a mirrored wall, a manicure table, and a few chairs in the waiting area. An air conditioner buzzed in the front window. Silk flowers, a candy jar, and piles of women's magazines, most of them current. A few sports magazines were included. Since Walt Hall, the only barber in town, had started rambling about flying saucers, a few of Sable's men had begun to drop by the Wak 'n Yak for their haircuts. It was a busy place.

## Cut and Dry

One wall was hung with framed photographs snapped over the years of Alice cutting hair, presiding over charities, laughing it up with her customers. Newer photos included Fanny and Katrina in similar poses. Ruby suspected that every woman in Sable passed through the Wak 'n Yak at least once in her life.

Ruby glanced behind the counter at the cash drawer Carly had claimed was as secure as his wife's silverware drawer. Just a wooden handle to pull it open, not even a lock. A pickle jar sat on the counter. *Donate to Sally Becket's surgery*, requested a label taped to its side.

A label had been attached on the same pickle jar last fall asking for donations to help Jesse. The results had been generous and Ruby suspected Alice had heavily supplemented the donations herself. The gift had paid for transportation to the special classes in Pere, for a tutor, and for the monthly drives to the therapist in Grand Rapids.

"Hi, Ruby," Katrina said, looking up from the curler she was winding in Mrs. Tzesni's gray hair, her long fingers expertly catching every silvery wisp. "Fanny's getting a cup of coffee. She'll be right back." She pinned the curler and made snipping motions at Ruby with her fingers. "You'd knock Hank the Hunk to his knees if you'd let me shape up your hair."

"You mean shear it off," Ruby amended. Katrina's black hair was snipped close to her scalp. On her, the style was citified and sophisticated. On Ruby, it would be a disaster of cartoon ears and pug nose.

"That's exactly right," Katrina agreed.

Mrs. Tzesni looked at Ruby from the corners of her sagging eyes as if her head were in a vise. "How's your father, Ruby?" she asked.

"He's fine," Ruby told her. Mrs. Tzesni knew better than Ruby did, she'd lived next door to Ruby's parents for forty years. Mrs. Tzesni's hobby was making preserves and jams to give away as gifts. When Ruby was a teenager, a batch of Mrs. Tzesni's grape jelly had sickened half of Sable. Mrs. Tzesni still gave away as much canned food as ever, except now the recipients discreetly poured the contents down their toilets and returned the glass jars with thanks.

"Oh my, but it's a shame about Alice," Mrs. Tzesni went on, wiping at her nose with a lavender tissue pulled from her sleeve beneath the smock. She nodded toward the navy curtain decorated with sunflowers that hung in the doorway separating the parlor from the back room. Ruby followed Mrs. Tzesni's gaze as if Alice's body still lay on the floor back there.

Katrina patted Mrs. Tzesni's shoulder, saying, "Now, now," and smiling at her reflection in the mirror.

Fanny, her hair sticking straight up in a curly ponytail, pushed her way through the curtain carrying two styrofoam cups of coffee. She handed one to Ruby. "Our coffee machine's on the fritz, this is from the Knotty Pine. Be careful, it's hot."

"Thanks."

As Fanny smocked Ruby and sat her in one of the chairs in front of the mirrored wall, Katrina guided

# Cut and Dry 111

Mrs. Tzesni to a hair dryer, turned it on and set a stack of magazines beside her. The dryer hummed and Mrs. Tzesni closed her eyes, retreating into a lulling state of sensory deprivation.

"How's business?" Ruby asked Fanny as she dampened her hair. Ruby had washed her hair at home. She'd laid her head in one of the scooped-out porcelain sinks only once in her life, and that had ended in panic at the sensation she was trapped, that her neck would break.

"It's great, well, better anyway. People were a little shy at first, with . . ." She nodded toward the back room. "Sometimes I still feel like we should be whispering."

"Carly said you were the one who found Alice?" Ruby asked.

Fanny's hand froze. "Almost. I opened up and something in the air felt like a storm coming. I stood real still in the door, just listening."

"So you saw items out of place in the shop?" Ruby prompted as she removed the lid from her coffee. Fanny had already added the perfect amount of cream.

"Not really." Fanny touched her blond hair, then her heart. "It was in here, a sense I had. I'm a little psychic. Sometimes I know who's on the phone before I answer it. I knew there'd been sorrow and pain in this building," she said, gazing sadly around the shop.

"Oh, cut it out, Fan," Katrina ordered, dropping into the empty stylist's chair beside Ruby and reaching for Fanny's coffee. "Tell Ruby how you saw Alice's shoe and freaked out and ran to the gas station." Katrina shook her head and sipped the coffee. "She was shaking so bad, Bob had to call the sheriff for her."

"Where was the shoe?" Ruby asked.

Fanny shot Katrina a pained look as if she'd stolen the punchline to Fanny's story, and pointed to the floor behind Ruby's chair. "It was her white slip-on. I knew she'd been wearing them the day before because I admired how easy she walked on them. Three-inch heels, and at her age, too."

"Then you didn't actually see her body?" Ruby asked, disappointed.

"Not then. Only after the sheriff got here." She hesitated and nodded toward the curtained doorway. "Only a little bit. I put a rug over the spot." In the mirror Ruby saw a tear sliding beside Fanny's nose. "Who could have done this to Alice? She never hurt anybody in her life. Not anybody. And all the good she tried to do for children."

"Because her own were such a disaster," Katrina offered. "That's what people do who have bad luck with their kids. They try to make it up to other people's kids."

Ruby thought of her own father and his open love for Jesse, certainly not a love she'd experienced when she was a child.

Fanny snorted in agreement. "Franklin and Roseanne are really kind of . . . weird. You weren't here to see it, Ruby, but they both lived at home until a couple of years ago. They stopped by the shop all the time to ask for money." She shook her head, her ponytail bobbing. "And Alice would just fork it over."

"Life in another dimension," Katrina agreed, humming the theme from *The Twilight Zone*.

"Roseanne smells like pickled herring," Fanny said.

"Pickled herring?" Katrina repeated, slapping Fanny's wrist.

Fanny dropped her comb and Katrina handed her a fresh one from a round plastic container.

"Somebody who knew Alice killed her," Katrina said to Ruby. "Somebody demented."

"Do you know anybody demented?" Ruby asked Katrina. "A sick person who could commit murder?"

Katrina shook her head. "Nobody any crazier than anybody else around here."

"I still think it was a stranger," Fanny said stubbornly, and Ruby sensed they'd argued the same point countless times since Alice's death.

"Who were Alice's enemies?" Ruby asked, following Katrina's line of conversation. "In sixty years, Alice must have made a few."

Fanny pulled the new comb too hard through Ruby's hair and Ruby winced. "Some people might have got mad at her because she gossiped—"

"Don't we all," Katrina interrupted. "But mostly people liked to talk *to* Alice. She was a better listener than Barbara Walters and I bet she knew more secrets than Father Doyle. She could have reeled off every tax dodge, surgery, who was drinking and who was poking who, divorce grounds and you name it, in this town." She paused. "But Alice wouldn't have shared any of the serious secrets, just the fluff."

"Then you two probably hear a lot of gossip, too?" Ruby asked.

Katrina waved her hand as if it were burning hot, and Fanny said, "Do we ever."

"Do you hear about Jumbo's affairs?"

Fanny and Katrina exchanged glances over Ruby's head. "You mean Tracee? Or before that?" Fanny asked cautiously.

"Just Tracee for now. Did Alice know?"

"If she did, she never said anything," Fanny said, finally beginning to snip Ruby's hair. Her face pinkened, darkening her freckles through the makeup. "Tracee had her nerve, coming in here to get frosted by Alice. That girl is a piece of work."

"Why do you always call Tracee a 'girl'?" Katrina asked, frowning. "She's older than we are."

"Because that's what she still thinks she is. And her name: two *e*'s on the end. It was plain Tracy with a *y* until she won the Miss Color Festival pageant." Fanny pursed her lips and made a snooty limp wrist.

The conversation was heading off in another direction and Ruby brought it back. "Did either of you see Alice fill out the deposit ticket for the day?"

"Sure," Katrina said. "She fills in the check side all day long to save time, whenever anyone writes one to the shop."

"And the cash?" Ruby asked.

"She totals . . . I mean, totaled, the hard stuff last,

# Cut and Dry

when we closed the shop. If there's any change, it goes in the jar."

"Did you see her total the cash the night she died?"

Fanny and Katrina frowned at one another and then, in unison, shook their heads. "We left before she did. She liked to wrap up the place by herself."

"What about Babs and her granddaughter?"

"They left the same time as us," Fanny said. "Katrina French-braided Susannah's hair—she had a piano recital—and Alice tinted Babs's hair." Her voice caught. "We left Alice here alone, defenseless."

"Didn't you usually?" Ruby asked reasonably.

"I guess so, but if only we'd known . . ."

Ruby let that comment go unanswered. That about summed up life in general: If only we'd known.

"You've got a lot of questions," Katrina said, narrowing her eyes. "Who are you working for? Carly? Or Jumbo, like everybody says?"

"I agreed to ask a few questions, that's all. No official capacity so you're not required to answer. You can talk to Carly if you'd rather, or Mac."

Fanny wrinkled her nose. Invoking Mac McCutcheon was the most effective tool Ruby had.

"Given the choice, you'd be my pick," Katrina said.

"Talking to me doesn't guarantee you won't have to talk to Carly," Ruby reminded her.

"But you might be able to run a little interference." She raised both elbows as if warding off an attacking line of football players.

"Then how about a favor?" Ruby asked. "Could you each write the numbers one to twenty on a clean sheet of paper? Four times. Once in a hurry, once carefully, both sitting and standing?"

"That's it?" Katrina asked. "Why?"

"So I can separate Alice's handwriting from yours. And do it in ballpoint pen, please."

"You got it," Katrina said, already rising and reaching for a purple Wak 'n Yak pen on the counter.

"Alice thought you two were pretty special to leave you the shop in her will," Ruby said as Fanny moved to Ruby's other side, swiftly snipping. "Don't take off any more," she warned.

Mrs. Tzesni had dozed off, her head tipped to one side against the bowl of the dryer.

"Oh, she did," Fanny agreed. "She said we were like daughters."

Behind Fanny, Katrina shook her finger at Ruby. "Don't even think it," she warned Ruby.

"Think what?" Fanny asked, her eyes wide. "Oh," she said, looking at Ruby in horror. "You wouldn't. Not us!"

"Don't be silly," Ruby said coolly. She glanced over at the wall of photos, from black-and-white to color, the Wak 'n Yak's history.

"Should I style your hair like Alice did?" Fanny asked Ruby.

Katrina snorted. "Don't bother," she told Fanny. "The only time I ever saw Ruby wear her hair the way Alice styled it was when she walked out the door. What did you do, go home and wash it out?"

Ruby felt her cheeks flush, and Fanny patted her

## Cut and Dry 117

shoulder. "That's okay, hon. Alice was always glad you came in."

Ruby paid cash for her trim, handing Fanny a twenty-dollar bill. "Tell me," she said, thinking of the $150 shortfall on the deposit ticket. "Did Alice take cash out of the day's proceeds for herself?"

Fanny shook her head. "I don't think so. She wrote herself a check when she gave us ours. Well, she might take out cash for coffee or donuts but she always wrote it down. She was fussy about money."

"What about when Franklin or Roseanne asked for money? You said she gave them cash."

"I saw her take that money out of her purse," Fanny told her.

"Then she deposited all the cash every night?" Ruby asked as she put her change in her wallet.

"As far as I know. On good days she'd take cash out of the drawer and put it in the blue dye until she went to the bank. She didn't like to keep a lot of cash out front."

"The blue dye?" Ruby asked.

"That's what she called it. An old box of dye that turned gray hair blue. She quit using it on customers years ago; there was a chemical in it that gave you cancer or lead poisoning or something. I'll show you."

Fanny led Ruby to the back room, giving a wide berth to a four-by-six green rug that appeared untrampled. "That's the spot," Fanny whispered reverently. Barely inside the back room, at an angle, as if Alice had been heading for the back door that led to the alley.

The back room held industrial-size jugs of shampoo and conditioner, boxes of dye and perms, packages of combs and curlers, holiday decorations, knickknacks that Ruby guessed were gifts from customers. A shop vac stood in a corner.

"Alice kept this place well stocked," Ruby said, looking at the crowded shelves.

"Actually, we're a little lower than usual," Fanny said, still in a whisper. "Alice bought supplies in Lansing every month. She would have gone next week. Katrina and I are thinking of paying the shipping to have supplies delivered instead."

"Alice *drove* to Lansing every month?" Ruby asked.

"Mm-hmm. She always left on Monday morning and came back Tuesday night. Those are our slow days. That's when she talked to congressmen at the capitol about those programs she lobbied for, too. And," Fanny added, smiling, "she shopped."

Fanny stretched to the top shelf and lifted down a box of dye that resembled every other box, except that the illustration depicted a very youthful woman with blue-tinged hair. "This is it," she said. She gave the box to Ruby.

Ruby lifted the flap. Inside lay a folded wad of cash.

"Oh," Fanny gasped when Ruby showed her. "Isn't that funny that Alice forgot to put it in the night deposit."

As Fanny slowly counted out the bills, smoothing and flattening each one face-up, mostly fives and tens, Ruby knew before she finished that the amount would be $150, exactly the amount that was short in the day's take.

As soon as Ruby stepped out the door of the beauty shop, she felt the first hints of the promised storm. The sultry day was still, heavy, as if all the air had been sucked inward in preparation for a big blow. The sun still shone, but to the southwest a solid line of featureless dark clouds hung at treetop level, like enemies stalking forward, preparing to storm over the ramparts. The leaves of the popple tree behind the gas station had somehow flipped in the dead air, showing their white undersides in surrender.

A few vehicles were parked along the street, but Sable was quiet, deserted-feeling. Everyone's gone home to close their windows and take clothes off the line, Ruby thought, remembering the propped casement in her loft, the open windows in the kitchen.

In front of the Sable bakery, a card table was set up on the sidewalk. A poster propped against it read *Every living thing has a right to life*. Two people stood beside the table, speaking earnestly, the smaller one in a white apron, their similar dark heads leaning toward one another.

It was Franklin and Roseanne Rolley, Alice and Jumbo Rolley's two children. Both were in their forties, and in a cruel trick that nature occasionally delighted in, Roseanne was built like her oversize father while Franklin the baker was smaller, finer-boned like Alice. He had thick lashes and thick wavy hair, as opposed to Roseanne's bristled lashes and thin hair.

Ruby slowed, then paused to glance at a display of watches in the window of the drugstore, trying to hear their conversation.

She couldn't make out the words of their exchange, only that Roseanne was the more animated of the two, leaning the upper half of her body toward her brother, her hands on her hips like a fairy-tale scold.

The word *Mom* reached Ruby and then a rusted pickup without a muffler rumbled past, thwarting all hope of hearing any more of their conversation.

She turned away from the window and saw both Roseanne and Franklin watching her, their exchange stilled. Roseanne's arms were crossed over her chest, Franklin's hands were beneath his white apron.

"Hi," Ruby said, pausing beside the card table loaded with brochures for various environmental causes, glimpsing a fox with a front paw pathetically caught in a trap before she glanced away. Neither Roseanne nor Franklin returned her greeting, only stood there regarding her, their faces similar in cold consideration. She longed to walk away but she remained beside the table, forcing herself to blandly smile at Franklin and Roseanne.

A blue pickup pulled in across the street in front of the hardware store. Ruby watched Dick Prescott climb from the driver's side, hiking up his pants as he bumped the door closed with his shoulder. Two beagles were tied in the pickup bed, their feet up on the rails, watching Dick, their tails wagging. Dick gave them each a pat before he left the truck and stepped up onto the curb.

## Cut and Dry    121

Ruby saw the outline of a person in the passenger seat, Babs's bouffant hair.

"It was nice running into you," she told Roseanne and Franklin—who hadn't moved, who still solemnly watched her without responding—and crossed the street. She had nearly reached the passenger's side of Dick Prescott's pickup when her attention was caught by Mac McCutcheon leaving the grocery store carrying a liquor-size brown bag. He strolled down the street, his free hand poised near his belt as if he were willing and able to pull his gun on the first bad guy who crossed his path.

Dick Prescott walked toward Mac, and Ruby watched the two men pass each other, both suddenly stiff-backed, heads high, not acknowledging each other. She couldn't see Dick's face, but McCutcheon's lip curled like a dog's eager to lunge for a throat.

Mac McCutcheon walked by Ruby and the pickup without seeing her or Babs, his knobby face red, his swagger saying *I dare you*.

"Hi, Babs," Ruby said through the open cab window, noticing how Babs's attention switched from Dick's receding back to Mac, her lips tightening.

Babs turned her dark blond head, frowned slightly, then smiled. A dimple appeared in the rouge of her left cheek. "Ruby, how are you?"

"I'm fine. I was wondering if I could come out and talk to you tomorrow."

"Is it about Alice?" she asked, tipping her head and smiling sorrowfully.

"Yes, if you don't mind."

"Sure, that's all right," she said, and then turned her attention back to the door of the hardware store, waiting for her husband to come out, as if Ruby weren't even there.

# Chapter 8

Ruby and Jesse sat on the cabin's screened-in porch watching the storm's approach. The sky turned blue-black, the clouds suddenly so dense, they blotted out the sun. It was only early afternoon, but the automatic lights at the public boat ramp across the lake flickered, then switched on.

The oppressive heat felt too thick to breathe, and yet there was an odor, so elusive that if Ruby sniffed, she couldn't smell it: the deliciously wicked smell of the devil's mad romp as the god Perkunas chased him through the world, Gram had always said.

Ruby had draped towels over the metal lawn chairs on the porch and she and Jesse sat side by side, too captivated to sip the iced tea Ruby had poured.

In the distance, thunder rumbled and bumped, rolling along the southwest horizon and gradually growing louder, soon accompanied by distant flashes of light.

Jesse leaned forward, her face rapt, neck straining as if she longed to take flight. Ruby couldn't help herself; she stretched out her hand and it hovered above her daughter's shoulder, ready to snatch Jesse back.

The wind arrived first, slamming across Blue Lake, frothing up waves that splashed over the wooden dock, bending trees and tangling branches in roars and whoops. Leaves tore loose and were plastered against the porch screen, branches broke and crashed to the ground. Spot whined and leaned against Jesse's leg, but she was too mesmerized by the storm to notice, so Spot moved to Ruby's side, pushing her cold nose into her lap until she stroked the dog's head.

It was still tornado season, but Ruby sensed there was no tornado in this storm, she couldn't have explained why, probably some sixth sense left from long ago.

Rain fell like hail. Cold drops sizzled on the hot earth and created a misty steam, more rain streamed from the roof in sheets. A yellow cat she'd never seen before streaked across the driveway and dashed beneath Ruby's car. "It's raining cats and dogs," she murmured to herself.

Then the thunder and lightning was upon them. Simultaneous and constant; it was impossible to assign peals of thunder to the corresponding strokes of lightning. It was terrifying; it was wonderful. Ruby hugged her legs and closed her eyes, feeling the mist of rain splatter through the porch's screen windows.

The storm raged for twenty minutes, and suddenly it was over. Thunder diminishing to mumbles, the southwest sky growing lighter, the rain a steamy patter. The yard was littered with branches and leaves,

# Cut and Dry

the bird feeder had blown down, and the lawn chairs on the shore had tumbled across the beach. One bobbed in the water against the dock.

"Good storm, don't you think?" Ruby asked Jesse.

"Do you think he's all right?" Jesse asked, pointing toward Johnny Boyd's cabin. The Barber cabin's porch was empty, which surprised Ruby. She would have expected him to be as interested in watching the storm as he was in watching them.

"I'm sure he's fine," Ruby told Jesse.

"Why are you sure?" Jesse asked.

"Well, I guess I'm not."

"Can we go visit him?"

"After a while. Maybe he's taking a nap."

"I'd like to go now," Jesse said, sliding to the edge of her chair and gazing through the porch screen at Johnny Boyd's cabin.

Why not? It *was* odd he wasn't in his accustomed front-row seat. She thought of Jesse's claim—which he hadn't denied—that he was sick.

"When the rain stops," she assured Jesse, "we'll take him the bottle of Tabasco sauce he asked for."

"All right," Jesse said, still looking across the lake. "He has a pirate flag."

"A skull and crossbones?" Ruby asked. "For his flagpole?"

Jesse nodded, shifting her gaze to the gentle rain at the tail end of the storm, willing it to cease and desist; she had things to do.

* * *

The sun returned but it was hazed, unable to pierce through the humidity and evaporate the rainwater. It remained, as if it had just fallen, in puddles and on leaves and flat surfaces, warming in the heat. The mosquitoes swarmed, viciously buzzing around them, riled by the storm.

Ruby paddled the canoe slowly toward Johnny Boyd's cabin, futilely waving the paddle every few strokes at the cloud of mosquitoes that circled their heads, keening in their ears, dive-bombing for blood. Mosquitoes buzzed Ruby, landing but rarely biting. They seldom did, something in her body chemistry repelled them. "It's a shame we can't bottle it," her aunt Magda had said once.

Jesse sat in the bow, still as a figurehead. The canoe was too small for both of them plus Spot, so Jesse had ordered the dog, "Go to Johnny Boyd's." Spot had frantically barked at them, racing back and forth along the shore and then disappeared, heading toward the road behind the cabin, her bark fading into the afternoon.

"Do you think she knows where we're going?" Ruby asked.

"I told her," Jesse said as if that settled that.

They were nearly across the lake and there was still no sign of Johnny Boyd. Ruby was beginning to share Jesse's unease. She had grown to expect his continual presence on the front porch of his cabin, she counted on seeing his still shape, the occasional glint of his binoculars.

"There she is," Jesse said, pointing toward shore.

## Cut and Dry 127

Spot, her tongue dripping, limped to the water by the disintegrated dock below Johnny Boyd's cabin and loudly lapped at the lake, glancing up at their approach.

They tied up the canoe and walked to the cabin through the overgrown grasses and weeds that brushed rainwater on their bare legs. Nothing moved around the outside of the cabin, no figure watched them from the open doorway.

"Hello," Ruby called out at the foot of the porch steps. The cabin interior was silent, shadowed. A puddle of rainwater stood inside the open door.

"Wait," Jesse said, touching Ruby's arm, listening.

"So all right, I've made a fool of myself," came Johnny Boyd's slurred voice from inside. "Come in if you want. Or go away. It'll make no difference."

The accent was more pronounced, the words lilting.

"I believe I'll come in," Ruby said. "It's Ruby Crane." She paused. "I've brought your Tabasco sauce."

"That's as good an excuse as any," he said.

Inside the cabin, Johnny Boyd sat on the floor, his back against his unmade bed, wearing a stained T-shirt and blue striped pajama bottoms. An open bottle of Jim Beam sat beside his leg, a quarter full. He raised his hand, palm toward Ruby, and said with exaggerated dignity, "I'm not a serious drinker, you see." He lifted the bottle from the floor and shook it. "I was thirsty and this was all I could reach."

"Should I shove this box of Spam closer to you so

you'll have something to eat, too, or help you up?" Ruby asked.

"Ah, now that isn't your run-of-the-mill sculptable Spam you're speaking of, my girl; it's the upper-class smoked variety." His gray hair was rumpled. He tipped his head, considering his options. Spam or Ruby. "You don't look very strong," he finally said.

"But it's how you use your strength that counts," Ruby told him.

"I've heard that," he said. "From down here, I had the impression I missed a good storm."

"One of the best," Ruby agreed.

"All right. I'll accept your kind assistance," he told her. "But can we spare the young lady the ordeal? Let her retain her illusions of the dignified gentleman who lives across the lake."

Jesse still stood in the doorway, Spot beside her, solemnly regarding Johnny Boyd.

"Can you wait on the porch, sweetie?" Ruby asked her.

Jesse nodded and disappeared.

"How long have you been down here?" Ruby asked as she hunkered beside Johnny Boyd, smelling his whiskey breath and perspiration.

"Not as long as it feels."

"Is anything broken?" she asked, touching his damp and pale forehead as she would have if she'd found Jesse on the floor, checking for fever, ignoring his amused glance. "Should I go for help?"

He shook his head. "Right as rain. I just can't find the energy to raise myself at the moment."

For a few brief months, when Ruby was trying to get herself straight, she'd worked in a nursing home in Oregon. She still remembered how to do it, at least her body did. Lift with your legs, not your back; foot against foot; pivot.

And he'd done it before, too; she could tell by the way he let her lead, leaning against her, not forcing any movements. "You've been ill for a while," she said, guessing.

"Off and on," he told her, sitting on his bed, taking deep and even breaths, slowing them through willpower, one hand on his chest. "Now more on than off."

"What's wrong with you?" she asked.

"Nothing worth talking about. What do I owe you for that?" he asked, nodding to the bottle of Tabasco sauce.

"You can pay me later," she told him, and then, seeing his defensive expression, said, "Don't worry. I won't forget. You just don't seem to have your wallet on you right now."

"Thanks." He lowered his hand to his leg. Every movement was economical, requiring as little energy as possible. "I had some time to think while I was reclining on the floor," he said. "And the subject of your local murder came up."

There was no mistaking the sudden sparkle in his eyes, the alert way he raised his head.

"I see," Ruby said. "Your cop's imagination was put into gear, wasn't it? And your conclusion?" She began opening the drawers of an oak dresser against the wall. Shirts, socks, and underwear as precisely stacked as Jesse kept her dresser, not at all like Ruby's tumble of clothes.

"No conclusion," he said, frowning as he watched her rummage through his clothes but not stopping her. "But it seems to me, a beautician is like a barber, only more so. Her customers confide in her. My first wife once said her beautician knew more secrets about her than I did."

"You're saying that secrets are a more logical motive than robbery in Alice Rolley's death?" Ruby asked, briefly wondering how many wives there'd been.

"In a small town like this. That's been my experience, anyway."

"I agree," Ruby said, and in a few moments she was telling Johnny Boyd about the bank deposit ticket containing numerals written by someone other than Alice.

"Whoever killed her knew her routine, knew her well enough to duplicate her daily habits," he said. A transformation had come over Johnny Boyd. He had dropped ten years, his gray hair crackled. He pulled himself to sit up straighter and his breathing relaxed into a natural rhythm.

"But they didn't know her well enough to discover where she kept extra cash," Ruby said, explaining about the blue dye box.

"Or else they *did* know and wanted it to appear as if they weren't well acquainted with her."

"But if they forged the deposit ticket, they were trying to go undetected," Ruby said.

"Unless it was a ploy in case the forgery was discovered," he countered.

"I don't think anyone . . ."

"Never underestimate the mind of a felon," Johnny Boyd cautioned. "Ah, there are some beauteously connived plots out there—worthy of honorary college degrees. Most murders are committed by an acquaintance of the victim."

"What would you do next if you were investigating Alice's death?" Ruby asked, laying out clean clothes on the bed beside him.

"What you're probably doing: talk to as many people as possible. Get a complete picture of Alice and her life and then poke holes in it. There's a slipup somewhere, you'll see it."

"You have a lot of faith in me for having spoken to me once in your life," Ruby said. She reached behind him and straightened the pillow at his back.

"Ah, but I've been watching you, don't forget. And besides," he added, grinning, "you handle a man well."

"So the fall was just a gimmick to get company?"

"Think of it that way, would you?" he asked.

"Tucking yourself away in a cabin in the woods isn't the honeymoon you thought it would be?" Ruby asked.

He shook his head and looked around his spartan cabin. "I'm discovering my own company isn't that interesting. Now there's a shock for a person who thinks well of himself, I assure you. I can't even hide from myself in my books."

"Would you mind if I chatted with you about the murder once in a while?" Ruby asked.

He leaned back his head, then smiled at Jesse peeking around the door. "I'll count on it," he said.

On her way to Babs's house, Ruby passed an abandoned farm where a tree grew through a window of the collapsing house and the fence along the pasture, which had long since been reclaimed by the forest, was built of silvery upturned tree stumps. Hundreds of them, intertwined roots, six to ten feet high, remains of the glory days of white pine–logging a century ago. Early recycling. Now the stumps and roots would be burned in huge, useless piles of slash.

Just past a field of corn that would definitely be knee-high by the Fourth of July, the driveway leading off the tarvy road into Babs and Dick Prescott's farm was gated like a western ranch, with a crosspiece fifteen feet above the entrance. A plaque mounted on the crosspiece sported intersecting rifles, just like Ruby had seen on western belt buckles.

Ruby glanced up at the plaque as she climbed from her car and unlatched the wooden gate, walking it open. The guns looked real, their barrels gleaming metallic blue, the rifle stocks polished. Were these just two of Dick Prescott's extras? Spares, maybe?

She braked on the other side of the gate and reclosed it, catching her thumb in the mechanism as she shut the latch.

"Damn," she said, sucking on her bruised thumb as she returned to her Pinto. Ahead of her, the driveway

## Cut and Dry

followed a curving line of willow trees that drooped over the lane. The lawn—at least an acre—was well tended from the road to the hundred-year-old two-story farmhouse and back to the white barn, cut short and trimmed along the edges. Done with a riding lawn mower, she'd bet.

Lightning rods spiked the roof peak of the farmhouse, the intact green glass bulbs an antique hunter's dream. Strips of blooming purple and bronze irises edged the sidewalk to the wide front porch. But like other Waters County homes, the preferred entrance was the back door off the kitchen, where plain daisies bloomed in lanky tangles.

Babs Prescott sat in a frame swing beside a maple tree in the backyard, the kind with two seats facing each other, propelled by feet pushing against the shared floor. She was dressed in shorts and a loose white blouse, cleaning green beans, pulling them from a bushel basket on the floor of the swing, breaking off the ends with her fingers and dropping them in a huge metal bowl on her lap.

Babs nodded to Ruby and motioned for her to sit in the swing seat opposite. Ruby did, rocking the contraption and experiencing the same sensation as climbing into a Ferris wheel seat.

"Are these beans from your garden?" Ruby asked, watching Babs's swift and mechanical movements.

"No. I bought them from the Beckets. Dick loves green beans, as long as they're whole, not cut up into pieces. If they're cut into pieces, he won't touch them. That's just the way he is: particular. There's my vegetable garden," she said, nodding toward a room-size plot of mostly tomatoes and zucchini. "I only grow enough for fresh vegetables during the summer."

Ruby nodded, thinking of her own weedy plot by the garage. She'd hoped Jesse would get involved in gardening, but the whole project had been too abstract for her daughter until Jesse discovered that tomato worms turned into hummingbird moths, and now the tomato plants had become feeding grounds for the gigantic green caterpillars. As big as cigars, the tomato worms were happily stripping the plants to sticks.

"I know Alice was a friend of yours," Ruby began.

Babs looked sadly at Ruby. She appeared younger without the eye makeup, her hair softer without spray. "She was, that's true, but she was a friend to a lot of people." Babs reached down for another handful of green beans. "All those good things people are saying about her are true, but she wasn't *really* close to anybody."

"She didn't confide in you?" Ruby asked.

"Not me or anybody else. She was a private person, but most of Sable didn't notice that. When people tell another person their secrets, they forget that the other person is only listening, not trading their secrets, too."

A gray and white goose waddled from behind the garage, its head low to the ground, following an insect through the grass. "You were one of the last people to see Alice," Ruby said. "Did you notice anything unusual?"

## Cut and Dry 135

"For instance?" Babs asked.

"I don't know. Was Alice nervous, on edge, upset?"

Babs frowned, her hands slowing. "No, not really. She was quieter than usual but I was her last appointment and she said it had been a busy day." Babs heaved a sigh and went back to the mechanical movements of snipping beans. "People think I should have stayed longer, don't they?"

"I haven't heard that," Ruby told her.

"They do," Babs insisted. "I know they do. If I'd stayed she'd still be alive, that's what they're saying." Babs absently pushed against the floor of the swing and the seats began moving back and forth, first jerkily and then in a faster pendulum that made Ruby's stomach queasy. "They blame me," Babs said, biting her lip.

"No," Ruby said gently, the way she used to talk to Jesse right after the accident, when he grew confused and panicky. She stiffened her legs against the swing's floor to slow it down. "No one's saying that, Babs."

"Maybe not to you."

"If the killer was watching," Ruby continued in the same gentle tone of voice, "waiting for Alice to be alone in the shop, he would have only continued to wait until you left."

"Maybe . . ." The swing slowed and Babs chose a bean biting off its end, slowly chewing. "Was it a robbery?"

"That's one theory. Fanny said the three of you left the shop at the same time? You and Fanny and Katrina?"

"Four of us," Babs corrected. "My nine-year-old granddaughter Susannah was with me. She had a piano recital that evening and Katrina French-braided Susannah's hair while Alice did mine."

"You didn't see anyone standing or waiting outside the shop? On the street?"

Babs shook her head. "I was in a hurry to get Susannah home."

"You all left by the front door?"

"Katrina, Susannah, and I did. Fanny locked the door behind us and left through the back. I think her car was parked on the alley."

Ruby made a mental note of that. Fanny hadn't mentioned they'd left separately. "Where did you go after you left the shop?" Ruby asked.

"To my daughter Darlene's house to dress for the piano recital. I'd left my dress there so I wouldn't have to come back to the farm. Susannah was in a tizzy, afraid we were going to be late."

"And then you went to the recital from Darlene's?"

"That's right. Darlene drove. Susannah played like a dream." Babs's hands slowed. "Did Jumbo really hire you to solve Alice's murder?" she asked.

"Jumbo asked me to look into her death, yes, but I told Carly I'd gather information for him."

"If you think you can work for Jumbo and Carly both," Babs said, shaking her head, "you're wrong."

"They both want to find out who killed Alice."

Babs looked over Ruby's shoulder, her face lighting. "Here comes Dick," she said.

Ruby turned. From the white barn, Dick Prescott

## Cut and Dry

exited through a side door, turning and padlocking it behind him. He wore green pants and an old military shirt. A rifle was slung over his shoulder. As he passed the row of kennels, several dogs began eagerly yipping and baying.

He stopped and spoke to the dogs, then strode toward Babs and Ruby with the self-satisfied stride a man affected when he considered himself armed and dangerous and proud of it. *Don't tread on me.*

"Hello, Ruby," he said, nodding, all business. The name tag on his shirt had been removed, a darker rectangle of fabric remained where it had been sewn on. The shirt's buttons were strained, and Ruby wondered if Dick had served in the military or had bought the shirt from the army surplus store in Muskegon. "Babs said you were coming out to see her. What for? Are you here representing the county sheriff?"

He placed a hand on Babs's shoulder, gently caressing her flesh, and a soft smile of pleasure curved Babs's lips. Ruby stared in fascination. For everyone there is someone, she'd read enough times.

"I'm asking a few questions for Carly," she told Dick, aware of the warning expression on Babs's face and the way she relaxed when Ruby didn't mention Jumbo.

Dick's face reddened. "I don't recognize the sheriff's jurisdiction over me or Babs. You tell Carly not to bother my wife. He's got no right . . ."

Babs placed her hand over Dick's. "It's all right, Dicky. I don't mind."

"Well, I do, and I say he butts out. Now."

"Don't scare her, Dick honey," Babs crooned, squeezing his hand. "She's just doing her job."

How many times had Ruby seen her own mother do the same thing? The soft, placating voice, hoping to soothe her husband's anger. Only she didn't recall seeing that tender expression that softened Babs's features on her mother's face. Mostly, it had been fear.

"Meddling, you people are always meddling," Dick muttered, and stalked off toward the back door of the house. "You've got no right."

"Has he been hunting?" Ruby asked, nodding toward the rifle bumping against Dick's back. "What's legal to hunt in June?"

"Dick doesn't have to follow the hunting seasons," Babs told Ruby. "This is our property. He can do what he wants here." She leaned over and patted Ruby's leg. "Dick's a little grumpy. Don't pay any attention to him. He's been mad at everybody who works for the government ever since the state declared the northeast corner of our property a wetland."

"I heard somebody mention the wetlands at Alice's funeral," Ruby said. "What's that about?"

Babs gazed toward the long, low cowshed behind the white barn. "We increased our beef herd by ten cattle so Dick tried to drain the wet corner of his pasture for more grazing land. Instead, because it covers more than five acres, the DNR, well, it's the Department of Environmental Quality now, decided it was a wetland and now we can't touch it. *Our* property. Dick can hardly stand it."

"Did Roseanne Rolley bring it to the state's attention?" Ruby asked.

Babs laughed. "No, but she'd like to have. She merely took up the charge. Roseanne . . ."

She spoke with the tone of mental headshaking that people used when they referred to those out of step with the community of mankind.

"How would you describe Alice Rolley?" Ruby asked.

"Dead," Babs said, following it immediately with a horrified gasp. Tears filled her eyes and she lowered her head, wiping her face on the shoulder of her blouse. "Oh my God, I don't know why I said that. It just came out. Please, I'm sorry."

"No, it's my fault. I should have used the past tense. How would you have described Alice?"

Babs ran her hands through the bowl of snipped green beans, letting them fall through her fingers like pirates' gems. "Generous, private. She might have loved her kids too much; that's an easy crime to commit."

"Did she love her husband, Jumbo?"

"She did once." Babs flushed. "Don't ask me if she knew about Jumbo and Tracee. I couldn't tell you that."

"But everyone else did?"

"Most everyone."

Babs made a motion to rise from the swing. "I'll stick some of these beans in a bag for you, Ruby."

Ruby started to protest, but Babs continued, "They're easy. Just parboil them before you put them in your freezer." The swing shuddered and swayed as Babs stepped off it. "Putting up food makes you feel rich, doesn't it?" she said over her shoulder. "Like when you can always find Scotch tape and extra batteries in the house."

As Ruby turned around her Pinto and headed back down the willow-lined driveway, she saw Dick Prescott in the front yard, running an American flag up the gleaming white flagpole that stood in a bed of red, white, and purplish-blue petunias.

# Chapter 9

A legal-size envelope came in the mail, with Ruby's name and address written in large angular letters with a curious downward hook at the end of each word, almost like a diacritical mark. There wasn't any rural delivery at Blue Lake and Ruby had to pick up her mail at the post office in Sable. She stood in the empty lobby, considering the envelope. One word stood in place of the return address, filling the upper left corner: *Rolley*, it said.

"Your dad hasn't picked up his mail in two days," the postal clerk told Ruby from the counter as he watched her check the back and front of the envelope. "He doing okay?"

"As far as I know," Ruby told him, tucking the envelope inside a grocery flyer, out of sight.

"Are you on your way over there?" the clerk continued. He drummed his fingers on the countertop, frowning.

"I wasn't planning on it."

"Just a second," he told her, and disappeared behind the bank of brass postal delivery boxes, returning with a meager bundle of mail. "Why don't you be a pal and take this to your dad? It makes me nervous when somebody skips coming in for a few days. You never know . . ."

"If he . . ." Ruby began, and then, seeing the clerk's stern expression, said, "All right," reluctantly taking the mail: ads, a doctor's bill, a copy of the Lithuanian newspaper that came from Chicago wrapped in brown paper.

"Thanks. I appreciate it." He smiled at Ruby as if she were proving herself to be a good daughter after all. "Let me know if he's sick or anything, okay? Just so I don't look for him."

In the post office parking lot, Ruby sat in her car, all the windows rolled down. A slight breeze stirred the leaves of the chestnut tree planted between the parking lot and the sidewalk, and she was loath to leave its shade.

She glanced at her watch; Jesse would be at her tutor's for another hour and a half. Part of the tutoring, Jesse's favorite part, included music lessons on an electronic keyboard, a recommendation by the therapist both to improve Jesse's dexterity and to encourage any musical abilities. For the moment, Jesse responded to printed more than performed music. "The notes mean what they say," she told Ruby, with a frown of consternation.

Her father's mail she placed on the passenger seat and removed the envelope she'd tucked in the grocery ad, slitting it open with her index finger.

It contained a check for five hundred dollars from

## Cut and Dry 143

Jumbo Rolley. Severance pay, Ruby thought as she held the pale green check, just as Tracee had promised. "Jumbo does what I say," Tracee had vowed. Then Ruby saw the slip of paper still in the envelope, a three-inch square from a notepad.

*An advance,* the note read, *In case you have expenses.* It was signed *J.R.*, the handwriting the same angular letters as on the envelope, with the odd little downward hook. So Tracee hadn't got her way on this one after all. Ruby checked the postmark date on the envelope and realized it had been mailed that morning, probably when Jumbo picked up his own mail. No zip code, and Ruby imagined him slipping the envelope into the "local" mail slot, his name written so large on the envelope that the curious clerk had certainly indulged in a few moments of speculation over *that*.

The check was written on Jumbo's personal account: Leo P. Rolley. While the penmanship was the same as on the envelope, it was more deliberate, the way penmanship often was whenever money or legal actions were involved, carefully formed by a man who wasn't simply dashing off a five-hundred-dollar check on a whim. He knew what he was doing: paying for services he expected to see rendered. Exactly what *did* Jumbo believe he was purchasing?

She slipped the check back into the envelope, then removed it again and looked at it. Five hundred dollars. She folded the check in half and put it in her wallet next to a one-dollar bill. She'd compare Jumbo's numbers against her photocopy of Alice Rolley's deposit ticket. She didn't anticipate any similarities, but she wouldn't take that for granted.

Ruby's father lived only four blocks from the post office, too far for him to walk in his condition. Albert Connelly, who was older and nearly as feeble, usually drove her father wherever he needed to go. They were a sight other drivers tried to avoid, creeping along the roads in Albert's aged brown oversize Dodge, two old men in decades-old gentlemen's hats, Albert's eyes barely rising above the steering wheel.

Ruby parked on the strip of gravel in front of the house, glancing once at the window of her old bedroom above the porch. Almost twenty years had passed since she last stepped from that room, on her way out for good. She doubted if a vestige of herself remained inside, and if any did, she wasn't interested in coming face-to-face with relics of her confused and belligerent past.

The porch swing where her father often sat was empty, the front door stood open to the screen door, and Ruby thought of Johnny Boyd lying on the floor of his cabin. She swallowed once and mounted the familiar front steps, noticing the leaves blown into the porch corners from the storm, then rapped smartly on the screen door, jarring it in its frame. "Hello?"

"Don't break it down. I'm right here," he said from the shaded living room. After the glare of the sun, she couldn't distinguish him from the silhouettes of furniture.

"The clerk at the post office gave me your mail,"

## Cut and Dry

Ruby said through the screen. "He's worried because you haven't picked it up in two days."

"Doesn't miss a trick, does he?" her father grumbled. "Nosy as an old lady."

"Old ladies aren't necessarily nosy," Ruby said.

He grunted and said, "Well, bring it in."

It was curious how many couples bought furniture when they were first married and then never replaced it. Time had stopped forty years ago in her father's house. The only new piece was the green recliner chair where he sat, the type of chair that electronically lifted its seat, boosting the sitter to standing. Plants were missing. Her mother had sought solace in plants, growing them in vigorous profusion until every window held a jungle, or building elaborate vases of flowers of vivid colors and wild contrasts. Sending out futile signals.

The house was clean, tidy, smelling of emptiness, stripped down to utilitarian purposes: no scatter rugs on the floors, nothing pretty or silly, the furniture probably hadn't been rearranged in years. A stack of newspapers was piled beside the recliner. Dark varnished woodwork and dusty blinds. An old man's house.

A newspaper folded back to the crossword puzzle sat on her father's lap; she'd never seen him work a crossword. He was white-haired, shrunk by age and mildness. This angry, raging man undone by mildness. If only her mother could see it.

"Why didn't you pick up your mail?" Ruby asked, setting it on the lamp table beside him. The house was cool without air-conditioning, its old thick walls forming a refuge in the heat, as it always had.

Her father scowled, then an agitated look of confusion crossed his face. "I'm waiting for a phone call," he said.

"If you aren't here, whoever it is will call back," Ruby said. She remained standing, allowing herself the pleasure of looking down on his wrinkled face and white hair. "Or you could buy an answering machine; they're cheaper every day."

"It was Phyllis," he said. "She's . . ." Again the confused look. "Will you call her?"

"I don't even have her phone number," Ruby told him. "We're not in the habit of chatting."

"She's your sister, Ruby. Just give her a call. She's been . . . upset."

"What about?"

Her father shook his head and wiped his mouth with the back of his veined and spotted hand. "She doesn't say anything's wrong. It's in her voice."

Phyllis was the older, the more beautiful, the more successful, her father's favorite. "Believe her, then," Ruby said curtly. "I won't promise to call her."

"Think about it." He shifted in his recliner, then coughed a wet cough, pulling a white cloth handkerchief from his pants pocket and wiping his lips.

When Ruby didn't answer, he said, "I heard you're hunting down Alice Rolley's killer."

Ruby wondered who'd told him. "I'm only doing a little legwork. Carly's shorthanded."

Her father tapped the head of the cane that leaned

against his chair and laughed a short bark. "Not just shorthanded. His ass is in a sling. If Carly doesn't solve Alice's death p.d.q. he can kiss his job good-bye. He'd better be Joe Friday on this one or he'll get voted right out of town on a rail this fall."

"I thought the general consensus was that he was getting voted out of the sheriff's office anyway," Ruby said.

"Maybe. The people grumbling the loudest expected him to raise his dad from the grave. Nobody's a chip off the old block unless we're talking bad apples." He frowned as if it pained him to ask Ruby for information. "You have any ideas about who killed Alice?"

"Not yet. I'm just gathering facts."

"Alice was one of your mother's friends a long time ago," he said, claiming his little corner of the tragedy that surrounded Alice Rolley. "Her girl Roseanne and my Phyllis were in the same grade."

Ruby felt a twinge of the old sorrowful jealousy at the way he said "my Phyllis."

"What was Alice like as a young woman?" she asked.

"Couldn't say. Who knows what a woman's like? Never what you think. Handsome. Held tight to those two kids after she lost the first one. She couldn't let them out of her sight and ruined them both, I'd say. Roseanne and Franklin didn't amount to squat in my book."

When Ruby was little, she'd believed every family

had a dead baby in their history. There'd been a boy between Phyllis and herself who'd only lived a day.

"Franklin Rolley does well at the bakery," Ruby said. More than one person had claimed that Franklin's piecrusts were "to die for."

Her father shook his head. "Who'd have ever expected Jumbo Rolley's son to end up being a baker? A three-dollar bill, that's what he is. He doesn't even look like a Rolley."

"Franklin looks a lot like Alice," Ruby said, tamping down the rising hot sparks. Milder or not, her father still could rile her with a few brief sentences. "Pushing all the right buttons," as Mary Jean liked to say.

"A boy shouldn't look like his mother," her father said, as if Franklin's bone structure had been his own decision. "A boy should look like his father and a girl should look like her mother. And Roseanne, she could break Franklin in half, built like a football player. You see the shoulders on that woman? It isn't natural."

Her father was getting warmed up, thumping his cane on the floor like a nineteenth-century crank. "I'd better get going," Ruby said, turning toward the door.

"Wait," her father said, suddenly mild again, his voice softening. "I've got something for Jesse." He glanced around the living room as if searching for a gift, then leaned forward and pulled his wallet from his hip pocket, removed a five-dollar bill and gave it to Ruby. "Tell her to buy a chocolate malt to keep cool."

"I will," Ruby said, putting the bill in her billfold next to Jumbo's folded check.

## Cut and Dry

"And call Phyllis," he said as Ruby opened the screen door.

She didn't respond to his request and heard his grumbling voice as she descended the steps to her car.

Carly was just leaving the sheriff's office as she pulled into the parking lot. He walked over to her car when he saw her, his tie off and the top two buttons of his shirt undone in the heat, but his head covered by his cap.

"I tried to call you a few minutes ago," he said. "Are you here to see me?"

"That's right."

"We can sit in our outdoor café," he said, pointing to the picnic table on a circle of mowed grass. It was shaded by an oak tree in a corner of the brick buildings that housed both the sheriff's office and the county jail, the jail distinguished by the spiked barbed wire topping the block walls. "Want anything to drink?"

"No thanks."

Carly sat on the edge of the bench and Ruby sat opposite him, the plank table between them. He removed his glasses and wiped them on the fabric of his brown shirt. "I heard you went out to see Babs this morning."

"How'd you know that?"

Carly shrugged. "The usual channels."

"I feel like I'm wearing a radio collar," Ruby said. She related her conversation with Babs Prescott, then added, "And Dick Prescott said to warn you to leave his wife alone, that he doesn't recognize your jurisdiction. He was in fine form, flexing his muscles and grunting. Babs said he's been in a bad mood lately."

Carly shook his head. "Dick's always been a pissant when it comes to the law, but he can't get past that wetlands issue. Says he's not going to pay his taxes this year or renew his driver's license. He's already refused to buy a fishing license and God knows what'll happen during deer season." One corner of Carly's mouth raised. "Just my luck his last act of civil obedience will be to cast a vote against me before he tears up his voter registration card."

"*Did* Roseanne Rolley have anything to do with his pasture being declared a wetland?"

"No," Carly said, laughing a little. "The fool applied for a loan to drain the property and the bank called in the big boys to take a look at it. The rest is history. Dick opened that can of worms all by himself."

"Babs said that on the night Alice died, she and her granddaughter and Katrina left by the front door while Fanny left by the back."

"I'll ask Fanny about that," Carly said.

"Did you know Alice drove down to Lansing every month for beauty supplies?" Ruby asked.

"No. Is that unusual?"

Ruby thought about Alice's making the nearly four-hundred-mile round trip every month by herself to pick up stock. "It's a long way."

"She probably got a good deal. Alice was a frugal woman."

## Cut and Dry 151

Driving close to two hundred miles each way, spending the night in a motel, and eating out just to get a little better price and save shipping costs didn't qualify as frugality in Ruby's mind.

"Besides," Carly continued, "Alice had that other business in Lansing. She's been tied up in lobbying for kids' programs and day-care centers for years. Knowing Alice, there were a couple of congressmen who ducked behind their desks when they spotted her coming their way."

"Fanny mentioned Alice's trips to the capitol, too. I didn't realize she was so dedicated."

"One of her pet projects," Carly said. "She thought she could benefit the most kids by badgering the people who hold the reins."

"She's probably right," Ruby said. "Who's our state representative?"

"Tsk-tsk, Ruby. You don't know? It's Bernie Woktoski."

"Still? That's who was in office when I was a kid. A Kennedy type, right?"

Carly laughed. "Not anymore. Time has caught up with good old Bernie. Age has a way of stripping off the veneer." He slid over on the bench, away from three yellow jackets that had landed on a shiny spill on the table, buzzing and twitching their antennae.

"Jumbo sent me a check today," Ruby told Carly, "an advance payment for looking into Alice's death. Do you feel I'm getting into a conflict-of-interest situation?"

"No, I don't," Carly said carefully, scowling toward

the police cruiser careening into the parking lot too fast, spraying up gravel. It was Mac McCutcheon and he braked the cruiser with the hood pointed toward them and turned off the engine, making no move to get out. In fact, he leaned back and laid one arm across the back of the seat, his mirrored sunglasses reflecting the day. Ruby felt the prickly sensation of being watched.

"You've been upfront about telling Jumbo you'd share information with me," Carly said, still frowning at Mac. "And as long as you don't strike off on your own . . . Curb *that* tendency, Ruby," he warned. "Go ahead and cash Jumbo's check. One of us should get decent pay for this."

After Ruby left Carly she phoned Congressman Bernard Woktoski's home office from the pay phone by the Shell station, getting the number from the operator.

"He's still in Lansing," said a woman who sounded too relaxed to be a secretary, giving her the Lansing office number. "The session's running late this summer and they're busting tail to get out of there by the Fourth of July."

"Thanks," Ruby told her.

"He'll be grouchy as an old bear," the woman warned.

Next she stopped by the Wak 'n Yak. Three customers were in various stages of beautification. Familiar but unidentifiable instrumental music played on a radio hung over the washbasins.

# Cut and Dry 153

"I have a quick question," Ruby told Katrina, who patted her customer's shoulder and set her comb on the counter.

"Fire away."

"I'm going to Lansing for a couple of days. Do you know which motel Alice stayed at when she drove down on her buying trips?"

"She never said," Katrina told her. "Sorry."

"Maybe Fanny knows," Ruby suggested.

Fanny left off adjusting a hair dryer and said, "I don't know either, not the name. But she always left phone numbers. Check last month's calendar."

Katrina flipped back to May. The third Monday of the month had two phone numbers listed, neither of them identified. Ruby recognized Alice's handwriting, the numbers elegantly formed, even though Alice had probably written them from a standing position.

Katrina pushed her notepad toward Ruby. "Take both numbers. One of them's bound to be right. Business or pleasure?"

"What?" Ruby asked.

"Your trip to Lansing—business or pleasure?"

"A little of both."

Katrina nodded sagely. "Do you intend to walk in Alice's shoes down there? You're thinking there's more to her trips than beauty supplies and bothering congressmen?"

"For instance?" Ruby asked.

She winked at Ruby. "I know we're talking Alice Rolley here, but who knows?"

"Did she ever mention Bernard Woktoski? He's a congressman."

"Not to me. Hey, Fanny," she called. "Did Alice ever tell you about a congressman named Bernard Whatchamacallitoski?"

Fanny shrugged and pointed to Alice's wall of photos. "No, but that's him at Alice's Cut-In."

"One of her fund-raisers," Katrina told her. "Eons ago."

It was a photo at least twenty years old, with Bernie as Ruby remembered him: slender, blow-dried hair, sitting in a chair with a towel draped over his shoulders, Alice holding scissors above his head, everybody smiling.

When Ruby picked up Jesse, Cheryl, the piano and electric keyboard tutor, was on the front porch slipping her keyboard into its nylon case. "Jesse has perfect tempo—very controlled," the red-haired woman said. "She'll be ready to perform in my next recital."

"I thought your students had their recital a week ago," Ruby said.

Cheryl's hand paused mid-zip of her keyboard case. "The night Alice Rolley died." She sighed. "That was the summer recital. I hold them twice a year, summer and winter. You'd be surprised how quick twice-a-year comes around."

"Babs Prescott's granddaughter is one of your students?" Ruby asked.

Cheryl grinned. "Susannah?" She glanced around the porch and said in a lower voice, leaning toward Ruby, "Her parents are positive she's the next female

# Cut and Dry    155

Van Cliburn. Unfortunately, they've convinced her of the same thing. Poor little kid, all the makings of a prima donna, except the talent."

Ruby pulled into the Dairy Queen on the way out of Sable so Jesse could buy her favorite malt: chocolate mint.

Five people stood in front of them and in a minute, three more behind them. From Memorial Day, when the stand opened, until Labor Day, when it was boarded over for the winter, the Dairy Queen was the most profitable shop in Sable, busy from morning to night. Its parking lot had been expanded again that spring. Ruby gave Jesse the five-dollar bill. "It's a gift from your grandfather," she said.

Jesse folded the bill in half and put it in her shorts pocket. "He gives me presents because you won't take anything from him," she told Ruby.

"Did he tell you that?" Ruby asked.

Jesse shook her head. "But if I buy your ice cream, too, he'd feel happier."

"I'll pay for my own," Ruby told her. "You save your change for the keyboard you've been wanting."

Ruby longed for the comfort of a crackling fire but the evening was too warm. She laid three logs on the grate anyway and then she called the first of the two numbers Katrina had given her.

"Central Casting," a female voice answered.

"What's Central Casting?" Ruby asked.

There was a few seconds of silence, then the female

voice answered patiently, disdainfully. "We're a beauty supply wholesaler. Whom do you wish to speak to?"

"I'm sorry. I must have the wrong number," Ruby said, jotting down *Central Casting* beside the phone number.

"I thought so," replied the voice, briskly cutting the connection.

Ruby hung up. Jumbo Rolley's check sat next to the telephone, smoothed flat. She tapped it with the eraser end of her pencil before she dialed the second telephone number. It was answered by an older-sounding woman. "Crown Inn. How may I be of assistance?"

In a split-second decision, Ruby responded, "I'm calling to make a reservation for Alice Rolley for next Monday. She'd like her usual room, please."

Ruby heard the soft clicking of computer keys. "That reservation's already been made, ma'am. Would you like it changed at all?"

"No thank you. Could I have your address again?" she asked, furiously jotting on her piece of notepaper.

# Chapter 10

Like mother and child, the sister-and-brother duo of Roseanne and Franklin Rolley appeared on the doorstep of Ruby's cabin.

It was evening, but not late enough to be completely dark; a pink and gold sky backlit the trees along the western edge of Blue Lake, and to the east the sky had already darkened to denim blue. Jesse had gone to bed early, more tired than usual from her afternoon of tutoring, as if a spring inside her had wound down. Ruby had finally learned not to panic but to truly believe these episodes were temporary and if she allowed Jesse to shut down for a while, the spring would rewind itself.

Spot had been uninterested in the Rolleys' arrival, not even leaving Jesse's room to investigate. "Some watchdog," Ruby grumbled as she answered the door.

Franklin stood a step behind and to the side of his sister, letting her take the lead, deference apparent in every atom of his body, from his rounded shoulders and wide-eyed attention on Roseanne to the way he held his hands clasped behind his back: constrained.

The differences in their height and body size were accentuated by their being together. Franklin could fit beneath Roseanne's chin, a slender shadow in his sister's presence. Behind them was parked a yellow pickup.

"We've come to talk to you, Ruby," Roseanne announced with brusque formality, her small eyes piercing into Ruby's, demanding not requesting. Roseanne had things to say and she intended for Ruby to hear them.

"My daughter's just falling asleep," Ruby told her, including Franklin in her glance. "Do you mind if we sit outside? The mosquitoes aren't too bad if I light the candles."

Roseanne shrugged and Franklin remained silent, curiously peering past his sister's shoulder into Ruby's cabin.

"I've got a lighter," Roseanne said, and then, as if she cared that Ruby might suspect she smoked, said, "I only carry it for campfires."

Ruby led them around to the front of the cabin where two lawn chairs sat in the center of four tall citronella candles on top of bamboo stakes set in the ground. They were marginally effective at discouraging mosquitoes. Ruby rarely lit them.

While Roseanne held her Bic to each candle, Ruby retrieved a third lawn chair from the shore and Franklin, looking like a man without a mission, sat down and watched the two women, his hands between his knees.

The candles flared, smoked and wavered, and then

steadied to yellow flames that illuminated their faces and gave their eyes tawny glints.

"What's this about?" Ruby asked.

"You know," Roseanne said, choosing a chair and ordering Ruby, "Sit down."

So that she wouldn't feel like she was facing an inquisition, Ruby moved her lawn chair closer to Roseanne's, positioning it to avoid the lumps in the lawn. Both Rolleys intently watched her, their expressions identically rapt.

By candlelight, Roseanne's features were softened, but the shadows flickering around their circle enlarged her size. Ruby brushed away the sensation of being small and in the presence of a stern schoolteacher.

"We know what our father did," Roseanne began in a strong, loud voice, then blinked as if she'd surprised herself with her own volume.

Ruby sat back, wondering if Alice's death was about to be solved before her very eyes, right here on her front lawn. She waited, her body still, not taking a breath that might interrupt Roseanne. The flame nearest Franklin guttered, and for a moment he slipped into deeper shadow, his eyes deepening so the resemblance to his mother was more eerily marked.

"And we don't want you involved in investigating our mother's death," Roseanne finally finished, her voice more normally pitched. "Whatever our father's already paid you, we're here to pay you the same amount. Tell him you've changed your mind."

Ruby was disappointed. No confession, nothing that

simple. "Did he explain why he'd hired me?" she asked.

Neither sibling answered, and Ruby asked, "He didn't tell you he'd hired me, did he?"

"People are talking," Roseanne said.

"Who told you? Tracee?"

She'd hit an open sore. Roseanne jerked her head and gazed at Ruby with distaste, her small eyes bright. "You've talked to Tracee? Is she in on this?"

"In on what?" Ruby asked.

But Roseanne wasn't listening. She squeezed her big hands into fists and hit her thighs. Once, twice. Her words burst forth on a single breath. "That pygmy brain. She's worse than a street whore; doing it while my mother was alive. Taking a stupid old man for every penny she can. The whore, spreading her—"

"Roseanne," Franklin interrupted in a lazy, low voice. "You're becoming redundant."

Ruby peered sharply at Franklin in the shadows, wondering if she'd misjudged him.

Franklin was four years older than Ruby, enough of a difference during her youth that she viewed him as a member of another, older generation. She remembered him but only because of his presence as a faded, solitary figure, not because of anything significant he'd ever said or done. If he hadn't recently come to her attention again, she doubted she'd even recall his name.

But Roseanne, as well as being physically conspicuous, had been her sister Phyllis's classmate. Roseanne's size, her passion for horses, and her emotional

# Cut and Dry 161

outbursts made her memorable. When Ruby had overheard Phyllis and her friends discussing her, it was usually to the tune of "Can you believe what Roseanne Rolley did this time?"

Ruby let the subject of Tracee drop. "But don't you agree with your father?" she asked. "He wants to discover who killed your mother."

"The sheriff is in charge of the investigation," Roseanne said, jabbing a finger toward the ground. "Carly will solve it."

"Hopefully," Franklin murmured.

"He's the sheriff," Roseanne continued. "Legally the law. You're . . . well, you're not."

"I see," Ruby said, beginning to understand. "It's not that someone outside the sheriff's office is involved; it's that *I'm* involved, right?"

It might have only been the candlelight that made Roseanne appear to blush. Franklin gazed at the faint afterglow still lingering to the west, removing himself once again from the conversation.

"I . . . we're telling you to stay out of it," Roseanne said.

Ruby rubbed her hands over her legs, suddenly chilled. She glanced across the water toward Johnny Boyd's cabin, glimpsing a glowing dot that expanded briefly and diminished. She wouldn't have expected him to be a smoker any more than she would have Roseanne.

"Is there a test I should have taken first?" Ruby asked, catching the fleeting grin on Franklin's face. "An assessment of my ability to distinguish right from wrong? Maybe an analysis of the percentage of income I've donated to charity?"

"You *were* the charity," Roseanne said in a low voice. "My mother's charity case."

"But I'm not yours," Ruby said. "And I won't take any of your money, either."

Ruby watched the light in Roseanne's eyes flare, her forehead furrow and shoulders square, realizing that Roseanne wasn't averse to a battle, that she probably even enjoyed a chance to engage in a good fight, maybe even a physical confrontation, experiencing that rush as her senses sharpened with a few jolts of adrenaline.

"Always the smart mouth," Roseanne sneered, the last of any civility draining from her voice as if a plug had been pulled. "You and your sister."

"Phyllis?" Ruby asked. "What does Phyllis have to do with this?"

But Roseanne went on. "Our father hasn't got the sense to leave this to the sheriff but *you* can back right out of it. That's all I'm telling you to do. Don't dirty our mother's memory by bringing in his whores. The whole town doesn't need to have what they're guessing confirmed by you."

"I'm not a gossip," Ruby said.

"And you're saying my mother was?" Roseanne challenged.

Ruby stared at her. Roseanne leaned forward as if she were about to leap from her chair and wrestle Ruby to the ground and strangle her by candlelight.

The fact that Alice Rolley had been a gossip hadn't even crossed Ruby's mind.

"I'm only telling you that my work is confidential."

"Nothing's confidential around here," Roseanne said, leaning back. She stared at Ruby, her face so distorted by rage that Ruby wanted to look away, but she held her gaze, goose bumps rippling down her arms. Roseanne's hands shook; her jaw jumped as she gritted and released her teeth.

"You're not listening to me," Roseanne accused her. "You don't care about the family's feelings."

"If I didn't care," Ruby said, "I wouldn't be involved. Your mother was good to Jesse and me. I'm grateful to her."

Roseanne sniffed in disbelief. "If that's true, let Carly handle her death. You stay out of it." She rose to her feet, knocking the chair backward. It would have tipped over if Franklin hadn't grabbed it and righted it on the rough ground. "Let's go, Franklin," she ordered.

He gave Ruby an unreadable glance and stood, following his sister.

"If you won't play fair, Ruby," Roseanne said, already moving into the darkness. "Don't expect me to."

Ruby didn't answer, didn't rise from her chair, suddenly weary to her bones, feeling as if she'd just outrun a dangerous animal and landed in temporary safety.

She listened to their pickup grumble away through the trees toward Blue Road, wondering what confidences Franklin and Roseanne were sharing by the light of the dashboard: frustration? Anger? Cooking up another, more extreme, plot to discourage Ruby?

One of the citronella candles had burned low, the flame drowning in its own wax. She watched it gutter as she wondered again why she'd come back to a place where the past was so bound to the present, some people couldn't separate the two. Was that what the word *home* meant?

The phone rang, jangling the soft darkness. Ruby didn't move. It wouldn't wake Jesse, who'd gone to sleep with music playing through a set of earphones, a curious form of insulation for her daughter, like white noise.

Five, six, then ten rings, and finally an even dozen before the caller hung up. She didn't have an answering machine, couldn't stand such an intrusion in her life, and callers frequently let the phone ring beyond reason, certain if they waited long enough, the mechanical voice would click on.

The evening was silent again except for the night sounds around Blue Lake. A frog croaked, a mouse rustled in the brush. Laughter floated over the water from a bonfire across the lake.

She'd slipped Jumbo's check into her pocket when Roseanne and Franklin knocked on her door. Now she took it out and smoothed it on her leg, then rolled its corners, thinking.

She wasn't convinced that Franklin agreed with his sister. Ruby detected a touch of amusement in the enigmatic man, as if he was humoring Roseanne, a role he'd played all his life.

Tracee Ferral didn't want Ruby investigating Alice's death, either, because she didn't want her own name linked to Jumbo's. Was that Roseanne's real reason too? Bringing her father's philandering into the open, so soon after her mother's death? Why did everybody care except Jumbo?

She stood and blew out the candles and sat in the comfortable darkness for another hour, feeling the dew settling around her, now and then catching sight of movement in other cabins and Johnny Boyd's flaring cigarette.

Ruby was asleep, but his touch was so familiar she wasn't even startled, only felt a luxurious arousal, both to wakefulness and to his hands on her body.

Hank Holliday slipped into bed beside her, his long body naked. "Mmm, you're warm," he murmured.

"You're back," she said, turning to face him.

"Like a thief in the night," he said against her neck. "I have to leave before dawn. The loggers from hell are arriving at sunup and I'd better be right there watching their every move or they'll rob this poor guy blind."

"You drove all this way, just to . . . ?" she asked.

"Just to," he said, his words muffled as his lips moved down her throat.

They hadn't seen each other in a week and sleep was secondary. She lay with her head on his shoulder, telling him about the past few days, beginning with the forged deposit ticket and ending with Roseanne and Franklin's visit.

"Roseanne showed up at a foresters' meeting last spring." Hank said. "She's dead set against the introduction of the *Entomophaga maimaiga* fungus to kill gypsy moth caterpillars."

"Is that the stuff you call bug Ebola?" Ruby asked.

"Mmm-hmm," he said, kissing the top of her head.

"I thought the fungus was already here."

"It is, but it's a slow migrator. If you take a few shovelfuls of dirt from beneath an oak tree where the fungus has already killed the caterpillars and spread the dirt beneath a tree infested with gypsy moth caterpillars, you've done the job. Add a rainy spring like the springs common here along Lake Michigan, and the fungi go to work. When the conditions are right, the success rate is phenomenal. It could put the gypsy moth experts in the unemployment line."

"So what's this *Entomophaga* critter been doing the last twenty years while the gypsy moths have been running rampant?" Ruby asked, smoothing her hand down his lean chest.

"Good question. It was actually imported from Japan in the early 1900s. Maybe it was adapting to our climate, or waiting until the gypsy moths hit critical mass. Whatever, it's finally giving us a chance to save the oak forests."

"Roseanne should be a cheerleader, then," Ruby said. "Saving everything on earth is her mission."

"She stood up at the meeting and predicted the

## Cut and Dry

fungus was an exotic that would mutate, go on the rampage, and create ecological disaster. The world won't end with a bang but in a giant pile of slush."

"*Can* this fungus mutate?" Ruby asked.

"When it runs out of caterpillars, it goes dormant." His arm tightened around Ruby. "You went up against Roseanne Rolley tonight, huh? I would have liked to have seen that."

"I could stage a rematch," Ruby offered. Lying there together the day's events lost their sting; the tragedy of Alice Rolley was muted.

"No thanks. *I* wouldn't want to go one-on-one with her. But what harm would it do if you *did* back out of this investigation? Let Carly handle it?" He turned on his side, facing her. "You've got the natives riled and you're not making that much headway," he said. "You don't always have to finish what you begin, Ruby. There's grace in knowing when to bow out, too."

# Chapter 11

"Was that you smoking out here last night?" Ruby asked.

Beginning with *Hello* and *How are you?* felt superfluous when she'd been aware of Johnny Boyd watching her every move since she paddled away from her own dock.

It was early morning, not long past sunrise, and Hank was gone. She'd been awakened not by his leaving but by his absence, unable to fall back to sleep. Her body felt relaxed, pleasantly worn.

"You have good eyes," Johnny Boyd said.

"When you live in the woods, flames catch your attention, no matter how small they are."

"I'll be catching your attention a lot then." He nodded toward a cardboard tomato soup box behind his chair. She looked inside; it was three-quarters filled with neatly stacked packs of unfiltered Camels.

"Manly," she commented.

"I haven't done this in ten years," he said, smiling with remembered pleasure. "There is not a vice on this earth that is closed to me at this point."

# Cut and Dry

"As long as you can do it sitting on your front porch," Ruby commented.

He laughed, the corners of his down-sloping eyes crinkling. She pulled a jelly jar containing a red wood lily from a brown bag and set it on the table in front of him. The lily's petals glowed. "I picked this near the cabin," she told him.

"Gorgeous," he said, touching the delicate bloom. "Did you grow it?"

"Not me. It's wild and probably protected. Don't get caught."

"It would be the least of my sins," he said. "You're out early. Where's Jesse?"

"Still asleep. I like a paddle early in the morning." She nodded toward Blue Lake, where a fisherman sat in his rowboat off a weedy backwater, his line angled in beneath the lily pads, perfectly still.

"I've seen you."

He looked tired; his eyes were red-rimmed, the flesh around his mouth pale. "Have you been up all night?" Ruby asked.

"Sometimes the sleep won't come," he told her, shifting in his chair, his mouth tightening as he moved. "But I can doze off whenever I want. I catch up."

Ruby sat on the edge of the porch and pulled up her legs, leaning against a railing post. "I also brought you an early tomato I rescued from Jesse's caterpillar farm and some fresh cherries." She nodded at the brown bag she'd set on the porch.

His voice lowered, a touch of the irritable cop's.

"Thanks. But don't turn me into your charity case, would you?" reminding Ruby of Roseanne's calling *her* Alice's charity case.

"This isn't charity," she told Johnny Boyd with a touch of irritability herself. "This is excess. If I thought you'd bother cooking it, I'd dig around in the weeds for an oversize zucchini."

"Now *there's* a vegetable I've never been able to understand."

Ruby laughed. "Vegetables don't seek our understanding, just a little space and nourishment."

"What we all want," Johnny Boyd said. "You had company last night."

Ruby felt her cheeks burn. This was prying, an invasion in her life, but he went on to say, "I saw you sitting by the light of your bug candles in your yard. Looked cozy," and she relaxed, realizing he hadn't been referring to Hank's late-night appearance, but to Roseanne and Franklin Rolley.

She was so relieved, she blurted out the circumstances. "Roseanne and Franklin Rolley stopped by to order me to quit investigating their mother's death. Or else."

He raised his thick eyebrows. "That's interesting. What reason did they give you?"

"Murky reasons. I'm not the law, they knew me when, gossip. They offered me money to *not* do what Jumbo offered me money *to* do."

Johnny Boyd frowned at the dissipating mists along the shadowed shores of Blue Lake. "Most people," he said slowly, "who've lost a family member to a violent death don't care who's investigating the murder, as long as it gets solved."

"You mean most people in most places," Ruby said. "Life is different here. Pasts and family connections get all twisted around the axle." She smiled at the image. "Hard to move forward."

He rolled his eyes at her, then asked, "Roseanne and Franklin are both Alice's children? Not a son and daughter-in-law?"

"That's right. And in their forties. Both single. They've spent their entire lives in Sable. Franklin lives in a trailer on his parents' property. Roseanne's the dominant one, in every way."

"I don't buy their reason for wanting you to butt out," Johnny said. "And neither should you. What are they afraid you'll discover?"

Ruby rubbed her cheek against her knee. A fine stubble grew on her legs. "For one thing, Jumbo, their father, has kept himself busy over the years having affairs with much younger women. Supposedly Alice and Jumbo quit sleeping together eons ago."

"And they don't think anybody else knows that?" Johnny asked.

"I guess not. Real Babes in the Woods. Maybe Alice didn't mind about the affairs. She styled the hair of at least one of Jumbo's girlfriends. She might have encouraged him, or even arranged trysts for him, I don't know."

"Ah, it always comes down to the basic impulses, doesn't it? Sex, jealousy, greed."

"That's what Ron Kilgore, my old boss, always says: " 'Check the messy stuff first.' "

"Is he a cop?"

Ruby shook her head. "Nearly a lawyer. He kept failing the California bar exams so he opened a detective agency. I was his secretary."

"And he got you involved in forgery detection?"

"He did and it changed my life. I still do jobs for him." The Darrow case sat on the table in her loft, momentarily on hold. She'd promised to get it back to him by next week.

Johnny Boyd flinched and, in a move Ruby guessed was involuntary, touched beneath his rib cage. She hadn't noticed it before but his abdomen was distended. She opened her mouth to ask him if he needed a drink of water or medication and caught the cold, warning look in his eye and closed her mouth again.

After a few seconds he said in a slightly breathless voice, "As I said, there's more to the Rolley kids' attempt to discourage you than the fact that you were a lively teenager. I'd pursue that angle; see what you find. The brother is pretty weak?"

"Maybe," Ruby said, remembering Franklin's grin and his admonishing his sister not to be "redundant." "Or else it's an act he performs in Roseanne's presence—trying to keep the peace."

"Work on him a little. Turn on the charm and see what he spills."

"He may be immune," Ruby speculated.

"No one's immune to a beautiful woman."

"So then we must have passed the test?" Mary Jean asked over the phone.

"You did," Ruby told her. "Leaving Jesse with you the first time was harder on me than on her."

"Told you."

"I'll be back Tuesday," Ruby told her, "so if she can stay with you and Barbara from Monday morning until then, I'll trade you: you can leave Barbara here on one of those excruciatingly embarrassing nights when you're sleeping with her father."

"It's a deal," Mary Jean agreed enthusiastically. "So you're hot on Alice's Lansing connection?"

"Can you keep it to yourself? God knows what that news would stir up around here."

"Can do. But I'll bet you ten bucks you're going to find Alice had a romance in the works in Lansing. Jumbo had his on the side so why not Alice? Traveling to Lansing once a month for twenty years is too suspiciously regular, like those people in that play who meet every year to roll around in bed. What was it called?"

*Same Time Next Year.* I thought you were positive Alice *didn't* have any romantic entanglements."

"I've changed my mind," Mary Jean said. "I know her better now that she's dead, you know what I mean? I *want* her to have had some fun."

Franklin Rolley worked at the Sable Bakery from four in the morning until one-thirty in the afternoon. It was two-thirty when Ruby passed the Rolleys' ranch house on property that hadn't been farmed in years and pulled into the narrow driveway that led to Franklin's travel trailer.

His trailer was positioned in front of two maple trees, occupying its own corner of his parents' property, a square of pasture cordoned off by a six-foot fence of chicken wire, a hundred yards down the road from the house, its view partially blocked by a row of poplars. The two maples were leftovers from the days when farmers clearing their land had left strategically placed trees in their pastures, oases to rest their plowhorses.

Ruby parked beside Franklin's yellow Toyota pickup and got out, surveying the tidy blue and white trailer, its wheels invisible behind white aluminum skirting and well-tended beds of bright red flowers. A row of elevated wooden cages with vetch growing around them stood in the shade of one of the maples, and Franklin—still in bakery white clothes—moved between cages carrying a white plastic bucket. He paid no attention to Ruby's arrival.

"Hi, Franklin," Ruby said, rounding the trailer and approaching the pens.

Franklin nodded and bent over to unlatch a mesh-screened door. The crown of his scalp showed through his thinning hair.

"Rabbits?" she asked, bending down to peer into a dark cage. Her sister Phyllis had raised two rabbits one summer. Ruby had been jealous until the doe had birthed her babies and eaten them. She shuddered at the memory of the scattered tiny pink bodies.

The odor around the cages was strong, musky. Close-set eyes peered from the back of the enclosure, as if the animal had pressed itself into the farthest corner. She heard a soft snort, like a harsh breath.

"Minks," Franklin said, scooping dry food from the plastic pail into a crockery bowl.

"Do you raise them for fur?" she asked, straightening. There were mink farms farther north in Michigan in the colder areas where the pelts grew more luxurious, but not as many farms as there had been: huge complexes of cages and controversy.

"Not for fur," Franklin said. He chuckled lightly. "But don't tell Roseanne that."

"You enjoy tormenting your sister," Ruby commented. "Is she against furs?"

"Of course she is. What kind of question is that?" Franklin raised up and flexed his skinny shoulders, turning his narrow face toward Ruby. "If an issue smacks of ecological slash environmental slash human or animal rights, Roseanne's ready to grab whatever protest placard is appropriate and march on somebody—anybody."

"Even her own brother?"

Franklin stood the scoop in the mink food and raised his eyebrows. "Why not?"

"Because she's always pushed you around?"

"Because she *thinks* she's always pushed me around."

"But she actually hasn't?"

"When dealing with Roseanne," Franklin told her as he relatched the door, "I learned as a tyke to look agreeable and lie low when she thunders off on one of her missions."

"Is that how you run all of your life?"

Franklin shrugged and set down the plastic bucket, picking up a hose and shoving it between the wire mesh, filling water bowls. "Nobody bothers me and I don't get in anybody's way. It's just a happy-go-lucky old world."

He turned off the hose that snaked from beneath a deck attached to his trailer. The deck was half finished, a stack of two-by-fours were balanced on top of open joists. "You're building a deck," Ruby commented.

"A deck?" Franklin laughed. "A deck is a porch somebody was too lazy to finish. This will be a porch. Silas Shea's building it. I just hold the dumb end of the tape measure."

Ruby followed Franklin to a wooden shed at the end of the row of cages. The door was open to bags of food, extra feeding bowls and waterers, containers of mink medicines, all neatly arranged along the walls.

Ruby pointed toward the row of poplars that obscured the Rolleys' house. "You live so close to your parents, you must have seen them pretty often."

"Yeah, pretty often. Sunday dinner sometimes. Mom brought me dinner three or four times a week."

"Did she do your laundry, too?" Ruby asked.

"I don't have a washing machine," Franklin said without any defensiveness. He poured the excess dry food from the plastic bucket into a brown feed bag, then turned and leaned against the shed.

# Cut and Dry

"Were you warning me the other night, too," Ruby asked him. "or just Roseanne?"

Franklin reached out with the animal food scoop and touched Ruby's arm lightly, sliding the scoop down to her elbow. "I told you: I'm agreeable and I don't get in the way."

Ruby didn't step back; she gripped the handle of the scoop, pushing it away from her arm. "No," she told Franklin. "You told me your habit was to *look* agreeable and let Roseanne have her way. Why is Roseanne afraid of an investigation into your mother's death?"

He turned and dropped the scoop into the empty bucket and set them both inside the shed, closing and latching the door. "Elementary, Dr. Crane. She killed Mom and she's terrified you'll figure it out."

"Seriously," Ruby said.

"How about this: Mom was a saint; Dad's a philanderer. She's afraid Dad's messy life will spill over on Mom. My sister loves a sacred memory." Franklin walked beside her, moving around toward the front of his trailer, and Ruby had the sensation of being herded toward her car.

"Did you ever go to Kalamazoo or Lansing with your mother?" Ruby asked.

"On her buying trips, you mean? A couple of times when I was a kid. It was boring. She could shop for hours."

"Did Roseanne go with her?"

"Roseanne? You've seen how she dresses, straight

out of Farm & Fleet. She's no shopper." He stopped beside the metal steps that led to his door.

"Did your mother have enemies? Anybody who'd want her dead?"

"Maybe. She probably gave a few bad haircuts in her time. What is this: *Twenty Questions*?"

This was useless. Ruby took a step toward her car and Franklin made no move to accompany her. "Call me—or Carly—if you remember anyone who quarreled with your mother or who held a grudge against her, would you?" she asked Franklin.

"Are you talking to Roseanne today?"

"Not today but maybe later, why?"

"Just wondered." He paused and said the only serious thing of the whole visit. "I wouldn't cross Roseanne if I were you."

Hank called on Sunday morning while Ruby was packing an overnight bag for Lansing. "I'm coming your way this afternoon—quick job for a guy—can you and Jesse come with me?"

"Where?" Ruby asked.

"Into the deep, dark, and dangerous woods," he told her.

"We'd love to."

Hank drove into the driveway after lunch, looking frazzled, his dark hair uncombed and a prickly growth of beard on his chin. "I haven't had a shower in three days," he said, hugging Ruby and kissing the top of Jesse's head. "Can I?"

"Sure," Ruby told him. "Is the timber job done?"

# Cut and Dry 179

He shook his head. "I have to get back this afternoon but I promised I'd take some pictures at Hale's Rollaway so I'm sandwiching it in between."

"You're sandwiching me in, too?" Ruby asked.

He hugged her again, tipping her backward, intoning like a movie star, "I'm sorry, baby, but I'm a man on the run. Say yes and I'll buy a round of ice-cream cones on our way home."

"Yes," Jesse said for her.

Hank released Ruby and smiled at Jesse. "Okay, it's settled, then. I'll be right back." And he sprinted for the cabin.

Hale's Rollaway didn't exist. It was now just a century-old name, from a time before roads and semis, when logging outfits had rolled gigantic white pine logs down the steep banks into the Sable River to be floated downriver to the lumber mills.

In Hank's Jeep they bumped over two-track roads to reach the remote rollaway, scraping against branches and swerving around mud holes. Between swerves and dodges, Hank held Ruby's hand.

"What are you taking pictures of at the rollaway?" Ruby asked.

"The DNR caught some log robbers and I offered to play photographer, to see if we can spot where they were hauling out. It's a closed case but nobody wants a copycat repeat."

"They were cutting down trees by the rollaway?"

"Nope, raising logs that sank in the river on their way to the mill around the turn of the century. Thousands and thousands of them did." A pine branch smacked the side of the Jeep and he asked, "Are you okay back there, Jesse?"

"This is cool," Jesse said, sounding so much like Mary Jean's daughter that Ruby turned and looked at her in surprise. She was smiling, her arms around Spot's neck.

"Aren't the logs rotten by now?" she asked Hank.

"Not in this cold water. The wood loses some strength after so many years but it's prime panel and veneer wood, worth a fortune. They raise the logs, cut off the old log marks on the butts and then sell the logs."

"But we're talking about a hundred years ago," Ruby protested. "The mills that branded the logs with their marks are long gone."

"That's right, but when the mills closed, they sold their log marks to other mills, and those mills sold to others, and so on. So the logs are still officially owned and hauling them out of the river is stealing. Capital S."

"Deadheads," Ruby and her cousins had called the half-sunk logs that got in the way of their canoes on Sable River. Only a hazard, the idea that somebody might *steal* them a silly fantasy.

Now, the rollaway only appeared to be a sixty-foot-high bank that had eroded long ago; no trace of its previous life remained. They stood at its top, overlooking the peacefully winding river and the trees and shrubs tangling along its banks. Ruby imagined the scene: logs rumbling down the bank one after another

# Cut and Dry

and crashing into the river in giant plumes of water, filling the river from bank to bank, then floated and ridden by loggers to the mills.

"Trying to raise logs out of that looks like too much trouble to me," Ruby said, gazing at the steep banks.

Hank nodded. "It takes a dedicated thief to do it. A lot of the logs are buried under bottom sand now, but think of it." He swept his hand along the course of the river, east to west.

"This is all we have left of our old growth forests, under the water, right here at our feet. Rare and *very* valuable wood."

Hank pulled a camera with a zoom lens from a bag in the back of his Jeep. "The government buys nice toys," he said, inserting fresh film. He snapped two pictures of Jesse and Ruby and then walked along the edge of the bank, clicking the camera at the river below them.

Ruby walked beside him, gazing at the river scene, the way nature had filled in the past. "Take a few over that way," she told Hank. "Near that snag."

He lowered the camera and looked at her. "What do you see?"

"Just that the bushes are trampled. See how the slanted sunlight forms shadows?"

"Not really," he said, snapping where Ruby pointed.

"Oblique light really points out any anomalies."

"If you ever get bored with forgery detection," he told her, "you can start a second career as a tracker."

After shooting another roll of film, they walked back to the Jeep along a narrow deer trail. Hank kicked at a dried piece of scat and commented, "Coyotes. They're coming back gangbusters."

"I haven't seen any," Ruby said.

"They don't want you to, either."

"Jesse?" Ruby called. A minute ago she'd been a few feet behind them.

"Over here." Jesse stood in a meadow of bracken fern as high as her waist, so thick, she appeared to be rising from a dense green sea. The ferns parted and trembled in a line from Jesse to the edge of the meadow and Spot emerged, her tail whipping.

Ruby, Hank, and Jesse sat for a while in the warm golden sand at the top of the rollaway, drowsing and listening to the river. Jesse leaned against Spot, turning her hand and watching an orange and black ladybug crawl across her knuckle. Hank glanced at his watch and gave Ruby an apologetic look.

Ruby was about to ask him if they really had to leave already when she heard a noise in the trees behind them. Hank heard it, too, turning his head quizzically. He squeezed her hand and stood.

Low rumbling began in Spot's throat. The dog crouched, her hackles rising.

"Stay," Ruby told her.

Out from a dense growth of hawthorne, stepped a man in camouflage, his face painted in green and brown swirls, leafy branches sticking from his hat. He carried a rifle in both hands, poised to shoot. Jesse gasped and Ruby put her arm around her.

"What's going on?" Hank asked the man, casually

## Cut and Dry

walking toward him. Ruby knew Hank wasn't feeling as relaxed as his words sounded.

For a moment the man stared at Hank, then lowered his rifle, holding it beside his leg, out of sight. "Hey, buddy," he said, waving his hand in a friendly gesture. "Just a paintball game. Don't say you saw me." And he turned and disappeared, fading back into the hawthorne.

"Paintball?" Ruby asked.

"I've never seen a paintball gun like that," Hank said, looking at the still-shuddering hawthorne. Then he smiled and said to Jesse, "Let's go get that ice cream."

He was silent on the rough drive out of the woods, distracted, his tongue circling inside his cheek the way it did when he was thinking. When Ruby heard Jesse humming to Spot, she said quietly to him, "Who was that?"

"I don't know."

"It wasn't a poacher. A nut case? Survivalists? Militia on maneuvers? The First Americans on the move?"

"Any of the above," he said. "I'll be back in town for good in a couple of days and I'll find out."

"How?"

"Guys can't keep escapades like that to themselves. An hour in Jimmy's bar and a few well-placed questions should do it."

"Do you know anybody who belongs to one of those organizations?" Ruby asked him.

He shifted uncomfortably. "Not around here," he said.

"So who? Well, never mind. My question is *why*? What kind of person joins up?"

Hank thought a few more minutes, and when they'd pulled out of the two-track onto a two-lane gravel road, he asked, "Do you remember when you were a kid and you realized somebody else got a bigger piece of pie than you did, or cheated to get a better grade than yours and didn't get caught, or you got blamed for something you didn't do?"

"Yes," Ruby said, feeling the hot prick of memory. "I do."

"What did you do about it?"

"I got mad."

"Then what?"

Ruby shrugged. "I don't know. Kicked around and got over it, I guess. Did something else."

Hank took his eyes off the road and smiled at her. "The world's number one rule is that life isn't fair. Bad things happen no matter how good you are. Most of us complain about it but we finally accept it, grow a little more cynical and muddle along. But some people don't. The desire to fix it drives them crazy. They're determined to make the world an honest place to their way of thinking and the more they try the more frustrated they become . . ."

"And the more extreme," Ruby finished.

"Yeah, they march down a noble, doomed path."

" 'That way lies madness,' " Ruby said.

# Chapter 12

The Crown Inn, where Alice Rolley had stayed on her monthly trips to Lansing, was actually in East Lansing, closer to Michigan State University.

The motel was a two-story white stucco building near a residential area, optimistically Spanish with Moorish arches and tile walkways, set back from the street on a block of small one-story businesses, its front lawn green and well tended, croquet wickets in place, striped lawn chairs in geometric groupings, a motel that might have been featured in a tourist brochure thirty years ago.

*Welcome to the Crown Inn, your home away from home,* the sign on the unattended counter read. *We're here to please.* Heavy oak and blue-upholstered furniture filled the lobby, a rack of tourist brochures stood beside a table holding a silver coffee urn and a tower of styrofoam cups.

Ruby glanced through the plate glass window at the empty grounds, noting how the grass around the croquet wickets was unmarred, as if no one had ever played the game. Not seeing anyone, she pressed the buzzer at the front of the counter.

Immediately a plump middle-aged woman entered through the door at the back of the office, wiping her hands on a kitchen towel and chewing. Behind her escaped the brown odor of cooking meat.

"Sorry," she said, swallowing and pushing her glasses higher on her nose. "I didn't hear you."

Ruby had thought this through, even repeated it aloud during the morning's long drive, so now she smoothly said, "I'm here in Alice Rolley's place. I'd like the room reserved in her name."

The woman wiped her lips with the dishtowel and removed a registration card from behind the desk. "Alice isn't coming?"

Ruby hadn't expected Alice to be a personal acquaintance of the manager's. "No, she's unable to. You've known her a long time?"

"Six or seven years, I guess," the woman said, glancing at the card as Ruby filled it out. "Every month. She's a sweetheart, isn't she?"

"A very good-hearted person," Ruby agreed. "Coming to Lansing was . . . is a pleasant escape for her, I think. She loves to shop."

The woman laughed. "Oh yes, she always heads home with *bagfuls* of goodies." She picked up Ruby's registration card, reading aloud, " 'Ruby Crane, Sable, Michigan,' " and looking up at Ruby before she gave her the key. "Room 208. Just dial 0 on the phone if you need anything. I set out coffee and donuts in the lobby every morning."

Room 208, Alice's customary room, was at the rear of the Crown Inn, on the second floor, quieter and farther from street noise. Ruby turned on the air conditioner as soon as she entered. It groaned and clunked, then settled into a steady hum. The room was pleasantly nondescript, with forgettable art prints on the mauve and cream walls, one queen-size bed and a bureau, a color TV, the toilet sealed with a paper strip for Ruby's protection, complimentary shampoo and lotion in a basket on the counter.

A wide window overlooked an alley and into the backyards of fading Victorian homes of brick and wood, turrets and long porches, from a time when families were large and servants cheap.

For a moment Ruby considered calling Mary Jean to see how Jesse was doing, maybe just to say hello. She even picked up the telephone receiver, then set it down again. Mary Jean had the motel's phone number. It was just that Jesse felt so damn far away.

"Overprotective mother," she told herself, and unfolded the map of Lansing she'd bought at a gas station outside of town and spread it on her bed. First, she circled the Crown Inn's address, then the site of the beauty supply house. They were six miles apart; surely there were motels closer to the beauty supply warehouse than the Crown Inn.

Ruby traced her finger in a straight line down Michigan Avenue to the capitol building, a few miles in the other direction from the inn. The three locations formed a rough triangle on the map.

Her back and shoulder muscles were tight after the

long drive and she took a hot shower, standing beneath the pounding water until her skin stung. As she toweled off, Ruby imagined Alice enjoying the luxury of towels she hadn't laundered or put out herself.

Get a complete picture, Johnny Boyd had advised. Ruby combed her hair and left the motel on foot, walking block by block inside a rough square of shops near the Crown Inn, trying to see what Alice had seen. The usual businesses, a body-piercing parlor, a New Age bookshop, a gun shop. She wished she'd brought a photograph of Alice, and then grinned at the thought of leaning across counters and asking in her best detective tenor, "Have you seen this woman?"

Few people were out walking on the streets. The doors of shops that weren't air-conditioned stood open; heat rose from the concrete sidewalks. Ruby stood on the curb beside a young black woman holding two toddlers by the hand and waited for the traffic light to turn green, realizing this was a fruitless exercise. Had Alice Rolley even bothered to leave the Crown Inn on foot? Had she chosen the motel because it *was* out of the way? Quiet? A sanctuary after weeks of cutting hair and listening to customers' mole hills of secrets and problems, maintaining a public happy face? She might have spent the entire time in her room with her feet up, eating takeout and watching HBO.

Ruby gave it up, leaving the shopping district and wandering through the older residential area behind the motel, grateful for the cool shade of old maple

# Cut and Dry

trees, lenghtening her stride until she felt the pleasure of her leg muscles stretching.

"Sorry," a college-age girl called out, skimming close to Ruby on a bicycle and careening through a rusted iron gate into an old estate that had been divided into apartments. Bicycles littered the front porch, which had probably once held genteel wicker furniture.

She passed another house with a lawyer's nameplate hanging in the curved front window, then another, its front steps replaced by long ramps. A young boy sat in a wheelchair close behind a wrought-iron fence, frowning at Ruby, his head tipped unnaturally. She stopped, remembering Jesse's first weeks after the car accident. The wheelchair days were long behind them, but she'd never appreciated the usefulness and damned awkwardness of a wheelchair before then. Now, a chair caught her attention. She noticed details she hadn't known existed before Jesse's accident: footplates and backrest angles, brake mechanisms and tire sizes, remembering the challenge of getting a chair in and out of the car.

"Hello," she said to the boy.

He continued to stare at her, bobbing slightly to a speeded-up internal rhythm, a less intense version of Jesse's rocking when her senses grew overloaded. The rocking periods were diminishing with time, but there was no guarantee they'd ever end completely.

"I'm sorry," Ruby said softly to the boy. She reached her hand through the pickets and touched his slender wrist.

"Hey, Joshua, are you hungry?" a girl in a college sweat shirt called from the front porch of the house.

Ruby snatched her hand back from the boy and continued down the sidewalk. What was she thinking, *touching* a strange child?

An old woman waved to Ruby from the next house, an impeccable Victorian painted white and several shades of green, a bright, timeless house in the midst of decay and change.

Ruby returned to the Crown Inn; she'd been walking for forty-five minutes and she could definitely use another shower. The motel manager was weeding flower beds between the sidewalk and her lawn, kneeling on a foam pad and humming to herself as she dug out weeds with a trowel. "Hot day for walking around," she said to Ruby, sitting back on her heels and pushing back her straw hat with her gloved hand.

"Alice told me about a gift shop in the neighborhood," Ruby lied. "I thought she said she walked to it."

The woman frowned. "I can't think which shop she was talking about, not a *nice* gift shop around here, anyway."

"Maybe she's a more ambitious walker than I am," Ruby said.

"I don't remember seeing Alice walk anywhere; she drives."

"I must have misunderstood her description. This is a pleasant motel. How long have you owned it?"

"Eight years." The manager moved her foam pad farther along the garden. "My husband and I bought

## Cut and Dry

it but he died three years ago. It keeps me too busy to feel sorry for myself. My daughter helps me if I get in a jam. We get the football crowd during homecoming sometimes. *There's* a job, keeping the place together in the midst of those shenanigans."

"So Alice has been coming here as long as you've owned the motel?" Ruby asked. A drab little hummingbird zipped across the motel's lawn, its wings a blur.

"I think so. I didn't get to know her until a couple of years passed." She pulled a spreading mass of oxalis weed from the dirt. "I hate these things; they're worse than morning glory."

"Does Alice ever bring any friends with her?"

The woman looked up at Ruby, tamping down the oxalis in her plastic bucket of weeds and sliding forward. "Alone as far as I know. We have a coffee together sometimes in the evening but she doesn't stay in very often. She always pays for a single, but I'm not that nosy."

"You said she doesn't stay in very often in the evenings. Do you know where she goes?"

The manager braced both hands on the ground for support and stood, facing Ruby, her expression steely. "I don't tell tales about my customers. If you want to know what Alice does while she's here, you go ask her."

Near the capitol, Lansing's streets were all one-way, and within minutes Ruby was lost and confused, able to see the dome but not get to it. She was stopped from turning into oncoming traffic by a warning chorus of car horns. "I hear you," she muttered, and turned up a side street near a cathedral, keeping the capitol's elongated dome in her sights and parking at the first empty space she spotted: on a tree-lined street in front of a gently run-down apartment building, six blocks from the capitol. She didn't have enough change for the parking meter, so she folded a five-dollar bill inside a piece of notepaper and slipped it beneath her windshield wiper; it had worked before.

The closer she got to the gray capitol building, the more the foot traffic increased. Suited men and women, briefcases and quick-draw cellular phones. Snatches of conversation full of political talk—committees and bill numbers—as intelligible as a foreign language. Ruby didn't feel like the woman who'd recently returned to Michigan from fast-paced California; she felt like a woman who'd spent years buried in Sable, Michigan.

Inside the capitol's visitors' entrance, she stood blinking in the dimly lit corridor, waiting for her eyes to adjust, surrounded by dark wood and low light. Voices and footsteps reverberated from all directions; the air smelled of wood and paint and cleaning solutions.

She approached the dark information desk on her right. "Can you give me directions to Bernard Woktoski's office?" she asked one of the uniformed young women.

"I'll look that up for you," she said, turning to a

computer that was already being used by an identically uniformed woman, and then, in frustration, opened a well-thumbed directory with escaping loose pages. "He's on the lower level, the third office on the left."

First, Ruby did what she'd last done for eighth-grade government class: She took the steps to the next floor to gaze upward. Light streamed downward from the ornate dome high above and two small boys lay on their backs shoulder to shoulder, pointing upward and whispering. Men and women intent on their business simply stepped around the boys without notice, as if they were potted plants on a sidewalk.

Behind Ruby a tour began, and in the long corridors the guide's voice echoed, distorted to gibberish.

Ruby wasn't a very good tourist. She'd grown up in the middle of the love–hate relationship that Sable had carried on with its tourists. Now, whenever she had the opportunity to play tourist, she discovered she still harbored that touch of disdain—only now toward herself.

The lower level was less ornate but appropriately legislatorial: tall polished wood doors with frosted windows, echoing voices and creaking floors, the state seal everywhere.

Bernard Woktoski's office door stood open, and when Ruby stepped inside she faced drop cloths and ladders. "Hi." A man in white painter's coveralls rolling white paint on the wall looked down at Ruby and said without breaking a long sweeping stroke, "If you're looking for Woktoski, he's across the street in the White Pine Building. Second floor. If he asks, tell him we've been here since eight this morning and the whole frigging thing will be done by five tomorrow. Guaranteed."

"Will do," Ruby told him.

Bernard Woktoski's office was at the very end of the second-floor corridor in the White Pine Building. His nameplate hung askew on the wall beside the office door. Taped to the frosted glass was an illustration of a robin, the state bird, waving its wing in front of a map of Michigan. Someone had drawn a mustache on the bird's beak. An NRA sticker was adhered to the bottom corner of the window.

When Ruby knocked, the door was opened by Woktoski himself. Carly was right: All vestiges of the Kennedy influence were gone. Woktoski was now the caricature of a small-town congressman: beefy with thin hair combed over a bald spot, a rumpled suit, glasses, a florid face. If she tried, she could still find a trace of the eager young congressman having his hair cut in the photograph on the wall of the Wak 'n Yak. Physically, but not in the eyes. His eyes were those of a man who now only tended to business.

"Did you bring the Hodgeson brief?" Woktoski asked Ruby impatiently, clicking a ballpoint pen.

"No," Ruby told him, holding out her hand. "My name is Ruby Crane. I'm one of your constituents from Waters County."

The smile turned on, the pen went into his pocket. He pumped her hand with just the right amount of pressure: firm sincerity, an extra squeeze before he released it, talking rapid-fire the whole time. "Good to meet you. Come in, come in. Have a seat. Anywhere you can find a spot. My office is being remodeled and this is where they stuck me for the duration. Did you see it? We were supposed to be on recess before they painted but this session's run long and God forbid we tamper with the painter's schedule; democracy takes a backseat. I feel like a freshman in here. After all these years."

Ruby chose a Danish modern chair opposite his desk. There was a couch, too, but it and one other chair were covered with file folders and stacks of paper. The walls were bare, the decor temporary.

"This heat is something else, isn't it?" he asked, sitting down and wiping his forehead with a handkerchief. "The air conditioner at this end of the building isn't worth beans when the sun comes around. What can I do for you? Are you touring the capital?"

"I am," Ruby told him. "I'm also doing a little legwork for Sheriff Carl Joyce."

He looked at her blankly, tenting his fingers.

"Regarding Alice Rolley's death. I understand she was very interested in legislation involving children?"

He gazed over Ruby's shoulder, his face appropriately sorrowful. "What a rotten shame, her dying like that. I only knew her from her work down here, lobbying, I guess you'd call it, but she struck me as a fine woman. A real loss to Pere."

"Sable," Ruby corrected. "Alice lived in Sable, not Pere."

"Right, right. I've met her daughter, demonstrating

against clear-cutting, I think. Or maybe it was for the Kirtland's warbler." He shook his head. "She sure didn't take after Alice, did she? How can I help you?"

"Can you tell me more about the issues Alice was advocating?"

Woktoski nodded and removed his pen again, holding it over a yellow pad of paper as if he were about to take notes. "With present state finances, she was mainly fighting to *maintain* funding for programs: prenatal care, early-start programs, aid for handicapped children."

"All worthwhile issues, you're saying?" Ruby asked.

"Definitely, definitely." The pen moved on the pad and Ruby could tell by the movement of his hand that he was making *X*'s, crossing and recrossing his lines. "Begin with the children, I always say. They're the ones who'll be supporting us in our old age. If we don't give them a good start we'll all have a bad end. Don't you agree?"

"I do. I'm curious how much time Alice spent here in the legislature. Did she visit you every month when she came to Lansing?" A bowl of chocolate mints sat on the table beside Ruby; she took two and tucked them in her bag.

"Not every month. She'd stop in for five minutes or so." He laughed. "She called it 'status checking,' kept track of how I'd voted, and she didn't waste any time letting me know if she didn't approve, either."

"Only five minutes every couple of months? You're sure?"

"I know it doesn't seem like I'd remember, as busy as I am, but Alice has been a constant the past twenty years. But yeah, that's right. She'd zip in and have her say and zip out again, maybe every other month, sometimes less."

"Did she ever bring anyone else with her when she visited you?"

He thought, frowning and skewing his mouth to one side. "I don't recall anyone else, but then like I said, I only saw her for a few minutes at a time. Why? Is this part of her murder investigation?"

"We're just trying to build a complete picture of Alice Rolley, that's all."

"I'm sorry I can't be more help. She was always pleasant—persistent—but pleasant. How's her family getting along?"

"They're coping," Ruby told him. She glanced at a page of notes on his desk: loops and swirls she recognized as old-fashioned shorthand.

"A senseless death, that's what it was," he said.

"Did you ever see Alice socially while she was in Lansing?"

Woktoski leaned back in his chair, his eyes instantly wary. "Don't get any ideas, Miss Crane. I'm a happily married man."

"Do you think Alice made any enemies here?"

Woktoski's laugh was spontaneous. He laid down his pencil. "Alice? Not at all. She struck me as a woman who made an effort to get along with people who disagreed with her."

"You're saying she would have made a good politician," Ruby said.

"That's right," he agreed.

"Thanks," Ruby told him, picking up her bag and notebook and rising from her chair.

He rose and accompanied her to the door of his small office. "I'll be back in the district as soon as the session ends. We're all doing our best to close it out before the Fourth of July. I've got a parade up your way."

"I'll look for you," Ruby said.

At the door he shook her hand again and asked, "You didn't come down with Dick Prescott, did you?"

"Dick Prescott?" Ruby asked, half to herself, thinking of Dick's private flag-raising ceremony on his front lawn after she'd talked to Babs. "From Sable?"

"The same."

"Was he here regarding his wetlands issue?" Ruby asked.

"He and his lawyer stopped by this morning. I just thought you two might have carpooled. Guess not, right?"

"I heard his pasture was declared a wetland and he's fighting it," Ruby said.

"Yeah, no matter what you think of the Department of Environmental Quality or environmental issues, you've got to feel sympathy for the man; he bought the land, has been paying taxes on it for years. Now all of a sudden he's barred from using it and still has to pay taxes on it."

"Does he have a chance of changing the ruling?" Ruby asked.

"He has two chances," Woktoski said before he closed his door. "Slim and none."

# Chapter 13

The growling of her stomach reminded Ruby that she hadn't eaten since her early breakfast before she left her cabin. She exited the White Pine Building into the bright sunshine and walked to a cafeteria a block from the capitol, joining the line filing past the glass counters of food, everyone preoccupied, snatching their food with only fuel in mind, no time for restaurants and cafés.

"Ruby Crane?" a man's voice asked tentatively as Ruby reached for a piece of cherry pie. She turned and met the gaze of a slender, vaguely familiar man balancing a tray that held a stack of papers beside a hamburger and a salad.

"I thought it was you. You probably don't remember me. We met at Mina's funeral last year. I'm her cousin, Jordan Asauskas."

At the time, in the confusion and sorrow of the event, Ruby hadn't spoken to Jordan Asauskas beyond their brief introduction, but she remembered him from the funeral, hearing how he'd moved away from Waters County as a child and was now a state con-

## Cut and Dry

gressman from the other side of Michigan. Local boy makes good.

"Of course, how are you, Jordan?"

"Fine. Care to share a table with me? Save me from doing this?" and he nodded to the stack of papers.

"Sure."

She followed the small man to a corner table beside a silk ficus plant. Jordan Asauskas was fair skinned, small-boned like Mina had been, wiry, his stomach flat and shoulders square, his hair prematurely silver. She did a quick calculation; he had to be in his early forties. An aura of self-confidence surrounded him, with none of the bluster she'd observed in Bernard Woktoski.

"What brings you to Lansing?" he asked.

"Business and pleasure. I'm doing some legwork for Sheriff Carly regarding Alice Rolley's death, putting together a more complete picture of her life."

He nodded as he unloaded his tray. "Aunt Fay told me about her murder. A bad shock for Sable, I'm sure. Any progress?"

Ruby spread her paper napkin on her lap. "Not so much in finding the killer but I'm finding she was a more complex person that I'd realized. I talked to Bernard Woktoski a while ago; did she stop by your office like she did his?"

"I saw her once or twice a year. She wasn't in my district but she was a master at publicizing her agenda. Alice wasn't a battering ram, more like a cold draft you couldn't keep out. I admired her dedication."

Two men carrying trays of empty dishes toward the tray return paused beside their table, one of them natty, the other looking like a retired farmer. "How's the new committee, Jordan?" the natty one asked.

"A hot potato," he answered.

"Don't we know it?" the other man said, and they both laughed.

After they'd left, Jordan said in response to Ruby's questioning glance, "I'm the chairman of the new Subversive Organizations Committee; some people refer to it as SOC, as in 'Sock it to 'em.'"

"You're investigating militia organizations? Constitutionalists?"

"Among others, as if any of the really rabid members are going to volunteer to emerge from behind the bushes and testify to a government committee as to what they're all about." He cut his hamburger in half. "But we'll do our best to come up with some definitive answers, report their agenda, maybe slap a few wrists."

"Are the First Americans included in your investigation?" Ruby asked.

He raised his eyebrows. "They began down by Allegan two or three years ago. Have they spread into Waters County?"

"I saw an announcement for a meeting a few days ago."

He nodded. "That's the modus operandi. Get a bunch of disgruntled people together and light a fire under them."

"Are they dangerous?" Ruby asked. Her sandwich

was dry. She opened one of the tiny packets of mustard.

"Only they know for sure if they are," he said. "The First Americans are a big umbrella: little groups with their own agenda squeeze beneath it. Some set up alternative local governments, 'pure' and based on their own interpretation of the Fourth Amendment and the Uniform Commercial Code, opposing the legal government. They'll refuse to pick up government mail or buy licenses. Some of them won't even respond to their given names, afraid it means the government has them in its sights." He shook his head. "I heard of a court hearing where a man lost his daughter rather than identify himself when his name was called. These groups can make a mess in a district."

With the handle of his knife, he tapped the stack of papers he'd been carrying. "These are letters from concerned citizens."

"From which side?"

"Both. A lot of them decrying the taxpayers' waste of money for the investigation process, advising me to mind my own business, threats of doom and anarchy, harm to my family and all my progeny, the usual."

He bit into his hamburger and chewed, thoughtfully studying Ruby. Suddenly he snapped his fingers, swallowed, and said, "You do handwriting analysis, don't you? I remember Aunt Fay mentioned it after that timber-buying mess last year."

"Forgery detection," Ruby corrected. "Questioned documents, not personality analysis through handwriting. That's another field entirely."

He pulled a folder from the bottom of the stack of papers and held it out to Ruby. "Could you do me a favor and take a look at these letters? I pulled them because of the similarity in phrasing. Maybe you can detect whether they were written by the same person or by several different people who have a connection?"

"You mean people who belong to the same organization so they'd use the same phraseology?"

"That's right," he said, still holding out the folder.

"You want me to look at these now?" She glanced around the bustling cafeteria. "Here?"

"Could you? Just your gut instinct, that's all I'm asking. I can't let these letters leave my possession."

She reluctantly took the folder. "I'll look them over but my opinion's useless unless I have time to do a detailed analysis."

"Fine, fine. Go ahead," he said, and removed Ruby's dishes and tray, giving her more room on the table. She snatched back her cherry pie.

The folder contained a dozen letters written by various means: computer printout, typewriter—those Ruby set aside. Others were block-printed in pencil or written in ballpoint pen, one in bright blue felt-tip. Three were anonymous, four had names without addresses: common names.

"I don't suppose you were able to verify the existence of Jim Williams, Ronnie Sanders, or Rick Smith?" she asked Jordan.

"Names like that are too common. And most postmarks aren't from the town where the mail originates anymore, unless a letter's sent to a person in the same town. The mail goes to regional processing centers."

Ruby forgot about her cherry pie; despite the hurried situation and the clattering surroundings, she felt the familiar rise of excitement at the sight of the penmanship, the challenge of detection. Usually, all it took was a pair of sharp eyes and patience. Her stereoptic microscope and rulers were only necessary in the most detailed studies.

The language of the letters was inflammatory; here and there she spotted Old Testament exhortations: "Woe unto you." "God granted man dominion."

"These letters are very articulate," Ruby told Jordan. "Complete sentence structure, correct spelling."

"There's a plus for the Michigan public school system," Jordan replied as he peppered his salad.

She lined up four of the letters on the table in front of her, letting her eyes unfocus, viewing the rhythm of penmanship, the spacing between words, the positioning of the letter body on the page in relation to page edges, the comparative height of capital letters to small. A forger most frequently changed the slant and size of his penmanship, but it was invariably in the subtleties where he slipped up, in the spacing and letter heights.

"There are similarities," she told Jordan cautiously. "But unless you let me study them in my lab with better light and measuring plates, I can't say for certain."

"Show me some of the similarities," he requested.

Ruby turned the pages toward him. "See how the

capital *D* in the salutation of all four letters is different? Four different styles, but look in the body of these three letters and you'll see the capital *D* is very similar to the *D* in letter one." She turned two of the letters over. "And notice how the handwriting leaves an imprint on the back in some instances? The author might have been pressing harder on letters he wasn't comfortable writing, concentrating, attempting to create them in a different style. If you were to examine these pressed letters through a microscope you might discover they had a "drawn" quality, with unsteady lines and lifts as the writer tried to disguise his penmanship."

"Then you think the letters may have been written by the same person?" Jordan asked.

"Possibly," Ruby said, restacking the four letters. "Would that surprise you?"

"Not at all. It frequently happens when people are passionate about an issue and trying to have an effect, like stuffing the ballot box."

"Strength in numbers," Ruby commented as she replaced the letters in the folder.

"Exactly," he agreed. "It doesn't matter what you say as much as how many times you say it." He nodded to a well-dressed woman heading toward the door and carrying a bulging briefcase.

"Did Alice ever mention the First Americans to you?" Ruby asked. "Or any subversive group in Waters County?"

"No. I don't recall the subject ever coming up."

"You don't sound very thrilled with this committee," Ruby said.

He gazed off. "We don't know who's out there or what their intents are. But how far can you investigate and legislate before you find yourself treading on Rights to Privacy, Freedom of Speech, et cetera? It's a tightrope over an alligator pit. If we're not careful we could find ourselves fulfilling the militia's prophesies ourselves."

"How much of this need to investigate is because of the Oklahoma City bombing?" Ruby asked, seeing those haunting images in her mind.

Jordan clasped his hands together. His face sagged in sorrow. "Well, that bombing challenged how we protect our freedoms, especially when they threaten innocent people. How do we balance Free Speech against Conspiracy? It's too soon to say how it'll all shake out. The repercussions will go on for years." He nodded to the file folder. "Thanks for looking at these."

"You're welcome," Ruby said as she gave him the folder and reached for her cherry pie. Her impression was that yes, these letters had been written by the same person, although she wouldn't say so aloud.

"Did you know Alice Rolley when you lived in Sable as a kid?" she asked.

"Not really. I always spent a couple of weeks in Sable with my cousins during the summer. I guess I knew who she was. Then she did that Cut-In to raise money while I was a page in the state legislature." He laughed. "I was seventeen and I remember being embarrassed by a woman from my hometown cutting legislators' hair and calling me 'Jordie' when I was planning to be the political whiz kid."

"You never ran into her outside of the legislature?"

"No, but sometimes she'd drop notes in the mail to remind me of upcoming votes or to congratulate me on this or that: the reelection, the birth of our son. She kept up."

"What about her children, Roseanne and Franklin?"

"I knew who they were, sure, but they didn't run around with any of my cousins so I don't recall even speaking to them. They both still live at home, is that right?"

"Still in Sable, anyway," Ruby told him.

"Continuity," he commented.

After a second cup of coffee with Jordan Asauskas, Ruby left the cafeteria and walked back along the shady street to her car, pausing to pet a tabby cat that rolled to its back on the sidewalk in front of her.

A parking ticket was pinned beneath her windshield wiper and not only that, her five-dollar bill was gone, too.

Ruby sighed and removed the ticket, folding it half, wishing she had an expense account to charge it to. She unlocked the door and had just pulled it open when a woman's voice behind her screamed, "Look out, lady!"

Somewhere she heard a revved-up motor, dangerously close. Instinctively, Ruby slammed the door and flattened herself against her car. Behind her, tires

## Cut and Dry

squealed and a car roared past, brushing so close, she felt the rush of air, maybe its slightest touch. Her bag was knocked from her hands.

Footsteps ran toward her. "Are you okay?" The voice belonged to the same woman who'd called out the warning. She touched Ruby's arm and then pulled her away from her car.

Ruby turned around and looked into the eyes of a teenage girl in shorts and a T-shirt, a ring in her nose, short hair slicked back.

"I think so," Ruby told her, glancing down at the dirt across the front of her shirt where she'd pressed herself against her car. Her legs felt rubbery, useless. Her ears rang. On the street before her lay the scattered contents of her bag. Whoever had come so close to hitting her had turned the corner and was gone. "Did you see the car?" she asked the girl.

"It was blue, I think. Just a car. Let me help you." She knelt down and began picking up coins and Ruby's comb and lipstick. "Are you sure you're okay?"

"I'm fine, thanks for warning me." Ruby bent down to help scoop up the contents of her bag and nearly toppled over.

"I'll do it," the girl said. "You stand there and take deep breaths."

Ruby gratefully did as she was told, squeezing and opening her hands while the girl scrambled around in the street, holding up a hand to stop a car until she'd picked up Ruby's notebook from its path. She swore she'd felt the car brush against her. If it had been two inches closer . . .

"Is this yours, too?" the girl asked, holding up the parking ticket.

Ruby nodded.

"That guy looked like he was going to run you down," the girl continued. "He was parked back there by the fire hydrant and just pulled out like a maniac."

"Then you saw the driver. Was it a man?"

She shrugged and dropped the ticket into Ruby's open bag. "I didn't really see him, but it must have been, I mean, who else? You want me to call the cops? I only live a couple blocks away."

"That's okay," she said. "I'm fine."

"Okay, I guess that's cool," the girl said, and handed Ruby her wallet, grinned, and headed off down the block.

"Thanks again," Ruby called after her. The girl waved without turning back.

Ruby sat in her car with the windows rolled down, putting her purse back in order, breathing steadily, willing her shaking hands to be still. Her wallet was unsnapped and Ruby opened it, glancing in the bill holder; the only piece of paper remaining was the uncashed check from Jumbo Rolley; all the cash that had been in her wallet five minutes ago was gone.

"Shit," she said, and jumped out of the car. It had been a scam: the speeding car, the offer to help. She ran in the direction the girl had headed, pushing past a couple holding hands, peering up and down the street, but there was no sign of her.

○ ○ ○

Ruby stopped at a cash machine for more money, then drove back to her motel via the Central Casting beauty supply house, a long, low warehouse in the industrial section of Lansing. There was no point in stopping, but she did anyway, completing the entire circuit of Alice's monthly agenda.

So she was surprised when the girl at the front desk asked, "You wouldn't happen to be from Sable, would you?"

"Yes, I am," Ruby admitted.

She pulled a Post-it from the side of her computer screen and said, "Katrina at the Wak 'n Yak called and said you might drop in. She described you perfectly. Can you take this box of perms back to her?" She pointed to a large brown box on the counter.

"Sure," Ruby said, wondering how Katrina had described her, in beauty terms? Not enough makeup and hair that would look a heck of a lot better if it was short? "Did she tell you about Alice Rolley?"

The girl's face saddened. "She did. Alice was a nice lady."

Ruby picked up the box of perms. "Did she spend much time here?"

"No, always ordered ahead and just ran in to pick it up. That's all. Most people want their supplies shipped. Not many customers pick up so we got to know her better than our other clients."

After leaving Central Casting, Ruby drove the confusing streets back to the Crown Inn, detouring twice around road construction, thinking that picking up her beauty supplies was the least of Alice's chores on her monthly jaunts to Lansing. Her visits to the legislature didn't take much time, either. And the manager had said Alice was gone most evenings. Where? She considered the male love interest that Mary Jean had predicted, contemplating first Bernard Woktoski, the congressman, then dismissing the blustery man, unable to see the match from either of their perspectives.

She left the box of perms locked in her trunk and went to her room, waving at the motel manager in her office as she passed, anticipating a third shower, cooler this time. Then she might change into the dress she'd brought and go out to dinner to be waited on, just as Alice must have. No cooking, no dishes, thank you very much.

She unlocked the door of her room and reached inside to flick on the light, then froze in the open doorway, staring.

Her room had been ransacked. Her suitcase was dumped across the carpet, toiletries spilled and broken on the bathroom floor. She stood where she was, taking it all in without stepping inside. Her green dress had been pulled from its hanger and lay in a heap on the floor. Even from the doorway, she could see it had been raggedly slashed down the back, from neckline to hem.

# Chapter 14

Ruby stood there, scanning the mess in her room, then stepped back onto the motel's second-floor landing, leaving her door open. The air conditioner kicked in as the cool air escaped into the summer heat.

Whoever had trashed her room was long gone; she was sure of it. They weren't hiding in the shower or beneath the bed, waiting to leap out like a banshee and attack her with fists or knives. They'd done their business and slipped away. A job well done.

The afternoon sun beat against her back and still she stood there, noting how the motel furnishings were untouched—the spread wasn't even pulled from the bed—while her own possessions lay scattered, broken and destroyed.

This violation had been aimed at Ruby personally. *She* was the target, not the motel, not her possessions. Whoever had ransacked her belongings might as well have scribbled her name on the mirror in red lipstick: *Ruby, go home.*

In the parking area beneath her, a car pulled in front of a first-floor room. Doors slammed and exhaust fumes drifted upward. "It doesn't *say* 'nonsmoking,'" a woman's voice complained.

Ruby scrutinized the havoc as she would a sample of handwriting: searching for patterns and anomalies, telltale individual characteristics, the signature act that would ultimately identify the perpetrator. Slashed clothing, emptied and broken toiletries, her papers swept off the bureau to the floor. Her hair dryer was broken, the plastic in pieces. Someone had been furious.

Finally, she pulled the door closed and walked down to the office. The manager had already turned on the outside neon lights; a lamp was lit on the counter where she was helping an elderly couple sign in. She looked up at Ruby as she entered, and asked, her voice far cooler than earlier that day, "Did you need something?"

"I'll wait," Ruby said, motioning for her to continue registering the couple. She stood by the plate glass window and watched the rush-hour traffic stream by, everyone heading home, until the couple was gone and the office was empty again.

"Now what can I do for you?" the manager asked. "You look very serious."

"Did anyone ask if I was staying here?"

The woman shook her head. "No. No one."

"Did you see anybody go up to my room? Or somebody who wasn't registered hanging around the motel?"

"Why? What's happened?" She raised a hand to her

face, thumb on one cheek, fingers to the other, her eyes wide behind her glasses.

"Somebody broke into my room. They destroyed nearly everything I brought with me."

The manager gasped. "No! Oh dear. Oh my heavens." She glanced outside at a black sedan pulling in front of the office and looked beseechingly at Ruby. "Do we have to call the police?" She shook her head and slapped the countertop with the palm of her hand. "I'm sorry. What am I saying? Of course we have to call the police. But my business . . ." She nodded toward the man climbing from the black car. "A police car here, you understand; it won't look good. I've never had to call the police. Not ever. I run a nice honest establishment."

"I understand," Ruby assured her. "I'll ask them to park behind the office."

"And not to use their sirens or lights, either. Go ahead," she said hurriedly as the man from the black car opened the office door. "Use the phone in my apartment. It's on the kitchen counter," and she hastily opened the wooden door behind the desk and gave Ruby a gentle push into her apartment, closing it with a click behind Ruby as the customer said, "Hot one, isn't it?"

It was a tiny apartment filled with delicate and expensive antique furniture, at odds with the heavy Mission furniture of the motel. China teacups and saucers lined one shelf in the dining room, porcelain birds another; a miniature porcelain village sat in the middle of dining table. There obviously weren't any small grandchildren. She found the phone on the counter: a pale pink Princess model.

"The perpetrator's gone and no one's hurt," Ruby told the dispatcher after she explained the break-in. "Could you keep the response low-key?"

The office was empty of customers when Ruby left the apartment. The manager stood behind the counter, nervously eyeing Ruby, hand to her cheeks as before. "Are the police coming?" she asked through her fingers. "Will all my customers see them?"

"They're sending a plain car. Nobody will be any wiser."

"Oh, thank you." Then, as if her gratitude were out of place, she said, "I'm so sorry about your room. What did they take? Did they make a . . . mess?"

"No one else in the motel has complained?" Ruby asked.

"Why . . ." the woman began, then gasped.

"Maybe you should check the other rooms," Ruby suggested.

Her hands fluttered. "Oh no, you don't think . . ."

Ruby didn't, but she admitted to herself as she followed the manager, who bustled from one empty room to the next, throwing open doors and sighing in gratitude, that it would have been a relief to see other rooms vandalized, if hers hadn't been the only one targeted.

But the vandal hadn't been interested in anyone besides Ruby, just as she'd expected.

"Well, that's good news," the manager said. "I mean, for the rest of us. You checked in early; maybe you're the only one the thief noticed. Like I said, I haven't seen anyone sneaking around here."

The policewoman arrived in a plain car, no lights or sirens, but she wore a uniform. A couple stood beside their open trunk, watching avidly as Ruby and the officer walked up the steps to Ruby's room. The officer was petite with cool eyes and sharp, economical movements, glancing up at every word Ruby said, taking notes and asking Ruby if she had insurance. "What's missing?"

"Nothing that I can see." She picked up the torn dress. "Whoever did this was intent on destroying my belongings."

"Did you leave the door unlocked?"

"No," Ruby told her.

"Sometimes these doors don't shut the way you think they ought to."

"I shut it," Ruby said. "They're simple locks. A snap to open with a credit card, if somebody wanted to."

"Funny they didn't steal anything, at least your calculator or your hair dryer. You have any idea who it might have been?"

Ruby thought of the teenage girl who'd taken her money, hesitating just long enough for the officer to narrow her eyes. "No, I don't," she said firmly.

The policewoman tucked her notebook in her pants pocket and strolled around the room, lifting the bedspread, pulling back the shower curtain, glancing into Ruby's suitcase. "They might have been looking for money."

"Then why tear my clothes and dump out my lotion and shampoo?"

"Did you have any drugs?" the detective asked matter-of-factly.

"No."

She considered Ruby, tipping her head and rocking a little on her feet. "Are you a cop?" she asked.

"No, why?"

"Just something. Usually I can tell."

As Ruby could also, something in the eyes; the sharp watchfulness she'd noticed in Johnny Boyd's gaze, suspicion, maybe even a touch of paranoia. Did she now possess the same wary tenseness? All because she worked in forgery, making her living by *expecting* fraud and deceit?

As soon as the detective was finished and gone, Ruby tackled her damaged belongings. What wasn't ruined she threw in her suitcase. The rest of her possessions, including her torn dress and the ripped T-shirt she wore as a nightgown, her broken comb and hair dryer, she left piled in the center of the room. Then she carried her suitcase to her car and loaded it in the back beside the box of perms.

For now, Lansing had given up all the information it was going to. Once a month Alice Rolley had shown up for two days, spent a few minutes talking to congressmen and a few minutes picking up beauty supplies. That accounted for about one hour out of thirty-six. What else had she done? Gone shopping? Pampered herself? So why had Ruby, who was investigating Alice's sterling life, been the target of vandalism? A warning to lay off? "Well, get in line," she murmured, thinking of Tracee's and Roseanne's and Franklin's warnings.

"You're not staying?" the manager asked, clasping her hands tightly together on the counter when Ruby returned her key to the office. "I can send one of the girls to clean up your room. Or what if I give you another room? Wouldn't that be all right? There's one on the ground floor, closer to the office."

"No thanks."

"Are you going to another motel?" the manager asked, touching Ruby's wrist. "I hope not. I assure you; nothing like this has ever happened here, not since I've owned the Crown Inn, anyway. All these years: absolutely nothing."

"I'm not going to another motel," Ruby told her. "I've decided to drive back home tonight."

"Oh my." She shook her head. It'll be late when you get there. It's not safe to drive alone at night, especially for a woman. You hear all kinds of things."

"I'll be fine."

"And besides, you already paid for tonight," the manager said, then added doubtfully, "I could give you your money back, I suppose."

"Keep it," Ruby told her, turning and heading for the door. "Start a fund to install more secure locks on your doors."

The only gas station in Sable was a Shell station, so when Ruby spotted the familiar yellow sign on the edge of Lansing, she pulled in, brushing away the foolish sensation of familiarity, that she wasn't so far from home after all.

She drove across the cable in front of the full-service pump, hearing the *ding* inside the station, and stopped beside the self-service pumps. It was too late in the day for shadows. Dusky pink threads of clouds stretched across the western sky. It would be completely dark in an hour.

The man at the pump in front of her was filling a red gas can and nodded to her. A shiny jet ski hulked in the bed of his pickup. Ruby hated the machines, the way they buzzed and whined across Blue Lake like mad, water-bound hornets. Earlier in the summer a jet skier had drunkenly run into the end of a dock and drowned. Sometimes what you courted, happened.

She looked up from the whirling numbers on the gas pump at a blue pickup pulling in on the other side of the row of self-service pumps. A beagle sat in the front seat, its head out the passenger window. A larger black-and-tan hound stood in the bed, its nose up, sniffing the air with serious deliberation.

She eased up on the gas nozzle, watching the driver climb down from the pickup, his body momentarily hidden by the big vehicle. He came around the rear, ruffled the hound's ears, and unscrewed the gas cap. It was Babs Prescott's husband, Dick, the other Sable-ite whom Congressman Woktoski had mentioned seeing in Lansing. He wore slacks and a white shirt, the sleeves rolled up to his elbows; business clothes.

Ruby glanced at the pickup's cab, looking for Babs,

# Cut and Dry 221

but the passenger seat was empty, the beagle bouncing around the cab too freely for there to be anyone else up front.

"Hello," she greeted Dick as he inserted his credit card in the charge slot at the pump.

"Hello, Ruby," he acknowledged, nodding with an up-and-down tilt of his chin and punching in his code, no expression of surprise on his face; they might as well have been meeting at the pumps in Sable's own Shell station.

"I heard you were in Lansing today," she said.

"That right?" he asked her.

"It's a coincidence we're both here on the same day, isn't it?" Ruby asked.

"Not necessarily," he said. He jammed the nozzle into the gas tank and turned on the pump. "Legislature's closing down this week. I had a business appointment."

"About your farmland that's been declared a wetland?"

His jaw tightened and Ruby caught in his eyes the rage of the obsessed, the kind of anger that could blot out every other emotion. "You're just a little busybody buzzard, aren't you? Checking up on everybody left and right like you're the law of the land. Well, I have legitimate business here. Whatever you're up to isn't any of my beeswax."

"You wouldn't have been near the Crown Inn anytime today, would you?"

"Don't know it," he answered curtly.

"Did you ever run into Alice when you were in Lansing?"

He snorted, jerking his head. "Before the past couple of months, I hadn't been to Lansing since sixth grade, to tour the capitol." The automatic switch on the gas pump turned off and he pulled the nozzle from the tank. He paused.

"I'd lay off Alice Rolley if I were you, Ruby," he said, giving Ruby the mild look of a man who didn't need to give warnings, only advice that would doubtlessly be taken.

"Why?" she asked.

He shook his head and closed the gas cap. "Figure it out."

"I'm trying to, damn it," Ruby said as he took his receipt from the gas pump.

"Hey, lady. Are you pumping gas or what?" a male voice called from a car that had pulled in behind Ruby.

"Or what," she answered, squeezing the nozzle again and watching Dick Prescott drive away, both dogs with noses into the wind.

As the miles mounted up along the stretch of freeway between Lansing and Grand Rapids, she wondered how close Dick Prescott and his hounds were. All she could make out were headlights behind her, the quick outlines of vehicles passing her and their receding taillights. She wished she'd noticed how much gas he'd bought, wondering if he'd stopped at the Shell station because he'd seen her instead of because he'd needed gas. He hadn't been surprised to meet Ruby, that was certain.

Why had he, too, advised her to quit pursuing Alice's murderer? The warning hadn't been threatening like Roseanne's, more like a matter of common sense: Don't touch the stove; you might burn yourself. And if he'd been the one to trash Ruby's motel room, would he have made himself so conspicuous as to pump gas right beside her?

Ruby hit her fist against the steering wheel; if Dick Prescott had information to share with Ruby, she'd probably discouraged him by confronting him as if he were a criminal. Maybe Babs *had* seen something unusual the night Alice was killed. Maybe a congressman had let something slip to him about Alice.

Ruby sighed, taking one hand from the wheel to massage her temples. She changed the fading radio station, glancing at the minivan that whizzed past. And just maybe Dick Prescott *hadn't* seen Ruby at the station; he might have chosen the Shell station for its familiarity, the very same reason she had. He could have been too preoccupied with his wetlands melodrama to care that Ruby was coincidentally pumping gas right next to him.

She exited the freeway onto two-lane Highway 37, where traffic was sparser and vigilance more of a necessity. The highway cut through huge swaths of national forest land, and every couple of miles she spotted the bright reflection of eyes. Deer meandered along the highway, unafraid, stepping into the road without concern, taking the right of way and expecting her to grant it to them, which she did. Groups of three or more of the graceful animals cropped grass along the shoulders; once she counted a dozen following one after the other along the shoulder as if on a pilgrimage.

There were too many deer, Hank had told her. People fed them in the winter, hauling hay and carrots deep into the winter woods by snowmobile, keeping alive the ones who should have died from illness and predators, disrupting natural selection, but assuring that the deer hunters would take to the woods in droves in the autumn. "We're turning into a giant game preserve," Hank grumbled. "Fences around our houses and gardens to keep the deer *out*."

It was after ten and Ruby drove straight to her cabin on Blue Lake. She'd pick up Jesse and Spot at Mary Jean's in the morning. Eyes, for an instant caught in her headlights and glowing with malevolence, made her hit the brake before dissolving into a fat raccoon waddling across her driveway.

The cabin stood dark and silent, like most of the other cabins she could see around Blue Lake. The night was too warm for dew, smelling of leaves and lake water. The sound of the Pinto's hatchback being closed was an assault on the silence, audible clear across to the public boat ramp, she was certain.

Ruby left the cabin's lights off, unerringly finding her way across the wood floor without even brushing against her furniture. The glow of a three-quarter moon cast a shaft of green light through the window in the main room. She was beat. She'd driven close to

# Cut and Dry 225

four hundred miles, spoken to too many strangers, lost her cash and half the clothes and toiletries she'd taken with her. And still she didn't know much more about Alice than before she left Sable. She kicked off her shoes and poured herself a glass of whiskey, stepping barefoot onto the front porch.

A bat darted past the cabin, a flash of blacker erratic movement heading toward the lake, a tiny vampire caricature.

Johnny Boyd's cabin was dark. She stared at it until her unblinking eyes began to water, waiting for an instant's red glow of cigarette, seeing nothing, hoping he was able to sleep this night.

She felt behind her for one of the metal chairs and sat down, tilting back her head so her neck rested on the cool lip of the metal backrest, holding her glass on her leg, picturing Jesse asleep in Barbara's bunk beds.

On the ceiling above her, an old paper wasps' nest hung between the rafters, a pale silvery bulge in the darkness. She gazed at it, listening. Nights were never actually silent, only devoid of human movement. Nature carried on: leaves rustled, water lapped, frogs and whippoorwills mournfully called, nocturnal animals hunted and roamed. A continuous, well-balanced song.

Ruby raised her head, gripping her glass, reverie broken by a discordant note. Near the old pumphouse across the driveway, she'd heard movement too heavy to be a deer's. She silently sat upright and peered toward the dense trees. Was that a person standing at the edge of the woods or was she being spooked by a tree trunk she'd simply never noticed before?

No, in the breezeless night the shape moved forward, a single sliding step that shooshed in the dry grass.

She waited, her throat dry, as the figure took two more smooth steps toward her cabin, almost to her driveway. She thought of the man in camouflage they'd seen at Hale's Rollaway, the rifle he'd carried.

There was nothing on the porch to use as a weapon. She glanced at her nearly empty glass: useless. She contemplated screaming; would that frighten away the intruder or encourage him to make his move?

The figure reached the driveway. She attempted to pick out some distinctive feature to remember, for identification, but the shape was too indistinct: only dark movement in the moonlight.

Suddenly weariness overtook Ruby. She wasn't up for this. She stood, scraping the chair loudly against the porch floor.

"Mrs. Pink?" she called. "Is that you?"

The figure froze and Ruby called again, giving the intruder an excuse, an out, a reason to believe he hadn't been detected. "Don't run away, Mrs. Pink. Come in and have a cup of coffee with me."

Mrs. Pink would have come in. She snuck around, it was true, an old lady who shamelessly spied on the residents of Blue Lake, but she was too proud—or too sure of herself—ever to hide or make excuses when she was caught out. She blatantly admitted what she was up to, maybe even itching to let people know she was still capable.

The figure paused, then turned and slipped back into the trees, dissolving.

"Good-bye, Mrs. Pink," Ruby called, half smiling to herself: somebody believed they'd fooled her.

She sat down again and finished her whiskey, wondering who it had been. The person who'd trashed her motel room? Wondering, too, if whoever had invaded her property would return to finish the job.

# Chapter 15

Ruby was too jumpy to sleep, so she locked her doors and climbed to her loft and pulled out the Darrow job, the sales receipt for "one used oak desk" supposedly written by Clarence Darrow, and which she'd promised to get back to Ron Kilgore this week. Maybe if she did a preliminary examination, just to take her mind off Alice and prowlers.

*Paper is contemporary to Darrow,* Ron had written. *Verified by E. M. Jansen.* Emmy, one of the best. Contemporary papers were easy to come by. A favorite source was the end pages from books printed during the subject's time.

So she didn't need to worry about the paper, only the handwriting. Ron had included two photocopies of Clarence Darrow's signature, both showing how he formed his letter *a* off the top lift of the capital *D*, the remainder of his name hanging above the baseline.

The receipt, carefully encased in plastic, had been written in pencil. Forgeries were harder to detect in pencil. It was easier for the forger to retouch his writing, and pencil also made it tough for her to determine the direction of a stroke.

The pencil was smudged, as it should be if it had been written eighty years ago. The page had been folded; a deep crease down its center. And that's the spot where Ruby concentrated first, using a high-intensity lamp and a magnifying glass.

"Bingo," she said aloud. The penciled connection between *e* and *s* in the word *desk* was broken over the fold, indicating the writing might have been done recently, on a piece of folded paper. But this was only step one: Darrow himself also might have written the receipt on an already folded sheet of paper.

Next she concentrated on the strokes themselves, without attention to their formation or the words, poring over the lines with her magnifying glass. The first stroke of the date at the top of the page was the same width as the last stroke in Darrow's *w*. The words were most likely written with a mechanical pencil rather than a wooden pencil which made thicker strokes as the lead wore down between sharpenings.

Ruby's phone rang in the quiet cabin and she jerked upright, dropping her magnifying glass. She threw herself across the bed and grabbed the receiver off the hook, glancing at the softly glowing dial of her alarm clock beside the bed. It was a minute past midnight.

"The witching hour," she murmured, her heart thudding. Late-night phone calls, fire alarms, and screaming children; there was no way to stifle the mind's dread response.

"Hello," she said cautiously.

"You sound like you're still awake."

"Hello, Phyllis." Ruby sat up, reaching for her pillow and shoving it under her stomach. "It's midnight."

"Not here it isn't. Here it's ten o'clock. Midnight, the ghost is out. Remember that game?"

"Yes, I do."

Ruby's father had begged her to call Phyllis. "Something's wrong," he'd said. Ruby had spoken to Phyllis twice in the past year, and for the twelve years before that, only to answer the phone and pass it wordlessly to Jesse. But now, hearing Phyllis's rushed words, her overbright voice, Ruby agreed: something was wrong.

"I always found everybody, remember?" Phyllis asked gleefully. "None of you could hide well enough to escape me."

Controlled, forthright, no-nonsense beautiful Phyllis the engineer who'd been steadily climbing the Albuquerque engineering ladder for the past ten years, partner in the city's second largest firm. "A *real* success," as people tended to remind Ruby.

"How's Jesse?" Phyllis rushed on. She'd always kept in touch with Jesse, sending her gifts and phoning regularly, the only child likely ever to enter her life.

"She said you sounded funny the last time she talked to you." Through the loft window, Ruby could see the jagged outline of the oak trees against the lighter sky as the moon slid downward.

Phyllis laughed, cackled really. "I am funny. I've always been funny."

"That's not what she meant."

# Cut and Dry

"Oh, the old 'funny-odd, not funny-haha' adage, eh?"

"What's going on, Phyllis?" Ruby asked, shifting on the bed, making herself more comfortable.

"Nothing."

"Then why did you call?"

"No reason."

Ruby didn't answer and Phyllis continued, "No reason to continue this conversation then, either."

"Wait!" Ruby said, but the line was dead. Phyllis had hung up.

Ruby set down the receiver. She didn't have Phyllis's phone number, but she knew where Jesse kept it. The staircase from the loft was hardly more than a ladder and Ruby descended barefoot to the darkened downstairs, sure of her steps. She paused in the main room, gazing through the windows toward the lake, where the moon had slid behind the trees, wondering where the person who'd been sneaking up on her cabin was now. Home in bed, she was sure, but where? Whose home?

On the shelf beside Jesse's bed, tucked between a copy of *The Wind in the Willows* and a diary Jesse had begun and given up on, and which Ruby had truly never peeked inside, she found Jesse's address book with its carefully formed post-trauma penmanship. Letters sometimes transposed or written backward, the numbers as careful and laborious as a newly trained draftsperson's.

She carried the address book back to the loft and by the glow of her bed lamp, dialed Phyllis's number. It rang five times and Ruby was about to hang up, suspecting Jesse had mixed up the numbers, when Phyllis picked up the phone.

"Hello," she answered. Brisk and defiant.

"It's Ruby. We were disconnected." She pushed the pillows behind her, leaning against the wall.

"That's the truth."

"Do you remember Roseanne and Franklin Rolley?"

"I try not to."

"Alice Rolley's dead, you know. She was murdered a week ago."

"And the poor little dears are orphans. Who do I write a check to?"

Now *this* sounded more like Phyllis.

"Save your hard-earned money for a manicure," Ruby told her. "Did you and Roseanne get along?"

"Roseanne didn't 'get along' with anybody. She was spoiled rotten—what a waste on somebody so . . . unpromising. Her mother kissy-faced and poo-pooed and handed her anything she wanted. The unimaginative little brute's vision didn't extend beyond horses and chocolate bars."

"So you picked on her and she hated you," Ruby guessed.

"She stuck a melted Hershey bar in my gym clothes once. *No* reason. And I *never* picked on her," Phyllis denied. "I wouldn't have bothered."

Ruby had been the victim of Phyllis's scathing tongue often enough. Phyllis had hidden behind her perfect smile, high grades, and an uncanny ability to appear blameless, angelic even. Old ladies loved Phyllis.

"How well did Roseanne get along with her parents?" Ruby asked.

"How should I know? My impression was Mommy pampered her to make up for Daddy not giving a damn. He fooled around, you know."

Even then, Ruby thought. "What about Franklin?" she asked Phyllis.

"What about him?"

"Were he and Roseanne close?"

"God, Ruby, what do you think I am, the Waters County historian? I guess they were close. They had to get along with each other because nobody else did. Orphans in the storm or something. If you're asking me if they were a kinky incestuous duo, I don't know and couldn't care less. What's so important about Roseanne and Franklin Rolley that you'd call me in the middle of the night?"

"Why did you call me?" Ruby asked.

There was silence, then Phyllis asked in a softer, hesitant voice, "Did I?" Too uncertain to be a joke.

"Phyllis," Ruby began. "Are you . . ."

"Never mind," Phyllis said, stretching it out like a line in an old *Saturday Night Live* skit. "Gotta go now. Lovely chatting with you." And she hung up.

Ruby held the phone to her ear, hearing the distant buzz of some other midnight conversation leaking through the wires. Phyllis was over a thousand miles away. They hadn't met face-to-face in thirteen years. Phyllis's life was her own business. If she had a problem, she had the money and the means to correct it. Ruby couldn't be any help and neither did she want to be.

But still, she sat with the phone to her ear until the mechanical voice came on telling her to hang up, thinking unreasonably that Phyllis might somehow come back on the line.

In the morning, still scratchy-eyed from lack of sleep, Ruby called Carly early, knowing he'd already be in his office, and told him she'd returned from Lansing.

"Can you meet me for a cup of coffee in a couple of hours?" he asked. "A little chin-chat?"

"Sure," Ruby told him. She wasn't dressed yet, still sitting at her kitchen table, dunking a banana in a cup of coffee and making lists. Without realizing she'd remembered it, she'd written Phyllis's phone number at the top of the page, retracing it until it stood out thick and black. "The Knotty Pine?"

"I'll be there."

Ruby dressed in shorts and a T-shirt and paddled the canoe across the lake to Johnny Boyd's cabin, giving wide berth to two fisherman anchored at the midway point. As usual, Johnny Boyd sat on his front porch, watching her, not moving.

"Were you sitting out here last night?" she asked.

He nodded. "I saw you come home about ten-thirty. I thought you were spending the night in Lansing."

"I intended to but I had a very bad day and abandoned the plan."

"What happened?" A bowl beside his chair was half-filled with cigarette butts. Next to it sat a stale-looking sandwich with one bite taken from it.

"I'll tell you the gruesome details in a minute," Ruby said, sitting in the chair beside him. "But did you notice anyone around my cabin last night, after you saw me drive in?" Ruby told him about the figure skulking in her driveway.

"It wasn't Mrs. Pink?" he asked.

"No, she wouldn't have run away. Besides it was a larger person. Someone who stood straighter. Younger."

"I saw nothing." He scowled across the water toward her cabin, appearing troubled, contrite, as if he'd been derelict in his duties.

"Maybe Mrs. Pink has an apprentice." She gave a short laugh. "But while I was in Lansing, someone did break into my motel room and tear apart my belongings."

In Johnny Boyd's tired eyes Ruby saw the cool calculations common to his former life; removing himself from personal interest and concentrating on the crime itself. "Did you see them?" he asked.

"No."

"What did they take?"

"Nothing. But I didn't have anything valuable with me, either."

"But they vandalized your belongings anyway. Anyone else's room?"

"No, just mine," Ruby told him.

"Motel theft is more common than you'd believe. They might have destroyed your possessions in a rage because you *didn't* carry any valuables—you look like you would."

"Thank you, but this was too deliberate. It *felt* like I was the target, does that make sense?"

He nodded. "Who knew where you were staying?"

"My friend Mary Jean. Katrina and Fanny at the Wak 'n Yak might have guessed."

"And they could have mentioned it in the shop. If people are curious about your involvement in Alice's death, your whereabouts would be a primary interest."

Ruby sighed and leaned against the porch railing. "You're saying the whole county might have known where I was."

"Most likely."

"That sure deepens the suspect pool. Oh, look," Ruby said, pointing to a flying squirrel who'd just leapt from a silvery beech tree beside Johnny's cabin and soared across twenty feet of open space to catch himself on an oak branch. "I wish Jesse was here."

"She still has a chance," Johnny Boyd said, frowning at the drab little squirrel. "They're in the attic, probably whole families of them. They have square dances every night."

"I did see one other Sable person in Lansing," Ruby told him, watching as the squirrel leapt again, landing on the rear corner of Johnny's cabin. "Do you want me to send over a carpenter to seal up the attic?"

"Never mind. A carpenter banging around up there would be worse. Who'd you see?"

"Dick Prescott. He's trying to fight a ruling on his farmland; a portion of it was designated a wetland and now he's barred from using it."

Johnny Boyd shook his head slightly. "You can't fight city hall. Not because it's so powerful but because nobody in a bureaucracy has any real power. Any connection between Prescott and Alice Rolley?"

"No," Ruby said immediately, then amended, "at least I don't think so. His wife, Babs, had her hair tinted the day Alice died. You're not speaking of a romantic connection, are you?"

"Not necessarily. Maybe political?"

"They were on opposite ends of the spectrum politically. Alice wanted state-funded programs; Dick wants the state to butt out of everybody's lives completely."

"But you did run into him in Lansing," Johnny reminded her. "That's the seat of the state government."

"That's where his wetlands lawyer is. But you know," Ruby said, "Alice's evenings are unaccounted for. The motel manager said Alice usually left the motel in the evenings. Her congressmen say they saw her for only a few minutes, and then, not every month. I don't know how to find out where she was— or even if it matters."

Johnny leaned his head back. His lips were cracked and Ruby made a mental note to buy ChapStick in town. "Your motel room," Johnny said. "It was the room Alice usually stayed in?"

"For at least the last five years."

"The person who broke in might have been looking for Alice, not you. Maybe the destruction was aimed at *her* instead of you."

Ruby hadn't considered that possibility. With her finger, she absently traced the alphabet on the arm of her chair in cursive. "Once they got inside the room, they'd have realized Alice wasn't staying there."

"And got mad."

She drew out a European Z on the chair arm. "Maybe," she said thoughtfully, and glanced at her watch. "I'm talking to the sheriff in an hour."

A wistful expression crossed Johnny Boyd's face and she recognized his burning desire to be involved, an ache to get to the bottom of Alice Rolley's death himself, not through hearsay and proxy.

"Do you have to just sit here?" Ruby asked. "I could take you to town in my car, to Lake Michigan, out for dinner, you name it."

"No thanks," he said. "I'm surrounded by everything I need. And I'm too tired to want anything else." He spoke the word *tired* with finality, heavily, connoting exhaustion akin to paralysis.

"Just let me know, okay?" she said, touching his hand.

He surprised her by taking her hand; his grip was warm, strong, almost a grasp. "I will," he said, looking away and letting go of her, a meaningless agreement.

*   *   *

## Cut and Dry

Although she knew it would make her late, Ruby stopped by Roseanne Rolley's apartment on her way to meet Carly at the Knotty Pine.

Roseanne lived in a white three-story house that had been slashed and patched into five apartments. Its history was obscure; built a century ago by a forgotten timber baron. The house stood on the edge of town, fields beyond with room for Roseanne's horses.

Ruby parked behind a small blue VW Rabbit, the no-frills model with a bumper sticker that said *Love your mother* and a depiction of the earth.

Paint peeled from the walls of the house's wide front porch, exposing a pastel green layer beneath it; a couch fashioned from an old car seat sat beside a rocking chair between two doors. The leaded glass door on the left, hung with sheer white curtains and stickers of endangered animals—snow leopards, Kirtland's warbler, whales, and eagles—belonged to Roseanne. Ruby's hand was poised to knock when Roseanne herself jerked the door inward, dressed in jeans and a T-shirt, her ponytail undone and hair flat to one side of her head as if she'd slept on it.

"Now what do you want?" Roseanne demanded, holding the door barely wide enough to contain her body, her arm behind it as if she feared Ruby might try to ram her way inside. Behind Roseanne, Ruby made out carved plaster molding, an elegant but dusty chandelier, dark wainscoting, and flocked wallpaper. Piles of papers and books everywhere.

"Did you ever go to Lansing with your mother?" Ruby asked. "Do you know what she did there?"

Roseanne's eyes bulged; spittle formed at the corner of her mouth. She loomed over Ruby and Ruby took a helpless step backward. "I already told you everything I'm going to about my mother," Roseanne said in a barely controlled voice. Ruby felt Roseanne's breath on her face and took a second step back.

"Stay out of my family's business," Roseanne went on. "Do you hear me?"

"I'm trying to *help*, Roseanne," Ruby tried. "You may as well cooperate so we can find her killer. It doesn't make sense to waste precious time like this."

"Get out," Roseanne said, her voice dropping to dangerous lows. "Just get out of here." She made a fist and struck it against her own heart in a caricature of a Catholic *mea culpa*.

"Roseanne," Ruby tried again. "If you—"

"Get out or I'll kill you."

Roseanne slammed the door in Ruby's face. The opaque curtain on the door shuddered, and through it Ruby watched Roseanne's form recede deeper into the shadows of her apartment.

She stood there a moment, then took a deep breath and glanced at her watch. She wouldn't be late meeting Carly after all. Her exchange with Roseanne had taken less than three minutes.

A barefoot girl of five or six stood in the yard beside the blue car. She hugged a Kermit the Frog doll and intently watched Ruby, her dark head tipped as she twisted one of Kermit's legs into a spiral.

"That's a nice doll," Ruby said, pausing beside the girl.

"It's not a doll," the girl said indignantly. "It's a frog. Can't you tell?"

"You're right; it's definitely a frog," Ruby agreed, and as she raised her head she glanced into the VW Rabbit.

On the front seat lay a white bakery bag, its top open as if the driver had been eating pastry straight from the bag. Crumbs and flecks of powdered sugar dotted the seat. *Cheryl Lynn's Bakery* was printed on the bag, and beneath it: *Two great locations in Lansing.*

Lansing?

"Whose car is this?" Ruby asked the girl.

"I'm not supposed to talk to strangers," the girl said, suddenly coy.

Ruby held out her hand, "Well, let's not be strangers, then. My name's Ruby Crane. What's yours?"

"Jacqueline Bouvier Polowski," the girl recited in a high voice, her hand sticky in Ruby's.

"It's nice to meet you, Jacqueline. Do you know who this car belongs to?"

"The Roly Poly lady."

"Do you mean Roseanne Rolley?"

"Mmm-hmm," she said, pointing to Roseanne's door and twirling Kermit by one leg. "It's hers; she gave me a chocolate bunny for Easter."

While the girl chattered on, Ruby stood beside Roseanne's car, gazing at the curtained door of her apartment.

○　○　○

Carly sat in a wooden booth, a double order of onion rings piled high in front of him, mounded over with catsup like an ice-cream sundae. A glass of iced tea and two empty pink packets of sweetner sat beside it.

"Early lunch?" Ruby asked.

"Snack," he said, squeezing an onion ring in half and daubing it in catsup. "Help yourself. These aren't those frozen onion rings; Betsy cuts and batters these herself."

"Thanks but I'll stick to a cup of coffee. My stomach's still in breakfast mode."

"You don't know what you're missing." His open notepad and a ballpoint pen sat on the table next to his elbow. "Tell me about Lansing. Did you run into Dick Prescott?"

"How'd you know?"

"I heard he'd gone downstate to see a hot-shot attorney who specializes in water rights cases against the government. I figured he'd be around the capitol about the same time as you, flogging away on his own agenda."

"Well, *I* was on somebody's agenda. My motel room was trashed."

"Is that why you didn't stay?" Carly chewed thoughtfully.

"It took the fun out of a night on the town, especially after my best dress was shredded."

"Too much crime in the city," Carly commented, as if she should have been prepared for at least one break-in.

# Cut and Dry

"Then, after I got home, I caught somebody sneaking around my cabin."

"Not Mrs. Pink?"

"Not Mrs. Pink."

"And you're thinking that whoever broke into your motel room also showed up at your cabin? Dick Prescott?"

"Dick hadn't occurred to me."

Carly chewed, thinking, then gave a single nod in agreement. "Dick's too caught up in his own battles."

"Woktoski said he doesn't have much chance of reversing the wetlands ruling."

"That's the word going around. Now Dick's saying he's going to ignore the ruling and drain it anyway. It might have worked except he's made so much noise the State will be keeping an eye on him."

"He had his dogs with him," Ruby said.

Carly laughed. "Dogs come first with Dick. You know what he told me once? 'Dogs can't help the way they are, that's why I like them.'"

"His dogs come before Babs?" Ruby asked.

"Don't be too hard on him, Ruby. You can't judge men around here like you can men out in California or in the city. Dick loves Babs." Carly said the word *loves* self-consciously, like a prude discussing a fascinating but distasteful sex act. "You hardly ever see those two apart. But he *raised* those dogs."

"What about his family? Didn't he raise them, too?"

"He and Babs only had the daughter, Darlene. He dotes on her little girl."

"Susannah, the piano player?"

"That's right. Dick gave her one of his pups who wouldn't hunt."

"Touching," Ruby said.

"Think about it. It is."

She thought of Dick and his dogs riding around downtown Lansing in his blue pickup and suddenly remembered how the teenage girl who'd robbed her wallet had claimed a blue car had tried to run Ruby down. Could the girl have told the truth about the car and then just taken advantage of the opportunity to steal Ruby's cash? The vehicle passing so close to Ruby had been too small to be a pickup, at least one the size of Dick's. But now she knew that Roseanne drove a blue car.

"What's on your mind?" Carly asked.

"I had some money stolen in Lansing, too," Ruby told him.

"Other than that, how was the play, Mrs. Lincoln?" Carly asked, then raised his hand toward her, shaking his head in apology. "Sorry. Not your day."

She told him about Alice's unaccounted time, her evenings away from the motel, while Carly listened, jotting a few notes in his simple, rounded, almost feminine hand.

"Those stores stay open twenty-four hours a day down there," Carly said. "Maybe she was shopping. That's what Georgia would do if she had the chance. Back to the prowler around your cabin last night, could you see anything particular about him?"

"No, just a shadow."

"Big like Roseanne?"

# Cut and Dry

"I couldn't say."

"Or maybe smaller, like Franklin?"

Ruby paused with her cup halfway to her mouth. "Roseanne's brother, Franklin. You think . . ." she began.

"I'm not saying anything, Ruby, just that sometimes the Rolley kids act together. They always have. And with Roseanne warning you not to investigate their mother's death . . ."

"I'd say she *threatened* me," Ruby corrected. "Not warned."

"Roseanne's a lot of talk, don't forget that. I'd have a chat with Franklin."

"I will. I've already spoken to him once and I feel like I'm beginning to figure him out. Tell me what else you've found here."

Carly's onion rings were half gone. He ate them the way a chain-smoker smoked, always one in his hand. "Not that much. Fanny did leave through the back door while Babs and her granddaughter and Katrina left through the front. Fanny didn't see anyone in the alley. Neither door was locked, front or back."

"Babs said Fanny locked the front door behind them."

Carly shook his head. "Fanny told me she was going to but Alice told her to leave it, that she'd lock it herself."

"So whoever killed Alice could have come in either door," Ruby said.

"Looks that way."

"And everybody more or less has alibis," Ruby said.

"Tracee was home alone. What about Jumbo? Where was he? And what about Dick?"

A pained expression crossed Carly's face. "Dick was with Jumbo and then at his granddaughter's recital."

"Jumbo?" Ruby asked. "Before he went to Tracee Ferral's house? I thought he was at the mill."

"It seems a few of the men were meeting to talk about Dick's wetlands, or subjects along that line."

Ruby brushed her hands through her hair. "Are you saying Jumbo and Dick are involved in the First Americans movement?"

"They're just men talking, letting off steam. They were grousing long before the First Americans came to town. It's harmless."

"How do you know? Have you gone to their meetings?"

"No, but I stay up on them, who's there, what's being discussed. I'd know if the talk started turning into action. They're totally within their rights."

"With the Constitution to back them up?"

"That's right."

Ruby leaned forward, her elbows on the table. "Tell me about Johnny Boyd," she said. "What's wrong with him?"

Carly took a swallow of his iced tea. "He can tell you if he wants to."

"Come on, Carly. I'm his closest neighbor, at least the only one he sees. I've already picked him up off the floor once; what else should I expect? A heart attack? Fevers and delirium? Jesse's drawn to him, I want to know."

"It's nothing catching, if that's what you're worried about."

"Carly. Enough with the cop loyalty."

"Okay," Carly said, turning the salt shaker. "It's leukemia. He was diagnosed three years ago but it's been in remission. Now it's back and he's run out of treatments, or at least anything he wants done to prolong it."

Ruby nodded as she listened, closing her eyes to soften the words. Leukemia. That was why the sweating; not just the heat. And the distended abdomen: a swollen spleen.

"He's doing it his own way," Carly was saying. "Allow him that."

"He's not much for accepting sympathy," Ruby said. "Do you stop by to visit him?"

"Now and then," Carly said.

"I've been discussing Alice Rolley's death with him," Ruby said, and as soon as she said it she saw by the expression on Carly's face that he'd done the same thing.

He grinned. "He was in homicide in Cleveland. A good mind."

"Then I guess we can only benefit from his ideas," Ruby said.

"Plenty of crazy ones are floating around town, I assure you." Carly stared at the onion ring in his hand. "Some people say I'm dragging my feet." He paused while the waitress poured more iced tea into his glass. "The county's given me two terms as sheriff." He set the onion ring back on his plate. "Maybe it's time I did something else with my life anyway."

Ruby left him sitting in the booth, staring at the remains of his onion rings.

# Chapter 16

The aroma of fresh baked bread drifted onto the main street; Sable Bakery's best advertisement. When Ruby stepped inside, breathing deeply, the sparse shop was empty. It was strictly a takeout bakery: one glass counter and a cash register, no tables or coffee machine the way most bakeries were heading. A sign hung behind the counter reading *Franklin bakes cherry pies on Thursday! Order now.*

Franklin, dressed in baker's whites, including a white hat that he wore cocked like a natty sailor's, peered through the pass-through from the kitchen. He gazed through Ruby as if he'd never met her before; just an anonymous customer. "Martha ran over to the post office," he told her. "She'll be right back."

"I came to see you."

"If you were planning to order a cherry pie, I'm booked up this week. I can put you down for next Thursday."

"I can bake a cherry pie," Ruby said.

" 'Quick's a cat can wink her eye. She's a young girl

and cannot leave her mother,' " Franklin sang from the old folk song.

"Can I come back and talk to you?" Ruby asked.

"I don't know; can you?" Franklin asked.

Ruby stepped behind the counter and entered the kitchen through the swinging doors. Aluminum and steel pans gleamed. Shining utensils hung from hooks on the wall; the floor was spotless tile. Franklin stood in front of the marble-topped segment of a long wide table, rolling piecrusts. Behind him a bread hook was looping through pale dough to the drone of its motor.

"You look pretty professional," Ruby said, watching a perfectly smooth piecrust emerge beneath the swift sure sweeps of Franklin's rolling pin.

He paused in his rolling briefly and raised his eyebrows at her. "After twenty-three years on a job, even the most hopeless of us gain a little skill."

"I meant it as a compliment," she said.

"Noted," he said. "And accepted with gratitude."

"Were you sneaking around my cabin last night?" Ruby asked, trying the same direct approach she had with Roseanne, expecting the same results.

With floured hands, Franklin flipped the piecrust into an aluminum pie tin and swiftly crimped the edges. "Yup, I sure was," he said. "That was me."

"Are you joking?" Ruby asked him.

"Nope. You called out to Mrs. Pink. Nice move on your part. Allaying my suspicions, isn't that what it's called? You couldn't have confused me with Mrs. Pink even if it had been a moonless night and you were standing a hundred yards away. Were you trying to lull me into believing you weren't suspicious?"

"Yes. What were *you* trying to do?"

Franklin poured bright red cherries mixed with sugar, flour and spices into the crust. Fresh cherries; no glutinous prepared cherry filling here. "Just looking."

"For what?"

He shrugged, sprinkling a crumb crust over the filling. "Couldn't sleep. Maybe I'm Mrs. Pink's mad apprentice," and he hummed music from the sorcerer's apprentice scene in *Fantasia*.

"I already thought of that," Ruby said. "What did Roseanne tell you to look for?"

He dashed a handful of flour on the marble top, scooped pastry dough from a metal bowl and began rolling out another piecrust. "I *do* perform my own thinking once in a while, despite public opinion."

"I'm sure you do, but I'll bet not this time. What does Roseanne want?"

"You already know what my sister wants."

"For me to stop asking questions about your mother's death. So why poke around my cabin?" Ruby picked up a flour-smeared recipe card from the counter and Franklin removed it from her hand, shaking his finger at her.

"Cook's secrets," he said, placing the recipe card out of her reach and sight. "If you hadn't interrupted me, you might have found out. Ask Roseanne."

"I talked to her this morning. She's not interested in discussing the subject."

From the flash of irritation that crossed Franklin's face, Ruby guessed Franklin had frequently been caught playing Roseanne's pawn just as Carly had suggested. "This is ridiculous, Franklin. Tell me, would you? What were you looking for?"

"Just checking to make sure you got home from Lansing all right. That's where you were, right? A big day in the big city? Did you have a nice time?"

He was enjoying himself, she could tell, eating up the attention.

"Not particularly. But last night when you showed up in my yard, you thought I was still in Lansing. Did Roseanne ask you to trash my cabin, like she did my motel room in Lansing?" Franklin didn't even blink in surprise, only regarded her with mild interest. Ruby picked up a shred of pie dough and rolled it into a ball. "I want to talk this over with Carly."

"Go right ahead," Franklin invited. "Have a cozy little chat with the man."

The bell on the bakery door jangled and Martha entered, carrying a small cardboard box and a stack of mail.

"I'll see you later," Ruby told Franklin as she tossed the ball of piecrust dough into the trash can.

"Not if I see you first," Franklin said, laughing like a fifth-grader who'd just told a whopper of a good joke.

Ruby walked from the Sable Bakery to the post office. The postal clerk who'd given her her father's mail sniffed when he saw her enter the lobby, and turned his back to the counter. It was too obvious to ignore.

"Is anything wrong?" Ruby inquired of his back.

## Cut and Dry       253

He turned, frowning at her, his mild eyes hurt. "I was *not* trying to 'monkey around' in your father's life."

"Is that what he accused you of doing?" Ruby asked, spinning the brass dial on her post office box until it clicked open. Only an ad.

"It was just that he hadn't picked up his mail . . ."

"Don't pay any attention to him," Ruby said. "You know how he is. I appreciate it that you told me. He might have been sick and who would have known?"

"That man has a mean mouth," he called after Ruby.

A dog gave a single bark as Ruby let the post office door swing closed behind her, and she looked up to see a blue pickup pass by, with three hounds in the back. It was Dick Prescott and he was alone in the cab.

Ruby sprinted for her car and jumped inside, fumbling for her keys, then dropping them on the floor mat. "Clumsy, clumsy," she muttered, finally starting her car and spraying gravel as she pulled onto the street. The blue pickup was four blocks ahead of her, a green van between them, heading toward the river.

The three hounds stood in the back with their front paws on a toolbox, watching the upcoming scenery. In front of her the green van slowed, and Ruby floored the gas pedal, pulling into the left lane, blaring her horn when she belatedly realized the driver intended to make a left turn.

The van's driver slammed on his brakes, tires squealing, shimmying the van while Ruby veered helplessly off the tarvy onto the left shoulder, slewing dangerously in the soft earth as she fought to hold the steering wheel steady, finally bumping the car back onto the pavement. The driver of the van laid on his horn and gave her the finger, thrusting it out the window and over his roof.

"Ever hear of turn signals?" Ruby said aloud, leaving the van behind and closing in on the blue pickup. The commotion had attracted one of the hounds, who'd moved to the tailgate and was watching her, his tongue lolling.

Whether Dick Prescott had seen Ruby and recognized her or not, he crossed over the Sable River bridge and pulled into the two-track that led down to the public access.

The track's soft sand caught at the tires, rocking the car as if she were driving through sand dunes, five miles an hour, eating Dick Prescott's dust. She could see his figure swaying in the driver's seat, the rifle in his gun rack partially blocking her view.

In front of them the pines opened up to the wide clearing beside the river. For years it had served canoeists and hunters, or kids looking for a place to drink and make out in the backseats of cars. Remnants of buck poles and campfire rock rings dotted the treed perimeters of the clearing; beer cans were heaped in a pile beside a bullet-pocked trash can made out of an oil barrel.

The amber river swept past, filled with eddies and ripples, flowing black beneath the overhanging willow trees and pines. The low and sloping bank was tram-

## Cut and Dry

pled mud, mostly from canoeists putting in or pulling out of the river.

Dick Prescott braked and turned off his engine. Ruby did the same, suddenly hearing the river whisper and lap, a continuous sound like rustling silk. It was cooler here, and as she climbed from behind the wheel she inhaled deeply the smell of the water's cool passage, the odor of black mud.

The dogs whined, turning in eager circles, their eyes on Dick Prescott as he slammed the door of his pickup. He wore farmer's clothes: jeans and a T-shirt, his buzz-cut hair freshly clipped.

"Down," he ordered, and the dogs, whimpering in disappointment, dropped instantly to the floor of the pickup bed.

"If I let them out here," Prescott told Ruby, "they'd talk each other into wandering for a week."

"They look too well behaved for that," Ruby said, looking at the three hunkered hounds.

"Looks can fool you." He leaned against the rim of the pickup bed and patted the head of the closest dog. It closed its eyes in pleasure, its tail thumping the metal floor. "You have a reason to follow me?" he asked, his eyes hard on Ruby, his hands gentle on the dog.

"Last night at the gas station in Lansing? Why did you warn me to stay out of Alice Rolley's death? What were you about to tell me?"

"What makes you think I was going to tell you anything?"

"What do you know about Alice's murder?" Ruby asked.

Dick pulled a piece of straw from the pickup bed and broke it into pieces, letting them fall to the dark ground, slivers of gold. "Nosy, aren't you?"

"I'm only trying to do a job."

"Maybe that's the problem," he said.

"I don't understand."

One of the hounds whimpered and stood in the pickup bed until Dick Prescott raised his hand, palm toward the dog. The hound immediately lay down again, its head between its paws.

"Everybody knows Jumbo Rolley's paying you to investigate his wife's death," he finally said.

"I figured they did. What's wrong with that?"

"Do you know *why* Jumbo hired you?" Dick asked, narrowing his eyes at Ruby, then glancing around the clearing as if he expected eavesdroppers.

"Because Carly's understaffed and Jumbo wants to see his wife's killer caught as soon as possible."

"Not quite."

"Then why?"

"Carly's a disappointment as a sheriff."

"Because he's not his father, you mean?" Ruby asked.

"Partly. Carly and Jumbo never got along. Jumbo thinks Carly lacks balls and he's backing Mac McCutcheon for sheriff."

"Mac hasn't even declared yet."

Reluctance was apparent in every fiber of Dick Prescott's being. He didn't want to be here. He didn't want to be talking to Ruby; he'd rather be anywhere else. "He will. Jumbo's spreading it around that he was forced to hire you to get the job done."

"Discrediting Carly," Ruby said. "He's saying Carly couldn't solve his wife's murder without outside help? Without *my* help, which he's paying for?"

"That's right." One of the hounds hopefully pushed its nose against Jumbo's arm. "And he's milking it for all it's worth."

"Why are you telling me this?" Ruby asked.

Dick shredded another strand of straw and watched it drift to the ground. Then he watched a branch float past in the river. "Two reasons: Babs wanted me to tell you. She figured nobody else would."

"Then why didn't she mention it when I visited your farm?"

"She was going to but I guess I interrupted the conversation. She doesn't like to think about . . ." He paused. ". . . Alice's death, but she wants the murderer caught without it becoming a political game." A softness crossed Dick Prescott's face as he spoke of his wife. His eyes relaxed, a smile played at the corners of his mouth. It was so personal, Ruby glanced away into the trees.

"So now I've told you." He stepped away from the pickup. "And that's the end of my duty. What you do with the information is your own business."

"Wait a minute," Ruby said. "You told me there were two reasons. What's the other one?"

Prescott's face reddened with the same deep rage Ruby had witnessed at the gas station in Lansing.

"Because Mac's a son of a bitch," he said. "The last person we need for sheriff."

"He used to be the game warden, didn't he?" Ruby asked. "And I hear you're into license-free living these days."

"My politics are private."

"But not too private. Were you and Jumbo really together at some kind of a secret meeting the night Alice died?" Ruby asked.

Dick Prescott froze. "That isn't any woman's concern," he said. "You just stay out of private matters."

"Secret meetings?" Ruby asked. "What do you do, dress up in white sheets?"

"White sheets?" He grunted and shook his head. "You're in the wrong part of the county for that kind of accusation. What in hell are you after, anyway?" he demanded. His eyes narrowed. "Exactly what is it you're investigating?"

"Alice's death," Ruby said.

"Like hell," he said. He turned and patted the dogs with both hands. "I've got work to do now. I don't have anything else to say."

"Just one question," Ruby said. "Is Mac McCutcheon related to Tracee Ferral somehow?"

"Couldn't say," he told her.

If what Dick Prescott said was true, and Jumbo *was* backing Mac to be the new sheriff, why had Tracee, who was Jumbo's lover, warned Ruby *not* to get involved, completely at odds with Jumbo?

"I think you could," Ruby said.

She stepped between Dick Prescott and the door of

his pickup, blocking his way. He raised his hand as if he were about to push her away from his truck. "God, woman. Lay off, will you?" He shifted on his feet. "Just lay the hell off."

The biggest hound rose to its feet and leaned over the bed of the pickup, growling, its hackles rising and lips curling.

Prescott's hand held, six inches from Ruby's arm, his tendons taut with restraint. He wanted to shove her, knock her down; she could feel it. She didn't budge and he licked his lips, then dropped his hand. "You'd better move," he said in a quiet voice.

Ruby waited long enough so it wasn't a concession, then stepped aside. The hound snapped its teeth at her as she passed.

She stood in the sandy track until Dick Prescott had slammed his truck into gear and roared out of the clearing, throwing up a cloud of fine sand.

"Hey!" Mary Jean said when Ruby arrived to pick up Jesse, making a V for Victory sign with her fingers. "The Carter farm sale is scheduled to close in two weeks. I'll hold my breath until then but once the ink's dry, care to celebrate with me?"

"Out of town?" Ruby asked.

"Pere, at least. My treat. We could even include Hank and Pete. Go wild and drink California wine."

"Sounds good to me. How'd it go with Jesse?"

"Perfect. They did girls things. I even caught Jesse giggling. The only weird thing she did was go to bed at eight last night and sleep straight through until nine this morning. They're upstairs watching a video."

"Thanks, Mary Jean. Really."

" 'S okay. But mark your calendar for next Thursday. Barbara's coming to your place and Pete's coming to mine. How was Lansing?"

"Unproductive," Ruby told her. She picked up a real estate booklet and fanned the pages, not really looking at the photos.

"Too bad."

"Are Jumbo Rolley and Mac McCutcheon pretty tight?" Ruby asked.

"They're friends, I guess. Why?"

"Do you know if Jumbo supports Mac for our next sheriff?"

"Over Carly, you mean? Probably."

"Okay," Ruby said, returning the ad to the table. "So then what's the story about Dick Prescott and Mac?"

"Bad, bad blood," Mary Jean told her. "I don't know the details but some incident left over from the days when Mac was game warden. You know how Dick hunts whenever, wherever? Mac tried to arrest him for shooting two bucks out of season or something like that. Supposedly, Dick beat the crap out of him."

"And got away with it?" Ruby asked.

"If it came right down to it," Mary Jean asked, "which one of them would you hate to run into on a dark night?"

Ruby thought. Both men postured and blustered,

# Cut and Dry

but Mac's bullying was the bullying of a coward, a man who preferred to push around women and weaker men. Ruby couldn't picture Dick backing down from anybody, no matter what their size or gender.

"Dick," Ruby said. "Even without his hounds from hell."

"Exactly. I think Mac feels the same way and it makes him *sooo* mad," Mary Jean said. "Oh. There are a couple of new rumors going around here."

"Theories two thousand eleven and twelve?" Ruby asked.

Mary Jean took a drink from a Diet Coke can and shook her head. "No, these are about you."

"Me? Now what?"

A bang sounded from outside and Ruby jumped, turning to look out the plate glass window. Smoke twisted upward from a spot on the street and two boys ran down the sidewalk, laughing.

"Those kids just don't quit," Mary Jean said. She chortled. "You're going to get a royal chuckle out of this. I heard you aren't *really* working for Carly; you're a bona fide undercover FBI agent and maybe . . ." She giggled. "Carly's even working for *you*."

"Carly would love that one. What else?"

"That you called your rich TV friends in California—"

"I don't know anybody in TV," Ruby interrupted.

"What's that got to do with reality? Anyway, you supposedly called your rich television friends and that show that hunts down real-life criminals is coming to l'il old Sable to do a story on Alice's death. Everybody's wondering when the auditions will be held."

"It wouldn't make any difference if I gave the money back to Jumbo *now*," Ruby told Johnny Boyd. "It's too late. The whole town knows Jumbo's paying *me* to solve his wife's murder because he doubts Carly can do it, so the damage to Carly has already been done."

"Here's a classic example of killing two birds with one stone," Johnny said. "He'll get his wife's murder solved *plus* give his own candidate for sheriff a boost."

Ruby sat on the floor of the porch beside Johnny, leaning against the leg of his chair. Jesse and Spot were curled together in the shade of an oak tree, Jesse reading aloud as Spot dozed. Jesse had found an anthill beside their cabin and now was avidly studying the life of ants.

They'd arrived at Johnny Boyd's cabin an hour ago. While Jesse had given him a long and serious explanation of anthill social organization, Ruby had thrown out his accumulated garbage, including the dead lily and the spoiled tomato and cherries she'd brought a few days earlier, then made sandwiches to leave in his refrigerator for him. The case of protein drink was open; his appetite was diminishing. Neither Ruby nor Johnny Boyd mentioned what she was doing.

"I walked right into this mess. Damn. Just damn. The last thing I meant to do was make Carly look bad. What a mistake." Ruby ran her hands through her

# Cut and Dry

hair, side to back, and gripped a thick ponytail wad behind her head.

"There aren't mistakes," Johnny said. "There are only unintended results."

"But why *doesn't* Tracee Ferrall want me to investigate Alice's murder? Why did she try to fire me after Jumbo hired me?"

"Jealousy?" Johnny Boyd suggested. His voice was low, quieter than usual, as if the volume were being slowly turned down.

"No, Tracee imagines other people being jealous of *her*; it wouldn't occur to her to be jealous of someone else. I bet Jumbo doesn't even know Tracee tried to fire me in his name."

"Then she's trying to keep a secret of her own hidden."

"I keep coming back to Mac McCutcheon," Ruby told him. "Jumbo wants him to be sheriff and Tracee doesn't. That's the connection."

"What gets the most attention around here?" Johnny asked. He rested his hand lightly on her head, smoothing the strands of her hair between his fingers. She felt the warmth of his skin and leaned against his leg.

"Scandal," Ruby told him. "The juicier the better."

"Then create your own scandal," Johnny said to her. "One the whole town will hear about. Better yet, the whole county."

She bit her lip, thinking about how much she detested scandal.

"There's nothing as interesting as sex and money to ninety percent of the world," he continued.

"Are you reading my mind?" she asked.

"No, but maybe you and I are part of the ninety percent," he said, touching her cheek.

The auto parts store was a cement-block building on the edge of town, surrounded by a large gravel parking lot where the desperate frequently repaired their cars. Spark plug packaging, old, frayed fan belts, and empty oilcans lay among the weeds at the lot's edge.

"Are you buying an auto part?" Jesse asked when Ruby pulled into the lot. Ruby parked a little way from the building with a clear view of the front door.

"I just need to talk to somebody inside," Ruby told her.

"I'll wait here," Jesse said, then frowned. "Unless you need me."

"Not this time."

She waited, watching cars and pickups pull in and out of the parking lot. Auto parts was obviously big business. Finally, when she counted eight customers inside, Ruby checked her scowl in the mirror, held her breath to make her face red, and marched into the store, brandishing a white envelope with Jumbo's name printed in large letters on the outside with a black felt-tip marker.

Three men stood at the counter. A woman browsed the floor mat section and a couple was studying road safety kits. A radio talk show, sounding like an evangelist's sermon, blared from behind the counter where

# Cut and Dry

metal shelves stacked with auto parts stood floor-to-ceiling and black rubber belts hung from the walls.

Tracee Ferrall was behind the counter, waiting on two of the men, a bright blue apron over a pink blouse and tight blue jeans. The smile she flashed at them was intimate, teasing. Rings and bracelets glinted under the lights.

Without excusing herself, Ruby shoved between the two men in front of Tracee and thrust the envelope forward. "Give this money back to Jumbo," she said loudly, dropping it on the counter with the writing facing the men, all the better to read.

The store's noise level dropped, voices cut dead by Ruby's tone of voice. Only the radio continued to blare, and in a few seconds someone in the back turned that down, too, all the better to hear.

Tracee's bright mouth fell open. "What?" she asked helplessly. The two men stepped back, their faces turning between Ruby and Tracee. The woman peeked around the floor mat display.

"You heard me," Ruby continued at the same voice level. "I don't want Jumbo Rolley's money. I'm not for hire just because he's trying to make Carly look bad in order to get his own man elected sheriff. I'm only interested in who murdered his wife, whether Jumbo is or not." Ruby turned and took two steps toward the door.

"But . . ." Tracee began.

"Why didn't you tell me about Mac McCutcheon?" Ruby asked in the store's complete silence. She was taking a chance on that one, but why the hell not?

Tracee raised a hand to her heart and Ruby knew she'd hit Truth in some form. Every eye was turned toward the two women. Voracious curiosity crackled the air.

"Wait," Tracee called, scurrying from behind the counter, elbowing past the men. But Ruby pushed open the door and stepped outside. It would have slammed behind her if Tracee hadn't caught it.

"Ruby. Wait, please."

Ruby strode across the parking lot with Tracee at her heels, stopping ten feet from her car, far enough from the building that those inside couldn't hear. Let the conjectures fly; she didn't intend to satisfy their curiosity so easily.

"Why didn't you tell me about Mac?" she repeated, still trying to bluff her way. A figure passed in front of the store's door, paused overlong and then moved on.

"It was so long ago . . ." Tracee told Ruby. "I hoped . . ." She bit her lip; her bosom rose and fell with deep breaths.

"But you were terrified my questions about Alice's death would throw the whole thing wide-open," Ruby said, shocked that Tracee couldn't see she was lying. "Is Mac connected to Alice's death?"

"No!" Tracee shook her head vigorously. She looked down at the gravel and said in a small voice, "Just to me. I didn't want Jumbo to find out."

"You and Mac McCutcheon . . ." Ruby said. "How long ago were you involved?"

"Right after I was Miss Color Festival."

"But Tracee, you already told me that. Jumbo must

know, and that was a long time ago," Ruby reminded her, catching the flash of annoyance on Tracee's face.

"Not *that* long ago," Tracee said irritably. "And there were . . . complications."

"Oh," Ruby said, beginning to see. She glanced toward the auto parts store and spoke quietly. "You got pregnant," she guessed and at Tracee's downcast nod, guessed again, "You had an abortion."

Tracee nodded again.

"You were young," Ruby said. "It's happened many—"

"You don't know Jumbo. He wouldn't forgive me for something like that. And I don't want it all brought up. The way people talk. It would ruin my . . ." She stopped, flicking at a stone with the toe of her sandal.

"Your chance to be the new Mrs. Rolley?" Ruby asked, realizing for the first time that in Sable, Jumbo Rolley would be a "catch." He was a good-looking man for his age and, even better than that, Jumbo meant money, comfort, a good future for someone like Tracee Ferral.

"But *how* would I have discovered that you got pregnant by Mac and had an abortion?" Ruby asked her. "Just by investigating Alice's death?"

"Don't say that word," Tracee said. "Please."

Ruby wasn't certain which word Tracee meant. She glanced around the quiet graveled parking lot. Jesse's head was bent over her book. The engine of a red pickup pinged. On the paved road, heat shimmered like a mirage. Slowly, it dawned on her how she might have discovered Tracee's connection with Mac McCutcheon.

"Did you go to Lansing with Alice?" Ruby asked, picturing it all those years ago. Alice and the young, frightened Tracee. "Did Alice arrange an abortion for you in Lansing?"

Tracee winced and Ruby guessed it was the word *abortion* that Tracee didn't want her to use.

"Alice Rolley?" Ruby asked, half to herself. Alice who lobbied for children's rights, who volunteered her time, collected money for children who were ill, and donated her energies to struggling mothers?

"She tried to talk me out of it, really hard," Tracee said, as if she were providing an excuse for Alice's complicity. "When she realized I wouldn't change my mind, that I might . . . try something else, she helped me."

"But why did you tell *Alice* you were pregnant?" Ruby asked.

"I was working in her beauty parlor part-time, I told you that, while I was in high school, like an apprentice. I got sick, you know, in the mornings, and she guessed."

"Did Mac know?" Ruby asked.

Tracee shook her head. "He still doesn't. I didn't love him. It was a stupid affair; he bought me things. I didn't know anything back then."

"Did you kill Alice to keep this a secret?"

Tracee gasped and clutched her hands beneath her breast. "Oh no. I knew Alice would never tell anyone.

And she's the only other person who knew. I was grateful to her. Don't tell anybody, please."

"After Alice took you to Lansing and helped you out of a jam like that," Ruby said, "then you had an affair with her husband?"

"It wasn't the same," Tracee said. "It was a different . . . issue."

Ruby couldn't help it; she shook her head in bewilderment. Tracee pulled herself taller, thrusting her shoulders back and bosom forward. "You think life should be easy, Ruby Crane: black and white, yes and no. But it isn't. Other people's lives are more complicated than yours."

"Sometimes," Ruby said, turning and walking toward her car, thinking about Alice and Tracee and realizing that Tracee had continued to go to Alice to have her hair done for the same reason Ruby had: to show her gratitude for Alice's help.

# Chapter 17

Heat lightning glowed along the eastern sky, continuous blooms as if from a distant battlefield, eerily silent. It was after midnight and Ruby stood on the cabin's porch, watching the muted flashes that were too far away to cast light. The night was still, breathless, too warm to sleep.

Not that she would have slept anyway. She rarely slept a night straight through, and never a deep sleep, always as if a corner of her consciousness stayed awake counting off the minutes, warning her it was nearly time to get up, chiding her for not going to bed earlier, listening for Jesse. And when she did awaken during the deep nights, she dared not lie in bed during that drowsy mad period between waking and sleeping. "That's when the devils climb in your head," Gram had always said. Instead, she read or sat in the dark, keeping the devils at bay.

Behind Ruby, inside the dark cabin, a fan whirred softly in the bedroom where her daughter slept uncovered, wearing one of Ruby's T-shirts. Jesse's sleep remained the drop into unconsciousness it had been since the accident, sleep so deep that each morning she awoke as if surprised to find herself on earth.

Just enough moonlight shone to see the mist gathered on Blue Lake and the occasional flare of Johnny Boyd's cigarette. Small comforts.

By suppertime, Ruby had guessed that most of Sable had heard a distorted version of her confrontation with Tracee Ferral. She smiled, wondering to what heights and depths the rumors had reached. Screaming and hair pulling? Ruby and Tracee rolling across the parking lot of the auto parts store?

But the more compelling fact remained that Alice Rolley had assisted Tracee in obtaining an abortion, not illegal, but surprising. Still, in a way it *did* conform to Alice's mission of helping children; Tracee had been hardly more than a child herself at the time. Tracee and Mac McCutcheon. Ruby could understand Tracee's not wanting *that* to get out.

Had Alice assisted other young women in Sable? Maybe even run an abortion procurement service? And had someone killed Alice to keep the past a secret, afraid Alice would ruin a reputation by telling?

Ruby made her way inside to the telephone in the dark kitchen and counting off the holes in the rotary dial with her fingers, she dialed Mary Jean's number.

"This had better be good," Mary Jean said, answering the phone in a perfectly wide-awake voice.

"It's Ruby. I knew you'd be up."

"Too damn hot. What's up? You need my brain this time of night?"

"You've lived here all your life, right?"

"Don't remind me."

"What rumors did you hear about Alice Rolley over the years?"

Mary Jean sighed. "Haven't we already gone over that topic? She gossiped; she adored her misfit children. Not that any of those attributes are rumors, just the facts, ma'am."

"Did she ever help young women?" Ruby asked.

"Spell it out, Ruby. I don't have a clue what you're talking about. Young women? What? Porno? White slave trade? Pimping? Alice the local madame?"

"Young women in trouble?" She said the words *in trouble* meaningfully, the way her mother had, realizing this was a silly conversation. Come right out and say it; quit the euphemistic innuendos. But she felt an unintentional responsibility to Tracee, the burden of a secret. Ruby was probably the only person in Sable who knew about Tracee's affair and abortion.

Mary Jean whooped. "She did? *Alice Rolley* helped girls who were preggers? That's news to me."

"I didn't say she did. I just wondered if that was in the rumor mill."

"Not that I ever heard."

Ruby caught the upbeat at the end of Mary Jean's sentence. "So what *did* you hear?" she asked.

"Nothing to do with Alice. Only that if a girl was pregnant and didn't want to pretend she was off visiting her aunt in Timbuktu for seven months, there was an alternative method, one your mother would never find out about. Think it was Alice ferrying young girls to an abortion clinic somewhere?" Mary Jean sighed. "Alice Rolley, friend of youth."

"I don't know. Probably not." And that was true. Maybe Alice had helped Tracee, but Ruby doubted arranging abortions was one of Alice's regular practices.

"Yeah, it doesn't quite fit the image, does it? Any other wicked rumors you'd like me to verify right now, right here in the middle of the night?"

"No, but thanks," Ruby told her.

"Give it a rest, Ruby," Mary Jean advised, stifling an audible yawn. "Go read a boring book or count to a million by odd numbers. You'll never get to sleep if you waste your time thinking."

Ruby hung up and in the dark cabin, made her way to Jesse's room, where she stood in the doorway for a few minutes. She couldn't hear Jesse's breathing over the whir of the fan but she felt the comforting presence of her daughter, a presence she no longer ever took for granted.

After losing her first child, Alice Rolley had loved the children she bore next too much, people claimed. Ruby could understand that. It made perfect sense to her.

She rubbed the back of her neck and turned from Jesse's room, thinking she might as well lie on the couch for a while until she was sleepy enough to return to bed in the overwarm loft.

Because of Jesse's fan, Ruby hadn't heard the door off the kitchen open, but now, a step outside Jesse's room, she saw the glow of heat lightning through the widening crack. She froze, then pressed herself against the wall, arms at her side, palms feeling the cool varnished logs behind her.

Jesse's fan spun, softening the sounds of the stranger sliding through the door and carefully reclosing it. Ruby heard its quiet click as it relatched. She held her breath. Someone was inside the cabin with her. She could see the outline in the kitchen, a formless shape. She couldn't make out any details: man or woman.

Where was Spot? The big dog had been outside when they went to bed. Ruby knew that sometimes she strayed into the woods, hunting among the trees. She willed Spot to come back. Now.

She didn't move, barely breathed, her mind stumbling over the possibilities: Franklin Rolley returning to finish his mission of the night before? Robbery? Or worse? Her being concentrated on Jesse; no one would hurt Jesse as long as Ruby was alive.

The tiny yellow beam of a penlight clicked on, its feeble golden shaft moving jerkily across the kitchen counters, pausing briefly at a stack of mail, then wavering and moving to the kitchen table. Whoever held the penlight was nervous, a realization that comforted Ruby only a little. Nervous people were as dangerous as determined killers; they were unpredictable, as liable to kill in panic as flee for their lives.

It wouldn't take the intruder more than a few moments to search the kitchen table, and if he didn't find what he wanted, would he move deeper into the cabin? Ruby stood in the passageway between the kitchen and the main room—or Jesse's room. Even a beam as frail as the penlight's would reveal Ruby's presence once it was flashed in her direction.

She wasn't about to hide and leave Jesse unprotected. So far, the intruder was unaware of Ruby's presence. His light bobbed across papers that were being roughly examined, then pushed aside, with no attempt at concealment. Whoever was in the cabin was hurrying, jittery and clumsy. The time for Ruby to make her move was now, while she had the advantage.

Ruby had known this cabin all her life and was able to traverse it as well in the dark as during the day. The light switch was on the wall ten feet away, just inside the kitchen door. In order to reach it, she'd have to pass by the stranger, risking discovery. If the prowler carried a weapon, Ruby didn't stand a chance. She was barefoot, wearing a T-shirt and panties, too far from anything that could double as a weapon.

She breathed quietly through her mouth, watching as the trespasser worked his way around the table toward her, the light held close to each object, which was then either inspected or passed over. He was nearly finished, nearly around the table.

When the back of the intruder's body was to Ruby, blocking the narrow bead of the penlight, she took four quick steps toward the kitchen door and unerringly laid her hand on the toggle of the light switch.

The overhead light flicked on. It wasn't a high-wattage bulb, but it filled the cabin as if a klieg light had been flashed over the scene.

Both Ruby and the stranger gasped, blinking at each other in the sudden glare.

In front of Ruby, the penlight still shining and pointing at Jesse's math homework, stood Roseanne Rolley, her small eyes squeezing closed and open, her lips pulled inward so her mouth formed a tight line.

Ruby glanced over Roseanne's big body clothed in a navy sweat shirt and dark pants, her hair back in a ponytail, a sooty smudge on each cheek like a commando's. She saw no sign of a weapon, only her penlight.

"Give me one good reason why I shouldn't call the sheriff, Roseanne," she said.

Roseanne took a bosom-heaving breath and clicked off her light. She straightened to her full height and raised her chin as if she were nobility under assault by the peasants. "I haven't done any damage," she told Ruby.

"Only because I stopped you. What are you looking for?"

Roseanne didn't answer, but she took two steps toward the kitchen door as calmly as if she'd just excused herself from a boring social visit. Ruby stepped forward and blocked her path.

"You're not leaving, Roseanne," Ruby said, thinking if Roseanne wanted to, she could swat her out of the way with one hand. "I want to know what in hell you're doing here."

"It's none of your business, Ruby Crane," Roseanne said, glaring down at Ruby.

"Are you out of your mind?" Ruby demanded. "Who else's business is it *but* mine?"

Roseanne's face reddened, and Ruby hastily said, "Let's talk this out, Roseanne."

"I don't have to tell you anything," Roseanne said.

"If you don't tell me why you're here, I *will* call Carly. I'll press charges. Trespassing at the very least. Explain it all to a judge if you'd rather."

The large woman put her thumbnail between her teeth in a surprisingly childlike gesture and considered Ruby. Her shoulders slumped and chin lowered. "Don't call Carly," she said in a low voice, gazing down at the floor.

"Then let's sit down," Ruby said, and beckoned her into the main room where she turned on the lamp beside the couch, a glow that dimly illuminated the room, gleaming off the log walls. Ruby sat in the rocker and Roseanne dropped to the couch across from her, slouching, her arms crossed as if she were cold. She'd smeared the dark blotches on her cheeks and now one eye appeared to have been blackened, an effect that somehow reassured Ruby.

"Franklin told me he was the one who was prowling around my cabin last night," Ruby said, "but it wasn't him, was it? It was you."

"I don't have to tell you anything," Roseanne asserted again.

"Did we just make a deal or didn't we?" Ruby asked her, leaning forward as if she were about to rise and head for the phone. "You talk or I call Carly?"

Roseanne rocked a little on the couch, back and

forth in nervous rhythm. "So what if it was me? You're digging around in *my* business."

"Your mother's business," Ruby corrected. "Not yours. But now that I've caught you burglarizing my house, I guess that makes you my business as well."

"Just stay out of our lives. Let the sheriff handle it."

"Are you supporting Mac McCutcheon for sheriff against Carly?"

"What does the sheriff's race have to do with my mother's death?" Roseanne's eyes narrowed.

"You tell me. Your dad supports Mac."

"So? Dad and Mac are friends. My father wasn't thinking straight when he hired you."

"Obviously you're not on the Sable gossip circuit," Ruby said.

"What do you mean?" Roseanne had uncrossed her arms and leaned forward, elbows to knees.

"I already told Tracee to give the money back to Jumbo. I'm only working for Carly now, not your father."

Roseanne's expression momentarily brightened; then her face hardened again. "So nothing's really changed. You're still investigating my mother's death."

"You broke into my motel room in Lansing," Ruby accused her. "That was more of a woman's work than a man's. To tear my dress and empty bottles of lotion and shampoo? Break cosmetics? A man wouldn't bother."

"I was home," Roseanne said stubbornly.

"I saw the bakery bag on the seat of your car," Ruby

# Cut and Dry 279

told her. "From Lansing. You can easily drive to Lansing and back in one day. I did."

"I don't have any reason to go to Lansing."

Ruby was getting nowhere. She sat back, holding her foot to the floor to keep the rocker from rocking, thinking she had nothing to lose. "Roseanne," she said finally. "I know your mother didn't just go to Lansing to pick up beauty supplies."

"You do?" The words came in a near whisper. Roseanne's eyes filled with instant tears that trickled over, tracking the black commando paint. "You do?" she asked again. "Have you told anyone?"

"No."

"Are you going to? It has nothing to do with her death."

"How can you be so sure?"

"That was forty years ago, almost fifty," Roseanne said, raising her hands to Ruby, as if pleading for reason.

Ruby was confused. *What* was over forty years ago? Tracee was thirty or thirty-one, at the most; she'd had her affair with Mac and her abortion when she was seventeen or eighteen. What was Roseanne talking about that happened forty years ago?

"Times *were* different then," Ruby said, urging Roseanne on, looking down at her hands, hiding her confusion from the other woman.

"They were," Roseanne said eagerly. "Now it would never happen. He'd have spent his life at home."

"Then why did she do it?" Ruby asked, feeling like

Alice in Wonderland, holding a passionate conversation, the subject of which she didn't have a clue.

Roseanne's voice rose plaintively. "Dad did it, with the doctor's assistance, of course. Remember Dr. Beers? They were trying to 'help' her, taking the decision out of her hands for her own good. Mom didn't discover the truth for five years, until after Franklin and I were born. I'm positive she never told him she knew and he still believes he got away with it."

"How long have you known?" Ruby asked.

"A week. I went through her papers two days after her death. He didn't care about her belongings. 'Take whatever you want,' he told me. Everything was in one box—a jewelry box Dad would never have bothered to look inside, beginning when she discovered he was institutionalized in Kalamazoo. He was already five years old—can you imagine how she must have felt? She kept a notebook, like a diary."

Kalamazoo. Alice Rolley had bought her beauty supplies in Kalamazoo for years before she switched to Lansing.

"Kalamazoo," Ruby repeated.

The baby who came first, the baby who was supposed to have died at birth, institutionalized without Alice's knowledge. She tried to imagine the shock of Alice's discovery, and couldn't. A baby she'd already mourned for and believed buried. Resurrected.

"That must have ended your parents' marriage," Ruby guessed. "When she found out."

Roseanne nodded. "They lived in the same house, that's all. He didn't understand why she turned cold on him. I remember them fighting when I was little and how he accused her of not loving him. He cried." She clasped her arms over her bosom again, gently rubbing her arms as if she were comforting herself. "People made fun of us because he fooled around. One affair after another."

"But there's a tombstone," Ruby said, still thinking of the lost child. "I've seen it. The plot's not far from my parents'."

"I know. Clever, wasn't it? Leo Junior. With a marble lamb on top. He arranged a quick graveside service and she couldn't go because she was still in the hospital." Roseanne shook her head. "We used to put flowers on the grave every Memorial Day: baby's breath."

"Why did she move him from Kalamazoo to Lansing?" Ruby asked. She heard Spot outside, sniffing along the door of the front porch, as unperturbed by Roseanne's presence as the night she and her brother had shown up without warning.

"She heard of an experimental program Michigan State University was running for the mentally handicapped, a home environment, an early group home. From the papers I found, she strong-armed them to enroll him." A slight smile crossed Roseanne's lips.

"Why did you break into my motel room?" Ruby asked.

"I was just so mad. And I'd warned you. I told you if you didn't play fair, I wouldn't either."

"Didn't you realize that tearing up my stuff would only make *me* angrier? That I wouldn't give up?"

"Some people would have."

"That was you who tried to run me down by the capitol, too, wasn't it? You risked a hit-and-run, you tried to *kill* me, just to keep your mother's secret?"

Roseanne looked down at the floor, her lips tight.

"Have you told Franklin about the baby?" Ruby asked.

Roseanne nodded. "But no one else knows, besides you. I couldn't stand seeing her dragged through the gossip mills. You know how people would talk: whether she really did know and if she'd willingly institutionalized her own son. All the good she did in her life would be overshadowed. She helped you, Ruby. Can you keep this from other people? For her memory?"

"You came here to go through my papers, hoping to find out if I knew?" Ruby asked.

Roseanne nodded, her face beseeching.

So simple a mission. Roseanne had been so single-minded, it hadn't occurred to her that destroying any written information she found in Ruby's cabin wouldn't erase Ruby's knowledge of Alice Rolley's secret. Ruby was reminded anew of the power of the written word.

"I can't promise," Ruby finally said. "But if this child doesn't have anything to do with your mother's death, I won't bring it up to anyone, not even Carly."

"It doesn't," Roseanne said, with such fierce certainty that Ruby wondered.

# Chapter 18

At dawn Ruby awakened Jesse and said, "Pack a couple of books. We, my dear, are going for one heck of a long ride."

Ruby almost believed Roseanne's story, but she made the three-hour drive back to Lansing anyway, windows open, Jesse watching the scenery or contentedly reading in the seat beside her, accompanying Ruby without question.

She drove Highway 37, the old two-lane road that traveled south through small towns and national forest woods of pine and hardwood. The farther south they traveled, the hillier and tamer the land grew and the heavier the traffic.

Before long they were caught in a long, irritatingly slow line of vehicles led by a motor home topped by a boat and pulling a trailer loaded with two all-terrain vehicles.

"Forty miles an hour," Ruby complained aloud.

"Is that too slow?" Jesse asked.

"It feels like it to me," Ruby said. As the caravan rounded a long, sweeping curve, in the rearview mirror she could see the traffic piled up behind them, ten or fifteen vehicles, bumper-to-bumper.

Suddenly the driver behind them blared his horn and whipped around the right side of their car, throwing up dust and dirt from the shoulder.

Jesse gasped and knocked her book to the floor, staring in terror as the car shimmied along the shoulder beside them and pulled back into the line of traffic two cars ahead. Horns blared and Jesse inhaled in quick wheezes of breath, like tiny screams, her neck corded and body stiff, both hands clutching the door handle, her face contorted in fear.

"Jesse," Ruby cried, reaching out her hand and gripping Jesse's shoulder. With her other hand she twisted the steering wheel to the right, bumping across the shoulder onto a wide shelf of grass next to a barbed-wire fence, jerking to a stop, the engine bucking and dying.

"Jesse," she repeated, unbuckling her seat belt and climbing over the gearshift to her daughter, enfolding Jesse in her arms.

"It's okay, sweetheart," she crooned, rocking Jesse's tense and shivering body in her arms until she gradually relaxed, her wheezing finally slowing to deep, steady breaths.

"Are you okay?" Ruby asked her.

Jesse nodded and Ruby wiped the perspiration from her daughter's face with the palm of her hand.

"What happened? Can you tell me?"

Jesse shook her head and said haltingly, "I don't know. I had a funny feeling."

There had never been an explanation for the one-car accident that had killed Stan and injured Jesse. No witnesses came forward; Jesse could recall nothing, not even the day of the accident. Had someone tried to pass Stan on the right?

Ruby sat in the car with Jesse in her arms, watching the traffic pass by, heads craned to look at their car parked so haphazardly beside the road. A convertible slowed and pulled onto the shoulder. "Are you okay?" a young man shouted.

"Fine, thanks," Ruby called out the window, waving them on.

Now Jesse pointed to the barbed-wire fence a few inches from her door. "That would have scratched up the car," she said calmly.

Ruby picked up Jesse's book from the floor and set it on her lap. "I think it would have caught us like a fishing net," Ruby forced herself to say cheerily. "You lost your page. Were you reading about ants?"

"It was page eighty-six," Jesse told her. "Praying mantids. They rear up like horses when they're threatened." It wasn't unusual that Jesse remembered the page number; she read every bit of print, from the top of each page to the bottom.

"I didn't know that," Ruby said. What she remembered was that the female mantid liked to bite off the male's head during copulation.

The rest of the drive was without incident and when they were close enough to Lansing that it was a local telephone call, Ruby stopped at a gas station and phoned the social psychology department at Michigan

State University. Without questioning her interest, the secretary gave her the addresses of their three group homes. Ruby didn't provide the name of Alice Rolley's son, certain that his last name wouldn't be Rolley but guessing that his first name was Leo, the same as on the tombstone.

She matched the three addresses against the Lansing map she'd saved from the Crown Inn, shaking her head and choosing the obvious one.

"Can I come in with you?" Jesse asked when Ruby parked in front of the well-kept Victorian home.

"Sure," Ruby told her. "We definitely need to stretch our legs a little."

The front yard with its tidy shrubbery and long, tire-marred wheelchair ramp was quiet, but laughter and voices sounded from the rear of the house. Ruby opened the wrought-iron gate and followed the brick path around the building, Jesse at her side. Lilac bushes with gnarled trunks as big as her thigh crowded against the house.

A college-age girl with short brown hair—a different girl from the one Ruby had seen two days ago—sat on the grass with two young adults, directing them in a clapping game. The boy who didn't talk, who'd watched Ruby through the iron fence from his wheelchair, sat beneath a tree, frowning at the leaves just above his head, his rocking subdued.

The college girl waved when she saw Ruby, bringing the clapping game to a close and rising to greet her.

"Can I help you?" she asked, brushing grass from

## Cut and Dry

her slacks, and before Ruby could answer, said "Hi!" to Jesse and shook her hand.

"I've brought a present for Leo," Ruby said, showing her the box of chocolates she'd bought at Paulas's Drug Store in Sable.

The girl laughed. "He'll love you for that. It ought to last him an hour, at least. You'll find him inside, in the TV room, right next to the office." Again she turned to Jesse. "You can stay out here with me if you like. I'll show you our new pond."

Jesse looked at Ruby questioningly. "Go ahead," Ruby told her. "I'll be back in a few minutes."

Before she went inside, Ruby scanned the buildings across the alley from the home, spotting the rear of the stuccoed Crown Inn, counting the windows and guessing that the room Alice Rolley always stayed in gave her a glimpse into the home's backyard, a few more precious moments viewing the son she'd thought she lost.

A redheaded woman older than the girl outside, but still young, dressed in a short jumper, sat at a desk in the informal office that had once been an ornate entryway, rock music playing softly behind her.

"I'm here to see Leo," Ruby told her.

"Rogers? Right there in the green chair," and she pointed to a room the other side of a curved arch. A TV stood in a shaded bay window silently playing cartoons to three residents who watched the bright images with varying degrees of interest.

Ruby cautiously approached the middle-aged heavyset man who sat in the green chair, his body soft and pear-shaped, his shoulders narrow and downward sloping.

He was older than Ruby; she'd known he would be, but somehow she hadn't prepared herself, had still expected to find a young child.

"Hello, Leo," she said, squatting at eye level beside his chair.

His hands were pudgy, his neck thick and his face flattish. He had clearly been born with Down syndrome.

" 'Lo," he answered eagerly, pulling at his thin hair, his voice mucousy. He smiled, thick gums showing in his wide mouth, and pointed to the candy box Ruby held, asking, "For me?"

"Yes, it's for you. A present." She opened the box and set it on his lap. He clumsily picked out a round chocolate, singsonging a slurred "Thank you, thank you, thank you."

Ruby sat beside him for several minutes, watching his simple messy pleasure, realizing there were no questions he'd be able to answer for her. Everything Roseanne Rolley had told her was true.

Leo smiled happily at Ruby and said in perfect imitation of the Campbell's soup song: "Mm-mm good."

"Good," she repeated. She helped him sort the fluted paper holders from his candy, then stood. "Good-bye, Leo," she said, patting his shoulder.

"Uh-huh, uh-huh," he responded, his attention on his candy.

"Are you a friend or relative?" the woman in the

office asked, sitting on the edge of her desk beside a row of stuffed animals.

"A friend of the family's."

"I'm Anne Meeker, the assistant director here," she said, shaking Ruby's hand. "I was sorry to hear about Leo's mother."

"How did you know?" Ruby asked.

"Her daughter was here two days ago and told us."

"Roseanne?" Ruby asked, wondering which had come first, visiting Leo or trashing Ruby's motel room.

"That's right. It was the first time I'd met her. She said she'd be the one visiting Leo from now on." Ms. Meeker smiled toward Leo. "He's our veteran resident. He's been in the program the longest of anyone, over twenty years. I was told his mother was instrumental in our funding during the early years."

"How long have you been working here?" Ruby asked.

"Almost four years. His mother visited every month. She always brought Leo loads of gifts." She nodded toward Leo, whose attention was caught by the television, his hand suspended over the candy box.

"Do you know what time of day Alice visited him?" Ruby asked. "Whether it was during the day or in the evening?"

"Both. She came back at dinnertime to eat with Leo and usually stayed until he went to bed."

"So she spent the entire evening with her son?"

"Usually."

So that explained Alice's missing evenings. No clandestine lover, no secret agenda.

Jesse was still in the backyard, gazing into the small rock-lined pool at the fat goldfish swimming in its depths. The college girl kneeling beside her rose. "We're discussing the merits of fish and bugs," she told Ruby.

"Insects are Jesse's latest hobby," Ruby said.

"Will she be coming to visit us?"

"Who?" Ruby asked.

"Jesse. I thought . . ." Her face flushed deep red.

"You thought I was here to find a place for Jesse?" Ruby asked incredulously.

"I'm sorry, but she's . . ." The girl stopped in confusion.

"Jesse's fine," Ruby said, louder than she intended, realizing that the other voices in the garden had stilled. "She lives with me and she's perfectly fine."

She took Jesse's hand and headed for the front of the house where her car was parked, leaving the college girl still apologizing behind her, and feeling the sting of tears.

The first time the phone rang after they returned to the cabin, Ruby let it ring, too tired to answer. It only rang five times, someone who knew she didn't have an answering machine.

She and Jesse sat on the floor in front of the cold fireplace, their backs against the couch and Spot stretched at their feet. They'd found a bowl of strawberries sitting on their front step when they came home and now it sat between Ruby and Jesse, half empty. Dinner.

This is perfection, she thought, bumping hands with Jesse as they both reached for another strawberry. She bit into the juicy berry, feeling the fruit sting her lips and the aching sweetness along the sides of her tongue.

Twenty minutes later when the phone rang again, Ruby answered. It was Hank.

"Honest," he said. "I'll be back the day after tomorrow. Late afternoon. Can you put Alice Rolley's death on hold so I can take you and Jesse to dinner?"

"I think it already is on hold," Ruby told him. "I've hit a dead end."

She heard him sigh. "That's okay," he said. "Let it rest for a while, Ruby. It's not a case *you* have to solve."

# Chapter 19

"So now I'm back to square one," Ruby said. "There's no trace of political intrigue, no clandestine romances. All I've found is a mother visiting her secret son every month."

A plate of Mexican casserole sat on the makeshift table beside Johnny Boyd's chair. He nudged the spicy food from one side of his plate to the other so the serving appeared diminished. Ruby wasn't fooled; he hadn't swallowed a single bite. He'd told her that food was losing its taste; only the strongest flavors held any appeal.

She'd presented the serving of casserole with fanfare, promising it was hot enough to make his tastebuds cry uncle, and then discreetly opened a can of thick chocolate protein drink and set it beside his plate. The can was half empty. There weren't any dirty dishes in his sink, only empty cans of protein drink in his trash.

"Maybe not square one," he said. "That's just one lead that took you in a different direction than you expected. But what did you learn?"

## Cut and Dry 293

Ruby leaned her head back against the porch post. *Her* plate was empty; she nudged it farther away with her foot. "What did I learn about Alice, you mean? Well, that she could keep a secret for forty years. She must have been devastated when she discovered her baby was alive, five years old and handicapped. She probably wanted to howl it to the world, but she didn't share the fact with a soul."

"What else?"

"According to Roseanne, Jumbo was probably telling the truth when he claimed he didn't notice Alice was gone the night she died. They lived in the same house as a matter of convenience and convention, but didn't have much to do with each other." She inwardly shuddered, thinking of the coldness of it: all those years. She wished she *had* found evidence that Alice Rolley had taken a lover.

"What about Roseanne and Franklin?" Johnny Boyd asked. Ruby noticed a purplish bruise above his wrist the size of a lopsided quarter. Another darkened his right knuckle. His T-shirt hung more loosely around his shoulders, although his abdomen was still swollen. The outline of his handgun was clearly visible at his waistband. Some habits refused to die.

Ruby rubbed her forehead, then squeezed her temples. "Roseanne's whole focus was protecting her mother's reputation, that's all. Shielding her memory from gossip about the lost child was more important to Roseanne than discovering who killed Alice. Jumbo's affairs weren't an issue, either. She knew the whole town was aware of Tracee and Jumbo.

"And the sheriff's race doesn't have any bearing. Neither Roseanne nor Franklin give a flying chicken who becomes sheriff."

Johnny Boyd nodded. "You're missing something," he told her, finally giving up pretense and pushing away his plate. "Did you find the connection between Tracee and Mac McCutcheon?"

Ruby bit her lip and gazed down to the shore of Blue Lake, at the graceful willow tree beside the old rotted deck, its branches shivering delicately in a breeze that didn't reach Johnny Boyd's porch. She sighed. "As a matter of fact, I did." Still she hesitated, until Johnny Boyd chided her.

"I'm not about to tell anyone, Ruby. I assure you, your secret will die with me." He gave a brief, humorless laugh.

Ruby looked into his face. He smiled, his blue eyes clear and distant.

"It's one of those small-town messes," she began, explaining how Alice had helped Tracee obtain an abortion years ago when she became pregnant by Mac McCutcheon.

Johnny whistled through his teeth. "And Tracee claims Mac doesn't know? A scandal like that might interfere with his chances at becoming sheriff."

Ruby shook her head. She'd already thought of that. "Not here. Opinions might come down hard on Tracee but nobody would blame Mac."

"Adam and Evil," Johnny said. "Boys will be boys."

"And girls will pay for it."

An orange and black monarch butterfly fluttered

across the porch and around the cabin. "They fly all the way from Mexico," Jesse had told her. "And on their way, they don't fly around buildings and mountains; they fly *over* them."

"But you don't suspect Tracee?" Johnny asked her.

Ruby rose from the porch and stacked their plates. "When you consider the facts, she looks like a possibility," Ruby conceded. "Alice was the only other person who knew about the abortion. Tracee is having an affair with Alice's husband and she's terrified he'll find out. She had the most to gain from Alice's death."

"I hear a 'but' in your voice," he said, then motioned toward his plate of casserole. "Scrape that off by the stump for the raccoons."

"Tracee genuinely regrets that Alice is dead. She's not a good enough actress to fake that."

"We're talking gut feelings here?" Johnny asked.

"That's right," Ruby agreed with a touch of defiance.

"And what does Carly think?" Johnny asked. He raised his eyebrows, then chuckled. "You haven't told him about the Tracee–Mac connection, am I right?"

"You are."

He shook his head. "How does anything ever get resolved around here?"

"Sometimes it doesn't. I'm going to talk to Jumbo again."

"Where will that get you?" he asked.

"I want to be sure Tracee passed along my message that I'm not working for him anymore. Then I'll try to find what you think I've missed. Can you give me a hint?"

"Don't have one. If it were me . . ." His eyes twinkled, drawing her attention away from the dark circles. "You aren't beholden to my advice but I'd go over Alice's last day again, minute by minute. Like I said, something's there that you're not seeing."

"Is this the way you operated as a cop?" Ruby asked. "Plodding along?"

"That's the way it's done. Tedious, time-consuming, detail by detail," he said. "Nine times out of ten, that and a piece of good luck solve the case."

"Not much glamour to it."

"No." An embarrassed expression crossed his face. "Could you do me a favor?" he asked.

"You name it," Ruby told him.

"I feel like lying down. I can get there under my own power, but if I had a shoulder to balance against, I'd get there a lot faster."

It wasn't as awkward as Ruby expected. She let him lead, remembering he was left-handed and moving to his left side, feeling the tremble in his arm over her shoulder, the sheer willpower that kept him going.

"Do you think it's time to notify your family?" Ruby asked as she helped him lower onto the bed.

"Nobody to notify," he told her. "I drove them away years ago."

"I can't believe that."

He looked at her coolly. "Well, believe it, because that's what I did." He lifted his legs onto the bed and lay back. "Thanks," he said. "One more thing?"

"Sure."

"Will you lay down beside me for a while?"

"What are you up to?" Ruby asked, only half teasing.

"Not much, my girl. Give me the back of your hand if I misbehave and I'm flat out."

He folded his pillow beneath his head and Ruby stretched on the bed beside him, feeling the scratch of the wool blanket against her bare legs, the feverish warmth of his body beside hers. He turned toward her and touched the inside of her arm beneath her elbow, just resting his hand there, and then put his face close to her hair.

"Ah, you smell like life," he murmured.

Northern Timber, where Jumbo operated the headsaw for hardwood logs, lay on the northeastern side of Waters County, the biggest mill in the county.

Ruby turned off the road onto the mill's acreage, following a logging truck loaded with bolts of red pine. It bounced into the mill yard, pieces of bark and dirt falling behind it.

Nothing grew around the mill: no grass, no trees. Just buildings, mangled ground, and logs being turned into boards and sawdust.

She'd been here before and knew the mill's layout. While the semi pulled its load of softwood toward the long metal building where red pine was cut into landscape timbers, Ruby parked in the lot beside the hangar-sized structure that housed the hardwood line.

The noise was deafening. Saws screamed, conveyors

clanked, heavy orange machinery rumbled across the rutted mill yard. The men she saw—no women worked here—wore sweat-darkened clothing and hard hats, their dusty faces red and perspiring, tending to business.

Ruby sat in her car a few minutes, going over what she planned to say to Jumbo. She'd assure herself that Tracee had given him back his money and also emphasize she was no longer investigating Alice's death for him. If anybody heard their exchange, so much the better. And Alice's last day; whatever he remembered, she wanted to hear again.

Mill regulations prohibited her from entering the mill alone, so Ruby climbed from her car, looking for someone she could ask to fetch Jumbo. Vehicles were parked haphazardly in the rough lot, everyone trying to avoid ruts and puddles. On two sides, gigantic stacks of oak logs waited to be sent through the saws. The piles towered above her, as tall as houses.

She cut between the mountains of logs toward the building where Jumbo worked, feeling the sudden comparative quiet as she was surrounded by giant tree trunks stacked like cordwood, whole forests racked up for eventual metamorphosis into furniture and flooring. Sap dried on cut ends, moss died on the bark, the shaded and cooler air smelled of dirt and oak. She watched her every step over the mangled earth; it was too easy to twist an ankle.

Nearby voices stopped her. Ruby froze, reaching out a hand and touching the strangely cool butt end of an oak log. Two men were arguing around the corner of the stack of logs, their voices heated, rising and falling between the rush and rumble of the sawmill.

Ruby caught only a few phrases: "don't give a damn," "She can't . . ." "it's time." She leaned forward, listening, hearing the soft vowels and nasal edges. One voice sounded like Jumbo Rolley's. She closed her eyes, seeing in her imagination the way his mouth twisted over *k* sounds. It was Jumbo's, she was sure of it.

The other voice was lower in timbre and she couldn't hear it well enough over the sounds of the mill to identify its owner, although she detected a certain familiarity. She waited, vigilant for more clues to the argument, but only heard snatches that made no sense. If they were discussing a sawmill problem, who was "she"?

Slowly, Ruby turned around and retraced her steps back to her car. She turned on the engine and backed up to a row farther in the rear of the lot, jouncing over an especially nasty rut that bumped her head against the roof, then pulled in next to a van so her car was partially hidden but she still had a view of the stacks of logs.

She spotted Abel Obert, the owner of Northern Timber, leaving the office building, hurrying toward a clawed crane in his curious scurry, slightly bent forward as if he couldn't get where he was going fast enough. A secretary stepped outside and lit a cigarette. A lighted cigarette within yards of the mill buildings felt too much like tempting fate to Ruby.

The sun beat down on the bare lot. Even with the

windows open, Ruby felt as if she'd been shoved into an oven. She found an old newspaper under her seat and fanned herself.

Within five minutes a man stepped from the very same aisle between the logs where Ruby had entered, without glancing left or right, and swaggered toward a four-wheel-drive Bronco.

He was out of uniform and his car was unmarked, but Ruby had no difficulty recognizing Mac McCutcheon. He didn't waste any time before starting his engine and leaving the lot.

She watched him drive out of Northern Timber, turning toward Sable on the paved road. What was it "time" for? Ruby wondered.

She was about to again look for someone to get Jumbo for her when her attention was caught by more movement near the stacks of logs. Another man emerged from the logs, a baseball cap pulled low. Ruby took her hand away from the ignition and watched. Here was someone who was so unused to sneaking around that he was as obvious as a naked man to the most disinterested observer.

Now he made his way furtively to the blue pickup Ruby hadn't noticed in the corner of the lot. A beagle jumped up from the pickup bed and wagged its tail. Dick Prescott rumpled its ears before he got in and followed in the same direction as Mac McCutcheon.

Jumbo, Mac, and Dick Prescott arguing with one another, half hidden in the logs at Northern Timber. Ruby puzzled over the unlikely trio and finally put her car in gear and left the mill without talking to Jumbo.

## Cut and Dry

* * *

Ruby called Carly at home. "What do Mac McCutcheon, Jumbo Rolley, and Dick Prescott have in common?" she asked.

"What do you mean?" She caught the caution in his voice.

"Come on, Carly. I saw the three of them today, hiding like bad boys in a bunch of logs at Northern Timber, arguing. They're an unlikely combination. Especially since I've heard Dick Prescott badmouth Mac, Jumbo badmouth Dick, and Mac sneer at everybody."

"That's the way it is, Ruby. People are friends, then they fall out and then they're friends again. You know that."

"Do all three of them belong to the First Americans?" she asked.

"I don't know. Maybe."

Ruby sat crosslegged on her bed and glanced at her bedside clock. It was eleven, only nine in Albuquerque. Phyllis's phone number was written on a slip of paper beside the phone. She traced over the numbers with her fingernail, then dialed Phyllis before she could change her mind. The phone rang six times before Phyllis's carefully modulated voice came on the answering machine advising the caller to ring her office or leave a message.

The machine beeped and Ruby lowered the phone, then pulled it back to her ear and said, "It's me. Call me if you want to," and hung up.

# Chapter 20

"Can I sit outside and read?" Jesse asked, pointing to the tipsy wooden picnic table that occupied the narrow strip of grass in front of the Wak 'n Yak.

"If you want to," Ruby told her. "Come inside if you get bored—or too hot. At least the beauty shop's air-conditioned."

Jesse nodded, already heading toward the picnic table, her complete attention on the procedure of seating herself and positioning her book.

The evening before, Ruby had made an appointment for early that morning so she could claim the attention of both Fanny and Katrina.

"You want the works?" Fanny asked as Ruby entered the shop. The crepe-surrounded photograph of Alice that had hung in the window was gone. The strip of black cloth had been removed from the bell on the door and it jangled cheerily behind Ruby. A return to normalcy.

"No thanks. I'd like to talk to both of you and an appointment seemed the best way to do it. My hair's fine."

"That's a matter of opinion," Katrina deadpanned in front of one of the big mirrors where she was applying mascara, ducking as if Ruby had thrown her bag at her.

The two women were dressed in similar fashion: short skirts and scoop-neck tops, Katrina's small waist circled by a wide belt and Fanny's more comfortable proportions by a narrower, less attention-grabbing chain.

Fanny grabbed Ruby's right hand and inspected her nails, tsk-tsking as she turned over Ruby's hand, front to back. Ruby's nose twitched at the strength of Fanny's perfume. "At least let me give you a manicure," Fanny said. "These paws look like a farmer's hands."

"An honorable profession," Ruby said, regarding her uneven and rough nails against Fanny's magenta sculpted nails. "All right," she agreed, "but no nail polish except clear."

"At least that's one baby step forward," Fanny said, shaking her abundant waves and curls. "You'd be surprised how many people judge you by the state of your fingernails."

"Then I *am* in trouble," Ruby said.

"Sit down over there and we'll get started," Fanny told her.

Ruby sat at the small Formica-topped table while Fanny gathered her tools. She was the first appointment of the day and the shop was spotless, smelling only faintly of hair chemicals.

"What I want to do," Ruby said as Fanny took her

left hand, "is go over every detail of Alice's last day, anything you can remember, no matter how trivial."

Katrina sighed and sat at a dryer behind Fanny, crossing her long legs. "Didn't we already do that?"

"And once for Carly, too," Fanny said, pouting her raspberry lips and crossing her eyes.

"One more time," Ruby said. "Especially the afternoon."

"The afternoon *is* easier," Katrina conceded, "because we've talked about it practically every day since Alice died, trying . . . you know, to figure out what we could have done different."

"And we can't remember a single solitary unusual incident," Fanny agreed, dipping Ruby's hand in a lukewarm solution, saying, "Soak for a few," and patting Ruby's wrist.

"Then explain to me again how the day was so ordinary," Ruby said.

Tripping over each other, finishing one another's sentences, Fanny and Katrina related the afternoon's appointments: cuts and sets, tints and perms, manicures.

"Do you remember any of the conversations?" Ruby asked.

"The usual chatter," Katrina told her. "Shelley's having hot flashes; Pam's daughter Carol won't speak to her since Pam called Carol's husband an alcoholic. Dan Smith thinks Al shot his Labrador for chasing deer. That kind of talk."

"Did Alice receive any phone calls?"

"Phone calls?" Katrina repeated. "Besides appoint-

# Cut and Dry 305

ments, you mean?" She poked the tail of a comb into her short tight curls, frowning. "I don't remember any. Nothing personal anyway. Do you mean did she get bad news on the phone? I don't think so. She acted the same as always."

"What about your customers?" Ruby asked. "Did any of them mention anything unusual? *Do* anything unusual?"

"No," Fanny said.

Katrina snapped her fingers. "Except for the pictures," she amended. "We've never done that before."

"What pictures?" Ruby asked. "The ones on the wall?" She nodded toward the wall that held Alice's hairstyling history, her gallery of "star" appointments and the charities she'd been involved in.

"Mm-hmm," Katrina said. "We were running a little late and Dora Durbas's sister-in-law came to pick her up—I'd accidentally turned the dryer too low—so while she waited for Dora to dry, she asked about the pictures. Alice gave her the grand tour, telling her who everybody was."

"Do you think we should stick labels on each one?" Fanny asked. "Like in a museum? Who's who before we forget. Just because it's our shop we won't take Alice's pictures down; they're part of the Wak 'n Yak's history," she ended fervently.

"It's not our shop yet," Katrina reminded Fanny.

Ruby watched as Fanny magically transformed her nails with swift swipes of an emery board, remembering Franklin's easy skill with his piecrusts.

"Would you mind telling *me* who's in all these photos?" Ruby asked.

"I can try," Katrina said, rising from the chair and moving to the wall. "Help me, Fanny. Alice just rattled off everybody's name."

"That's because she was in most every picture," Fanny said.

Katrina began at the top left, where young Alice stood in front of her shop holding a dollar bill: followed by a mayor, a cat commercial star who'd once spent a weekend on Blue Lake, Color Festival queens, then the long line of congressmen from Alice's Cut-In fund-raiser years. The youthful Bernard Woktoski and several congressmen either out of office or dead.

"Who's this little cutie?" Katrina asked Fanny, pointing to a photo on the bottom row.

Fanny squinted. "Oh. That's Jordan Asauskas before he was elected to the state legislature. He was an apprentice or something like that. Years ago."

"A page?" Ruby asked. She pulled her hand from Fanny's and joined Katrina, who held her finger beneath a framed photo of Alice standing over an embarrassed-looking teenage Jordan Asauskas. Ruby was sure if the photo had been in color, Jordan's face would be flaming red. This must be the incident he'd related to her, when Alice had come to the capitol and treated him like the young local boy he was trying not to be. He hadn't mentioned that he'd gone under her scissors, too. She wondered if he knew his youthful mortification had been displayed on the wall of Alice Rolley's beauty parlor for the past twenty years.

"Jordan was Mina's cousin, you know," Fanny said in that sorrowful yet respectful awe used in referring to those who'd known unspeakable tragedy.

"I remember," Ruby said.

"She wrote to him that day," Fanny added.

"Alice wrote to Jordan Asauskas?" Ruby asked. "On which day?"

"The day she died."

"How do you know?"

"I mailed the letter for her when I left the shop," Fanny said, "just before . . . it happened."

"Alice gave you the letter to mail?"

Fanny shook her head. "I always picked up letters waiting to be mailed and dropped them off at the post office on my way home. I've done it for years."

"Sometimes I did it," Katrina said.

"But mostly me," Fanny countered.

"Where did Alice leave the letters she wanted mailed?" Ruby asked.

"On the counter. See the little letter holder made from a bed spring? Alice said Franklin made it when he was in fifth grade."

The letter holder sat beside the appointment book, visible to anyone paying her bill. "Were there other letters to mail that day?" Ruby asked. "Besides the one to Jordan?"

Fanny skewed her lips to one side. "I don't think so. No, I'm sure there weren't because I remember reading who the letter was addressed to." She shrugged. "I'm naturally curious."

Katrina guffawed.

Ruby grew aware of the slow tingling at the back of her neck that she was accustomed to when she was about to break a forgery case: the sensation that the patterns and rhythms were coalescing and any second, the forger's blunder would jump out at her. She only needed to be patient, stay alert.

"Think," she implored Fanny and Katrina. "Who was in the parlor when Alice named the people in these photographs? Every person who was here."

"Well, the three of us, of course," Fanny said. "And Dora Durbas and her sister-in-law. Babs Prescott and her granddaughter, Susannah. Who else?" she asked Katrina.

"Mrs. Sams, but I think she was under the dryer."

Fanny nodded in agreement.

"Nobody else?" Ruby asked.

"That's about all this place could hold without busting open," Katrina told her. "Why?"

"I just want you to be positive, that's all."

"I am," Katrina said.

"Me too," Fanny added.

"Can I use your phone in the back?" Ruby asked. "I have to make a long-distance call but I'll charge it on my card."

"Sure," Fanny said. "But what about your nails? I'm not finished yet."

Ruby glanced down at her hands: one with sleekly

# Cut and Dry

shaped nails, the other still a "farmer's hand." "I'll make another appointment," she told Fanny.

"We'll have to start all over again," Fanny warned her.

Ruby glanced through the plate glass window to the front lawn where Jesse still read, her head bent over her book, statue-still.

"I'll keep an eye on her," Katrina said. "Go ahead."

"Thanks." Ruby pulled aside the sunflower curtains that separated the back room from the shop. The green rug covering the spot where Alice had lain still appeared pristine, as if Fanny and Katrina avoided the death spot like good children in a cemetery.

It took her fifteen minutes and three tries to reach Jordan Asauskas.

"He has a meeting in ten minutes," the secretary warned Ruby.

"That's fine because I only need two of his ten minutes," Ruby assured her.

After a sigh, the line clicked and Jordan's voice sounded in her ear. "Ruby, what can I do for you?"

"Did Alice Rolley send you a letter about the time she died?"

"No," he said, and Ruby felt defeated until he finished. "Not a letter, just a card."

"What did it say? Do you remember?"

"She congratulated me for becoming the chairman of the Subversive Organizations Committee."

"Was that unusual for her?"

"To send cards? Not at all. I told you she sent my

wife and me a card when our baby was born. Alice kept tabs on her elected officials."

"But that was all it said? No other messages?"

"No. Just 'congratulations.' "

"Thanks. How's the committe going?"

He groaned. "These groups are a hot-button issue, so hot I'm longing to jump back into the frying pan. A few of my associates believe the good of the many outweighs the constitutional rights of a few. I wish . . ." His voice wound down to a sigh. "Thanks again for giving me an opinion on those letters. I've received some more interesting missives since then, a few I'm curious about. Would you be interested in a legitimate forgery-detecting job? If I can shake loose some funds, that is."

"Just give me a call," Ruby told him. After she'd given him her phone number, she hung up, sitting for a few seconds with her hand on the receiver.

Fanny was just smocking a customer at a styling chair in front of the sink when Ruby left the back room.

"Do you remember," Alice asked Katrina, "when Alice was naming off everyone in her photos, did she mention that Jordan Asauskas was the new chairman of the Subversive Organizations Committee?"

Katrina pursed her lips. "She said he was some honcho or other but I don't remember if it was of the Subversive Organizations Committee. Want me to ask Fanny?"

"No, that's all right for now. I'll come back if I need to know."

# Cut and Dry

❖ ❖ ❖

Ruby leaned over and said softly to Jesse, "Are you ready to go?"

Jesse raised her head, blinking as if Ruby had shone a spotlight on her. Ruby watched as her daughter shifted mental planes, returning to Sable.

"Did you already talk to Fanny and Katrina?" Jesse asked.

"Yes, I did. In fact, it took longer than I expected. I'm sorry if you got bored."

Jesse pondered Ruby's words, the double vertical frown lines appearing between her eyes. "When I'm thinking about something else, it doesn't feel like you've been gone at all."

"That's true," Ruby said, sitting on the bench seat beside Jesse, thinking aloud. "Sometimes you believe only a minute or two has passed and actually it's been much longer." She absently felt her fingernails, one hand refined, the other rough, considering the tricks of time.

Jesse broke into her thoughts. "Should I read some more?"

Ruby kissed her cheek. "You are a genius. Do you have the patience for one more stop?"

"I'm a very patient person," Jesse said solemnly.

"And a very wise one," Ruby told her.

Ruby drove to a white rambler a block from the high school where two bicycles leaned against the front porch. Climbing roses tangled up the side of the house and sparrows splashed in a concrete bird bath. Beaver Cleaver and Wally could have been in the driveway shooting baskets.

Dick and Babs Prescott's daughter, Darlene, answered the chiming doorbell, holding an aluminum mixing bowl and wooden spoon. "My turn for Girl Scouts," she explained, raising the bowl. "Chocolate chip cookies." From deeper in the house came a faltering rendition of "Lara's Theme" being pecked out on a piano.

"I have a question to ask Susannah about the day Alice died," Ruby said, then, seeing Darlene's reluctance, lied easily. "Carly thought it would be less upsetting for her if I asked instead of him. You know how uniforms can upset children."

"Do you have to?" Darlene asked. In twenty years, she'd be a replica of Babs.

"It'll only take a minute," Ruby said. She smoothly stepped through the door past Darlene, smiling. "Don't bother. I'll follow the music," leaving Darlene at the door with her cookie dough, her face still doubtful.

The piano stood in a recreation room that had once been a garage. All the garage transformations Ruby remembered from her childhood were present in this one room: wood paneling and orange carpet, a plaid couch and chair, console TV, a pool table. A beagle slept on a pillow in the corner, Dick's dog who wouldn't hunt.

Susannah looked up as Ruby entered, perfectly willing to stop playing and talk to Ruby, eager even. She was a young Darlene, probably a young Babs, nine years old with glossy strawberry blond hair and freckles, her charm dampened by an imperious manner and calculating eyes.

"That was nice," Ruby told Susannah. The girl inclined her head in agreement and folded her hands primly in her lap. "May I ask you a question?"

"Is it about Alice Rolley getting strangled to death?" Susannah asked eagerly, her mouth turning upward in a smile. So much for the sensitive child.

"In a way," Ruby told her. "Do you remember where you and your grandmother went after you left the beauty parlor that day?"

Susannah put an index finger into her cheek in a studied pose. "We came here to get ready for my piano recital. We were almost late."

"Did you go anywhere else on the way home?" Ruby asked. "Did your grandmother stop at the store?"

"No," she said with a touch of impatience. "We were in a hurry."

Ruby glanced at the clock that hung over the pool table. It was an advertisement for Hamm's beer. Susannah, following Ruby's gaze, said, "My dad paid a lot of money for that clock. It's rare."

"Why were you almost late for the recital?" Ruby asked.

"Because we had to pick up my dress from Mrs. Brent."

"So you stopped at Mrs. Brent's on the way home?"

Susannah nodded gravely. "It has a velvet pinafore, in royal purple."

"I'll bet you were nervous about the recital," Ruby said gently. "You probably couldn't think about anything else."

"I was a little bit nervous," Susannah agreed. "I played my hands on my legs, trying to remember the songs." She showed Ruby, her fingers pressing imaginary keys. "But after I got to the recital, I was calm. Mom said I played beautifully."

"I'm sure you did. So on the way home from the beauty parlor, after Katrina had French-braided your hair, you stopped at Mrs. Brent's and your grandmother rushed inside to get your new dress, is that right?"

Susannah nodded and said smugly. "And a killer strangled Mrs. Rolley."

After she left Darlene's house, Ruby drove through Sable, passing the Wak 'n Yak and turning the corner so she could drive around the block. Mrs. Brent was a widow who had once mended costumes for Las Vegas shows and for the past thirty years had sewn for families in Sable who could afford it. Ruby braked in front of Mrs. Brent's, gazing past her white and green house to the narrow path that led alongside the garage to the alley. Mrs. Brent's house sat directly across the alley from the Wak 'n Yak.

# Chapter 21

"You look as determined as a bulldog," Mary Jean said after Jesse and Barbara had left her real estate office arm in arm, heading for the fountain at Paulas's Drug Store across the street. "What's up?"

"I'm not sure," Ruby told her, "but I'm going out to the Prescott farm to talk to Babs."

Mary Jean's eyes sparkled. She crossed her arms and leaned back in her chair. "Aha! You think Babs knows more than she's saying."

"Maybe," Ruby said.

"She knows who killed Alice?" Without waiting for an answer, Mary Jean went on, fingering the scar on her chin. "Did she see the killer hiding by the Wak 'n Yak after all? Or did somebody spill the beans to her?"

"You know I can't say anything yet," Ruby said. "And then only when Carly gives the okay. After that, I promise I will tell all."

Mary Jean threw up her hands. "Boring boring boring. Are you going out there with Carly? In his big bad police car?"

Ruby shook her head. "I'm going alone."

She'd called Carly's office, but he'd been out and the receptionist said he was away from his radio. She'd briefly considered waiting until he returned, but unlike Jesse, patience wasn't one of Ruby's virtues. She'd talk to Babs, keep it low-key, completely nonconfrontational. There'd be plenty of time to discuss Babs's story with Carly afterward.

"Okay, do it your own way, as usual," Mary Jean said. "One of these days, playing the Lone Ranger is going to get you into trouble."

"But not today," Ruby assured her.

"Whatever you say. When's Hank hitting town?"

"Later this afternoon. We're going out to dinner tonight."

Mary Jean held up her hands as if sun were glaring in her eyes. "Oh, that smile could blind. Miss him, huh?"

"You could say that."

"I just did, didn't you hear me?" Mary Jean glanced toward Paulas's Drug Store, where Barbara and Jesse had disappeared. "Okay, so the girls are mine for the afternoon. I'm spending the rest of the day chained to my desk so it's my pleasure to watch over the little darlings."

"Thanks," Ruby told her. "I appreciate it."

"Don't worry. You'll get yours."

Babs had no idea Ruby was on her way to see her. She might not even be home. Ruby turned onto the paved road that led to the Prescott farm, scattering two crows tearing at an unidentifiable bloody blotch on the pavement. A creek ran beside the road, tamed to a ditch years ago when farmers worried more about draining their land than irrigating it, long before wetland awareness.

What Ruby had discovered was circumstantial evidence, purely coincidental. With a few well-worded questions, surely Babs would be able to explain away Ruby's concerns without being aware that Ruby doubted her earlier story.

Ruby slowed as she approached Dick Prescott's farm, glancing at a small herd of black and white Guernseys grazing in the thick grass of a new pasture. The Prescotts' gate beneath the ranch-style crosspiece stood wide-open, hauled backward and latched to a post. Ruby turned in, passing beneath the crossed rifles.

The lawn was as cleanly cut as before, the farm serenely bucolic with its fruit trees and flowers and well-tended buildings, the gates and fences to the pastures beyond. Dick Prescott's American flag sagged from the flagpole in the front yard. Another swayed gently on a pole that angled out from the long front porch. God bless America.

There weren't any cars parked in the driveway; the garage doors were lowered, the white barn closed up tight. The farm felt deserted, no one home. Ruby was surprised that Dick and Babs had gone away and left their front gate standing wide-open.

She braked near the frame swing and got out, looking around as she straightened her shorts, leaving her bag on the passenger seat. The dogs in the kennels gave a few half-hearted barks, then, deciding that either Ruby was no threat or wasn't bringing any food, retreated in silence to the shady sides of their doghouses.

Near the back door of Babs's house a handmade quilt lay draped across the back of a lawn chair, as if someone had sat there wrapped in it on a cool evening. Ruby stopped to finger the muslin borders, briefly admiring the tiny even stitches of the leaf and feather quilting.

No sounds came from the house, no music or TV. Ruby knocked on the screen door, calling, "Is anybody home? Babs?" A tabby cat, which had been asleep in a wicker dog basket on the floor of the entry, gazed up at Ruby through the mesh, then stood and stretched, front paws out, tail end high.

"Kitty, kitty," Ruby said absently, peering through the screen into Babs's kitchen: painted white floor-to-ceiling cabinets, orange Formica-topped counters, plants hanging in the window over a deep porcelain sink, all of it as tidy as the exterior of the farm, exactly as Ruby would have expected.

She turned the handle on the screen door and wasn't surprised to find it unlocked. She herself usually left her cabin open. Until she'd added locks to the doors last fall, she couldn't remember there ever having been keys for the doors.

As she pulled open the screen door, the tabby cat slipped outside, brushing against her legs. "Anybody home?" she called again. "It's Ruby Crane."

## Cut and Dry 319

Only silence. Ruby stood in the center of Babs's shiny clean kitchen, hearing the tick of the cuckoo clock on the wall behind the maple table and somewhere in the distance, a chain saw. Sun gleamed off the water in two ceramic mugs sitting in the sink.

Ruby stepped to a calendar hanging beside the wall phone, drawn to it by the notes penciled inside the square of days. She immediately scanned the day of Alice's death: *Wak 'n Yak 4:00*, it read. *Susannah's recital 7:00*, the penmanship clumsily executed because of having been written on a vertical surface.

In stronger penmanship, another hand had written *meeting 7:00* on every Tuesday of the month. And Ruby spotted the same handwriting on yesterday's date: *North Tim, M & J*, the entry read. M & J. Northern Timber? Mac and Jumbo? So the meeting at Northern Timber between Jumbo, Mac, and Dick Prescott had been planned. To what end?

Lastly, she glanced at today's date: *Meeting, noon*, then looked at her watch. It was twelve-twenty. So that's where they were, at a noon meeting, a lunch meeting like the Rotary Club's.

Without moving from the calendar, Ruby looked into the adjoining room at the dining room set, probably manufactured in the 1920s and handed down from Babs's or Dick's parents. Nearly ever family inherited a similar set: the leafed table with its curved legs and six chairs, the buffet, and—if it survived—the china cabinet.

A sheet of paper lay on top of a manila folder on the table; she could see penciled handwriting: dark and slashing like the writing on the calendar. Dick's. She licked her lips but didn't move. Entering a neighbor's kitchen to drop off food or a gift was no big deal; most people did it at one time or another. But to wander inside for no reason and go beyond into the private reaches of the house was another matter: invasion or, at the least, unpardonable rudeness, making her as much a prowler as Roseanne.

Suddenly, Ruby heard the creak of the screen door. She spun around and faced Babs Prescott, her hair disheveled, wearing jeans with dirt-spotted knees and a sweat shirt with the sleeves torn off.

"I thought I heard a car," Babs said, letting the door slam behind her and rapidly moving toward the kitchen counter. "But I'm all wrapped up in a new hatch of chicks. I just came in to get a screwdriver. The thermostat on the incubator's stuck."

Babs jerked open a drawer next to the sink and pulled out a screwdriver, looked at the tip and murmured, "I need a Phillips," then pulled out a second screwdriver.

"I'd like to talk to you," Ruby said. "About Alice Rolley's death."

"Sure," Babs said, straightening and slamming the drawer closed. "You can come with me if you want, or wait here. There's a pitcher of lemonade in the refrigerator. Help yourself."

"Can we talk right now?"

Babs shook her head, striding across the kitchen toward the door. "Only if you come with me. This

# Cut and Dry 321

incubator can't wait; I'll lose my chicks. Buff Orpingtons."

The door banged behind Babs and Ruby hurried after her. Babs was across the yard, halfway to the barn, nearly running, the red-handled screwdriver held at her side, pointy end backward.

"Wait," Ruby called, but Babs ducked through a side door of the white barn. The plank door banged shut behind her, rattling the horseshoe that hung above it. Ruby pushed the door open, shoving her shoulder against it.

The door slammed closed and Ruby found herself wrapped in darkness. There were no windows, no lights. She couldn't make out any shapes, could only smell a faint old medicinal odor, like camphor. "Babs?" she called, moving her arms in arcs like a blind person.

There was no answer and Ruby felt sick to her stomach with dread. "Oh shit," she whispered, disgusted with herself, knowing she'd made a lethally stupid mistake. Where was Babs?

Slowly, Ruby reached behind her back for the door. She hadn't taken more than two steps inside, it would only take an instant to get back outside into the hot, blessedly bright, day.

Her fingers touched cloth, felt the resistance of warm flesh. "Babs?" she asked, wincing. Where was the damn screwdriver?

"Don't move," a man's voice warned close to her ear. "Not an inch, you nosy broad."

Ruby froze. The voice was too low to recognize, hardly more than a menacing growl.

"Dick," she tried, making her voice as coldly demanding, as purely reasonable, as she could muster. "Let me go," spoiling the effort by helplessly squeaking out the word *go*.

An object was shoved against her spine just above the waistband of her shorts, and Ruby had no doubt it was the barrel of a gun. "What do you want?" she whispered.

"The thousand-dollar question is," the man said so close to her that his breath feathered her hair, "what do *you* want?"

"Just let me speak to Babs."

"We can arrange that. Go forward."

"I can't see," Ruby protested. "Turn on a light."

The gun barrel jabbed harder into her spine. "Forward."

"It is you, isn't it, Dick?" she said, blindly stepping forward, her point of reference the gun at her back. She felt the give of the wood floor beneath her feet as she stumbled, her arms in front of her, groping.

"Stop," Dick ordered, and reached around Ruby to open a second door, then shoved her through it.

Ruby blinked, tensed to leap for cover. She was in a hay barn. Bales were stacked to either side of her, piled toward the rafters in walls two and three stories high. Light shone through the long cracks between the barn boards, making golden beams that crisscrossed the walls of hay and the rough-hewn floor. From somewhere high a dove cooed. The sweet fra-

# Cut and Dry 323

grance mocked her as she stood in this peaceful place with a gun at her back.

Babs stood against one wall of hay, in the alley between the two mounds where there was room for a tractor and wagon to pull straight through the barn, in one rolling door and out the other. She still held the Phillips screwdriver, turning it against her leg, point to handle and back again.

"Babs, what's going on?" Ruby asked.

"Sit down over there," Dick Prescott told her, pointing toward a hay bale set in the middle of the barn.

Ruby sat down, warily eyeing Dick and his gun. It was dull black, from end to end, like stealth planes capable of flying below radar, smaller than a hunting rifle. Dick pointed it toward her, standing with his feet spread in military stance, his blocky body clothed in a short-sleeved khaki shirt and jeans. The tightly baled hay pricked the bare skin of Ruby's legs like needles. She tried not to move.

Babs moved closer to Dick, her eyes following him as he circled Ruby's hay bale, swaggering, making low grunting sounds in his throat as he considered her, his fleshy arms glistening with perspiration. Or nervousness? Ruby watched him point his gun toward her. It wavered and she sensed indecision. He'd come this far; now what?

"Where's the chick incubator?" Ruby asked Babs.

"Isn't one," Babs said, her voice relaxed. "I buy them already hatched."

"You were very convincing," Ruby told her. "I was

completely taken in by your heart-wrenching tale of baby chicks in danger for their lives. The screwdriver was a nice touch. Was that in case I didn't cooperate?"

"Be quiet," Dick ordered, stopping in front of her. "I'm going to ask you some questions and I want straight answers."

"If you . . ." Ruby began, and Dick pointed his gun at her, jabbing the barrel forward for emphasis.

"I'll ask questions. You answer them. That's how we're operating now. Got it?"

Ruby nodded, pulling her legs in closer to the bale.

"Who are you working for?" Dick asked. Babs moved near enough to Dick to touch him, her face unreadable. She no longer held the screwdriver. Ruby couldn't see its outline in her pockets or on the floor. Finally she spotted the red handle emerging from between two bales where Babs had been standing.

"I do forgery detection for a detective service in California," Ruby told him.

"Now, again" Dick demanded, raising his voice. "Who are you working for today?"

"Unofficially, for Carly."

He strutted back and forth in front of her, kicking up bits of hay dust that hung in the shafts of sunlight. "You're just not getting what I'm asking. I'm talking about the bigger picture."

"What bigger picture?" Ruby asked.

A phone rang and Babs jerked, glancing toward a door across from the smaller door through which Dick had shoved Ruby into the hay barn. Dick shook his head and reached for a cordless phone sitting on top of a hay bale. He handed it to Babs. Somewhere nearby there was a phone set; they were too far from the house for decent reception. Inside the other door? Dick motioned for Ruby to be silent.

"Hello?" Babs said in a pleasant, happy homemaker's voice. Dick didn't take his eyes from Ruby. His head was raised, listening to Babs's every word.

"No, I haven't seen her at all." Babs glanced toward Ruby and she knew someone had called Babs, asking for her. Only Mary Jean knew she'd gone to Babs's farm. Ruby pressed her hand to her throat. Jesse. Something had happened to Jesse.

"I'll tell her if she stops by," Babs said into the mouthpiece. "Bye now," and she clicked off the phone.

"Please," Ruby asked Babs, ignoring Dick. "Was it Mary Jean? Has anything happened to Jesse?"

Babs handed the phone back to Dick as if she hadn't heard Ruby. He slid the phone into his hip pocket.

"Babs," Ruby pleaded. "Is Jesse okay? Was that Mary Jean? Is my daughter hurt?"

"Be quiet," Dick ordered, but behind him Babs slightly shook her head and Ruby slumped back on the hay bale in relief. But why was Mary Jean looking for her?

"So who are you working for?" Dick continued. "The FBI? The ATF?"

Ruby looked at him in surprise. "What are you talking about? The FBI, ATF? Babs knows the reason I'm here."

"You're damn right she does. She told me why you went to Lansing. You thought you were being cagey, spying on us and reporting to Jordan Asauskas and his committee. You're investigating the First Americans for the Feds, aren't you?"

"I only met Jordan—" Ruby began.

Dick cut her off. "It's too late to lie about it. I *saw* you in Lansing, remember?"

"Asauskas's committee is investigating *subversive* groups," Ruby said frowning. "I thought the First Americans was a peaceful organization."

A horn honked briefly outside and both Dick and Babs raised their heads. Ruby glanced around her at the towering walls of hay bales, the locked rolling doors. A wooden ladder climbed each side of the hay walls, ending before the highest bales. Dick and Babs blocked the path to the smaller doors. There was no place to hide, no escape.

The three held themselves still, listening as a car door slammed and barn doors opened. Two knocks rapped on the side door and Babs and Dick exchanged tense glances, moving a step closer to one another.

Mac McCutcheon entered the barn, dressed in his deputy's uniform. He looked at Babs and Dick, then at Ruby, shaking his head. "What in hell is going on?" he asked.

# Chapter 22

"You're late," Dick Prescott told Mac McCutcheon, glancing at his watch. "We said noon."

"Some kid's dog got tangled up with a raccoon. I had to shoot it." He stood in a stream of sunlight and patted the black holster that held his revolver. "What's she doing here?" he asked, nodding toward Ruby.

"Nosing around," Dick told Mac. "Just like Babs said she was."

"Looking for what?" Mac asked.

"What do you think? She's a government agent reporting to Asauska's committee."

Ruby kept quiet, watching the two men. The air vibrated with their dislike of one another, apparent in their stiff bodies, the challenging tones when they spoke, as if they were about to circle one another and shoot to kill. Babs avoided looking at Ruby, her eyes moving between Mac and her husband.

"And what do you intend to do with her?" Mac asked. "Stuff her in the wetland corner of your pasture? At least we know the government wouldn't disturb it to look for her."

Dick's face faltered and Mac continued, seizing the chance to grab the upper hand. "You're holding a gun on an undercover agent? Do you believe for one minute that if you let her go, she'll just go on home to her kid and bake cookies and forget about what took place here?" He pointed at Dick. "What *you've* done here? I'm a cop; I know what'll happen."

"I don't know," Dick said. "I didn't . . ."

"You sure as hell didn't." Mac waved his arms, then pointed his finger at Ruby while he spoke, jabbing it toward her the way Dick Prescott had jabbed his gun. "She'll have this place surrounded by tanks and snipers so fast we won't have time to say our Hail Marys before we're burned to crisps."

Ruby rose from the bale, but Dick waved his gun at her and she hastily returned to her prickly seat. "I don't give a damn about your First Americans organization or whatever it is," she told the men. "If you're making bombs out of fertilizer or stockpiling machine guns or plotting an overthrow of the Waters County government, it's none of my business. I'm not an agent of any kind."

"Babs said you'd deny it," Dick said. "That's the way you people operate. Dirty spying liars until you're caught; then everything's all innocent." His voice turned into falsetto mimicry. "It wasn't *me*. I don't know what you're talking about, mister."

"So that's why you were looking around?" Mac asked. "Hunting for weapons and bomb fixings?"

## Cut and Dry

"Babs caught her inside our house," Dick told him. He'd recovered his confidence and now spoke to Mac coolly, with more certainty. "In broad daylight. She didn't think anybody was home."

Mac gave Dick a sharp glance. "Did she find anything?" he asked.

Dick raised his eyebrows at Babs, who shook her head. "She was just looking at our calendar," Babs told him.

"Not a very good spy, are you?" Mac asked Ruby. "Getting caught like this, by a woman even, and not a very sharp one."

Dick's face flushed and he took a menacing step toward Mac.

"Calm down now, Dick," Mac said, casually moving his hand to his belt a few inches from his revolver. "I'm just talking. No harm meant." He turned back to Ruby and leaned down, looking her in the eye, thrusting his knobby chin forward. "I knew there was something fishy about the way Carly asked you to work for him on Alice's death and froze me out. It was all planned. You're an insider, aren't you?"

When Ruby didn't answer, he continued, "I've had my eye on you ever since you came to town. I thought there was something funny, a city woman coming back to her podunk hometown and then getting mixed up with the police right away. You didn't run away from home; you were sent away to get training so you could come back as an infiltrator. Didn't get away with it so easy, did you?"

"Mac," Ruby said, trying to hold his gaze, "this is

crazy. You know why I came back: so my daughter could have a quiet place to recover. If she hadn't been hurt, there's no way I would have even crossed the Michigan state line."

He stood straight and Ruby kept her eyes level, watching Babs standing so close to Dick. "Is that kid even your daughter? Or is she a front? You and Carly have been using Alice Rolley's death to investigate us, haven't you?" Mac went on. "In fact, I'll bet Carly has known right from the beginning who killed Alice. Some drifter, looking for an easy mark."

"No," Ruby said quietly. "We only discovered recently who killed Alice."

"Who?" Mac said. He touched her hair and she flinched. "If you're so damn sure of yourself, tell us who."

Ruby nodded toward Babs. "Babs did. She—"

Lights exploded in Ruby's head, pain seared through her neck. She felt herself tumbling and collapsing, and the next thing she was aware of was staring into the worn floorboards of the barn, shafts of hay piercing her cheek. Blood dripped from her nose onto the floor, one round drop at a time.

"I should kill you right now," Dick shouted, kicking her in the stomach with his booted foot. "How can you even say Babs's name, you traitor."

Ruby moaned, twisting herself into a fetal position as Dick continued railing at her. "You'd lie about anything, wouldn't you? You don't even know what the truth looks like you've been so filled with propaganda."

# Cut and Dry

"Take it easy," Mac said. "Let's think this through."

Ruby sat up, gasping and trying not to vomit. She rubbed her neck and shoulder, realizing her left arm was useless, hanging limp and tingling. She slid over to the hay bale and leaned her back against it, shaking her head to clear her vision, wiping at the blood on her lips with the back of her right hand.

"Dicky," Babs said quietly, wrapping both her hands around his arm and pulling him away from Ruby. "Mac's right. She'll report back to the FBI about your group. Once she tells them what we did to her they'll come after us." Babs's voice rose, turning frantic. "Let's leave now, honey, please. Leave her tied up here and let's go; didn't you say there were people who'd hide us if we were ever in trouble?"

Dick touched Babs's hand, his face twisted. "I'm sorry I got you into this, honey."

"If we hide her car here in the barn," Babs pleaded, nuzzling against her husband, "nobody will find her for days. We'll be long gone by then. We have to get away."

"Hold on," Mac said. "Stop this huggy crap. There's more at stake here than just you two. You're not the only members of this group, don't forget. We can't all hightail it out of town for fear one lone woman is going to talk."

"I'm not responsible for what happens to the rest of you," Dick told him.

Ruby could see where the discussion was heading; she had to take the chance. She gulped a deep breath and said, "Babs heard from Alice that Jordan Asauskas had been named chairman of the Subversive Organizations Committee. She spotted an envelope on the counter at the beauty parlor addressed to Jordan and thought Alice was reporting on the First Americans' activities in Sable."

"You're lower than a snake," Mac said to Ruby, holding Dick back by the arm. Ruby had no doubt that Mac was the only thing keeping Dick from beating her, or worse. "Trying to wiggle your way out of this mess you got yourself into. It won't work."

"What are we going to do?" Babs asked Dick. "You know she's lying. She's going to turn us all in. We'll go to jail."

"I'm thinking," Dick said, holding Babs against his side.

"Please, Dicky," Babs began again, close to sobbing. "Let's leave."

"And then," Ruby continued from her seat on the floor, struggling to keep her voice even, remembering that in the midst of hysteria the voice that was heard was the calmest one. "On the way home from the beauty parlor, after everyone had left except Alice, Babs stopped at Mrs. Brent's to pick up Susannah's dress. Susannah was too nervous about the recital to notice how long Babs was gone. Mrs. Brent's house is across the alley from the Wak 'n Yak."

"Your imagination has gone into overdrive," Mac said. "Don't pay any attention to her," he told Dick. "She's desperate and she'll say anything."

"Babs slipped through the shrubs and across the alley to the shop. Did you knock on the back door?"

# Cut and Dry

Ruby asked Babs. "Alice wasn't trying to escape from a killer through the back, was she? She was fighting her way to the front while you were strangling her."

"Kill her," Dick said to Mac in a flat voice. "I'll take care of her car." He squeezed Babs's shoulder and said in a soft, reassuring voice, "Don't get upset about this, Babs. Getting rid of her is the only way. We can't run off and go into hiding for the rest of our lives. We have to think of Darlene and little Susannah. Our life is here, in Sable. Everything will be okay."

Ruby saw the light in Babs's eyes. Babs wasn't the least upset that Dick intended to kill Ruby; she was hopeful. If Ruby couldn't talk, Babs would be free.

"Tell him the truth, Babs," Ruby said, "how you and Dick attended Susannah's recital in separate vehicles, so afterward you drove past the bank's night deposit and slipped in Alice's deposit bag. It was late and nobody saw you."

She bit her tongue to keep from screaming as Dick landed a vicious kick in her side, knocking her sprawling again.

"Shut up," he shouted.

She lay on the floor, gasping. From the agonizing stab in her side, she thought a rib might be broken. She tried to roll over and tears of pain filled her eyes.

"God, Dick," Mac said. "Make up your mind. Should I shoot her or do you plan to kick her to death?" His words were full of bravado, but even in her agony Ruby caught the distaste in Mac's voice. He didn't like this. She managed to sit up, holding her hand to her side.

"Let me go, Mac," she said, gasping, appealing directly to him. "You know I'm not a federal agent."

Mac pulled in his lower lip. "I don't know anything like that," he said, unsnapping the holster on his belt and removing his revolver.

"Do it," Babs told Mac. Her eyes were wild. Her hair seemed to crackle in a shaft of light that fell across her body. "She's a liar. She deserves to die."

Mac frowned at Babs, his revolver still loose in his hand, pointed at the hay-strewn floor in front of him.

"Honey," Dick said. "You shouldn't see this. Why don't you go in the house now?"

Babs's chest heaved with her breathing. Her face was flushed. She clasped her hands together, avidly watching Ruby. "Afterward," she said, nodding to Mac, giving him the go-ahead.

"Babs," Dick cajoled. "I don't think you—"

"Go ahead," Babs told Mac, ignoring Dick. "Do it. Another death doesn't matter now."

The life seemed to drain from Dick's face. He stood like stone, staring at Babs, his hand dropping from her arm, forgetting Ruby. "*Another* death?" he asked her. "What are you talking about? What 'another death'?"

Babs smiled, almost shyly, reaching out for the hand he'd removed. "I had to do something. I did it for you."

Ruby closed her eyes for a long moment, blinding herself to the revulsion on Dick's face. "Alice?" Ruby heard him whisper. "You did kill Alice?"

"She *knew* what you were doing," Babs said to him, her voice rising, her hands out in supplication. "She

## Cut and Dry

wrote a letter to Asauskas; I saw it on her counter. There was a stamp on it. Right in the beauty shop she told me he was the head of that committee. She was *taunting* me because she thought I couldn't stop her from informing on you. She wrote to tell him about you and the weapons and your plans. Don't you understand? If you were arrested and sent to jail, what would I do?"

"But then you discovered the letter was gone after you killed Alice," Ruby said. "Alice wasn't informing on you. She sent Asauskas a congratulations card because he'd been named committee chairman. Jordan told me. She *liked* Jordan; he was a local boy. Alice didn't know anything about the First Americans and if she did, she probably wouldn't have cared."

Dick took a step backward from Babs as if it were involuntary.

"Dicky?" she asked, breaking into sobs. "Don't. Don't leave me."

He didn't answer and she followed after him, matching step for step, her sobbing turned into keening, primitive anguish, her face raised toward the barn's ceiling. Above them, wings rustled frantically as birds fled from the barn.

"Jesus Christ," Mac whispered.

The sound of a car interrupted the tableau. Both Mac and Ruby heard it while Dick and Babs remained frozen where they were, facing each other, dazed and lost.

Ruby met Mac's eyes. "Jesus Christ," he muttered

again. His revolver hadn't moved; it was still pointed at the floor and Ruby felt a pinprick of hope.

"Ruby?" a voice called. It was Hank. Mac shook his head at Ruby, pressing his lips together. What was Hank doing here? He was walking straight into an ambush.

"Mac?" another voice called out. "You in there?" It was Carly. The odds were rising in her favor.

Mac's head jerked at the sound of Carly's voice, and Babs turned away from Dick, tears streaming down her face.

"You have to kill her now," she told Mac. "And everything will be okay. Nobody will know."

But Mac hadn't moved, his head still tipped, listening to the approaching voices.

"Do it," Babs ordered. Suddenly she lunged for his gun, grabbing his arm and struggling to pull the revolver from his grasp.

Ruby screamed with all of her strength, painfully throwing herself behind the bale of hay, screaming for real as she rolled over her ruined shoulder, her vision spinning to blackness.

Mac's pistol went off, filling the barn with sound, echoing from the rafters. Ruby remained where she was, huddled behind the bale of hay, her good arm covering her head. Doors banged. Scuffling surrounded her, grunts and the sounds of flesh meeting flesh, but no more gunfire.

Suddenly she was being lifted from the barn floor and she cried out from the pain in her side and shoul-

## Cut and Dry

der. "Shh, shh," a voice whispered. It was Hank, cradling her in his arms. "You're okay."

"How do you know?" she gasped.

"Because I've got you," he said. "Nothing else is going to happen." He gingerly set her down on the hay bale, running his hands across her body, searching for broken bones.

"I think my collarbone's broken," she told him. "And maybe a rib. Is anybody else hurt?"

Carly stood with his gun held on Mac, whose hands were raised in the air, his face defiant.

"Did Dick and Babs get away?" Ruby asked Hank.

He nodded toward the wall of hay. Babs lay on the floor, blood spilling from her neck, across her sweat shirt, and turning the golden hay beneath her red. Dick knelt beside her, rocking back and forth, one hand tangled in her blood-dampened hair.

Hank rode with her to the hospital, sitting beside her as the ambulance careened down the country roads, siren screaming and lights gyrating.

"Do they have to make all this racket?" Ruby asked Hank. "I'm not hurt that bad."

He smoothed back her hair. "They're having fun. They don't get much chance to use the lights and sound."

"Why did you come out to the farm?" Ruby asked. "Was that you who called Babs?"

He shook his head. "Mary Jean. I got into town earlier than I thought and stopped by her office after I didn't get an answer at your cabin. She was trying to track you down for me, all in the name of love."

"So you called Carly after Babs said she hadn't seen me? Wasn't that a little extreme?"

"Don't forget. I've watched you at work before, my love," Hank told her. "I'd already figured there was more going on than you let on. The whole thing just didn't feel right."

"You're a psychic knight," Ruby said. She closed her eyes; the sheets smelled antiseptic. "Is Babs dead?"

"That's right," Hank told her.

"A waste," she murmured, feeling herself drift off.

Albert Connelly drove Ruby's father to the hospital to visit her. From her bed, she heard the gravelly raised voices of the two old men as soon as they exited the elevator, talking over each other, reading off the room numbers, then whispering outside the entrance to her room. "This is it," she heard Albert say.

Ruby caught a glimpse of Albert's brown felt hat before her father entered her room alone, dressed in a black suit that was years old, probably his funeral-attending suit. He stopped beside her bed and folded his hands over his cane, his mouth stretched in a stiff smile.

"Sit down," Ruby said, nodding to the plastic and chrome chair.

"I can't stay," he told her. "Albert has an eye doctor's appointment." He gazed at the flowers on the bedside table. "You already have flowers," he said as if the bouquet Hank had brought her precluded his bringing any.

Ruby waited, watching him swallow and nod at the blank wall, then look at her bandaged side, everywhere but at her face. He was freshly shaven, smelling of shaving soap. She'd bet he still used a straight edge.

"You're doing okay here?" he finally asked.

"Fine," she told him. "They're letting me out tomorrow."

He twisted his cane. "That's good. Good to hear it."

"Jesse was here this morning," Ruby said.

"Jesse's a good girl," he said, still twisting his cane. "Phyllis called. She's going to phone you."

"When?" Ruby asked. A nurse peeked in, smiled, and left the room.

"She didn't say. She wanted me to tell you that."

"Thanks."

He shifted his cane to his right hand and turned toward the door. "I'd better go now."

"And thanks for coming to visit me," Ruby told him.

He kept on walking toward the door, saying without turning around, "I'm glad you weren't the one who got shot."


"He left these for you," Carly said, arriving at her cabin a week after Babs's funeral. He handed her a black plastic box the size of a large dictionary.

"And did he leave instructions?" Ruby asked. She sat in a lawn chair by the water. A breeze was finally stirring off the lake and the day whispered with stirring leaves and grass.

"Only that you could do whatever you wanted with them, and he hoped you'd scatter them, not dump them."

Ruby smiled and cradled Johnny Boyd's ashes to her body with her good arm. "How did you know he was gone?" she asked Carly.

"We set it up between us," Carly told her. He hunkered beside her chair, pulling up a piece of grass and rolling it between his fingers. "One cop to another. He'd rigged a flag he planned to raise on the day he chose to end it and I promised I'd drive past every day. That simple."

She remembered the new flagpole beside his porch where a flag never flew, and then Jesse asking her to stop outside Johnny Boyd's gate. "Could you see the flag from Blue Road, by his gate?" she asked Carly.

"That's right. Did he tell you about it?"

Ruby shook her head. "And the flag?" she asked, remembering another thing Jesse had told her. "Was it a pirate flag?"

Carly nodded and grinned. "A Jolly Roger."

"And you agreed with that plan wholeheartedly?" Ruby asked him.

"Yes, I did," Carly said without apology. "He had no doubts about what he wanted: to go peacefully at a time of his own choosing. I respected that." He nodded toward her sling. "How's the shoulder?"

"Better and better. Well, actually, damn awkward. Jesse's cooking. We eat toasted cheese sandwiches every night. I mean, every single night. I heard you'll be running uncontested for sheriff this fall?"

"That's the rumor. Even with Babs's death, people are grateful Alice's murder is solved. They feel safe again. Unmasking Mac and finding that stockpile of automatic weapons and grenades won the hearts of the populace."

"*All* the populace?" Ruby asked.

Carly sighed. "That depends on which side of the First Americans their loyalties lie."

"Still, two deaths have to give people pause, no matter what their politics are. Will Jumbo be indicted along with Mac and Dick?"

"I don't know yet. His involvement didn't reach the frenzied level of Mac's and Dick Prescott's."

Carly gazed at her so long and steadily that Ruby began to fidget uncomfortably. "What are you looking at?" she asked.

"Are you keeping anything back in this case?"

"I can't think of a single thing I should have told you that I didn't," Ruby said.

He shook his head and stood, finally saying, "You're more or less a loner."

"You've known that for a year," Ruby told him.

"You act alone when it would be wiser to have backup, or at least tell somebody what you're up to."

"I think better when I'm working by myself," Ruby told him. She shifted Johnny Boyd's ashes and watched Spot cross the yard and sit beside Jesse, his nose to her leg.

"I wish you wouldn't do that, Ruby, but . . ."

"Yeah?" Ruby asked.

"I'm grateful to you."
"You're very welcome," she told him.

At dawn, Ruby rowed one-handed into the center of Blue Lake, switching from oar to oar, slow progress with her arm bound in a sling close to her body.

The morning was still, the mists still hovered, moving outward from the shore as the morning warmed, dissipating in the sunlight, moving so quickly, they formed eerie shapes and wisps. Ruby was alone on Blue Lake. A duck paddled near a line of water lilies, its occasional dip into the water echoing delicately across the lake.

Johnny Boyd's cabin was closed, his chair and table gone from the front porch, the front door shut and locked. Once again it was the Barber cabin and she looked at it for a long time, feeling a bittersweet ache.

Ruby allowed the boat to drift, rocking gently while she opened the black plastic box and removed the container of Johnny Boyd's ashes. "Scatter, don't dump" had been his only message to her.

And so she did, scattering the dark ashes into the moving mists as if the ashes might drift along with them, disappearing into the sun.